ZOO

LIFE COULDN'T GET
ANY WILDER

Graham Marks

BLOOMSBURY

First published in Great Britain in 2005 by Bloomsbury Publishing Plc
36 Soho Square, London, W1D 3QY

Copyright © Graham Marks 2005
The moral right of the author has been asserted

This edition published in 2007

A CIP catalogue record of this book is available from the British Library

ISBN 978 0 7475 9127 X

All papers used by Bloomsbury Publishing are natural, recyclable products
made from wood grown in well-managed forests. The manufacturing
processes conform to the environmental regulations of the country of origin.

Typeset by Dorchester Typesetting Group Ltd
Printed in Great Britain by Clays Ltd, St Ives Plc

1 3 5 7 9 10 8 6 4 2

www.bloomsbury.com

This one's for my mum, who instilled a love of the story in me from the very start.

And, because these things – no matter what it says on the cover – are always the work of more than just one person, I'd also like to thank a few people, starting with my agent Maggie Noach, my publisher Sarah Odedina and desk editor Georgia Murray. Without whom, as they say.

Also, this book is about a journey, and to complete it I needed the help of a few good friends in the States. Up in beautiful, if rainswept, Seattle, a big thank you goes to Annabella Serra and Dana Batali for their friendship and hospitality (plus a hi to Clio and Sebastian); down in San Diego a tip of the hat to Blue Gehres, who knew exactly where I should be going; in LA, major thanks to Norman and Francie Moore for giving the wanderer somewhere so much like home to return to – and to Daniel and Sophie for being an inspiration – and finally, I must raise my glass to Maria Kwong for her advice, her repartee and for being there whenever needed, which was often.

'Everything you can imagine is real'
Pablo Picasso

'Machines were mice and men were lions, once upon a time'
Moondog

Chapter 1

La Jolla, San Diego, CA;
Wednesday February 26th,
5.05 p.m.

Mike Henrikson stood looking at the wrecked dark green '97 Volvo sedan. The front was completely trashed, radiator grille total history, driver's side fender pushed way back into the engine compartment, hood folded back like it was a starched cotton sheet to reveal wires and pipes and the stuff only mechanics really understood. The windshield was all busted up, too, and both airbags had gone off, the propellant leaving a faintly acrid smell in the air.

'Jeez, Tony. Just how damn fast was he going up this hill?'

'He wasn't speeding, Mike . . . the other vehicle, the white Ford van? That lady I was talking to said it shot out of the alley over there like a bat outta hell.' Henrikson's partner, Tony Matric, shoved some of the larger pieces of plastic debris off the road into the gutter. 'You can see the skid marks where the guy popped the clutch.'

'She said "bat outta hell"?'

Tony looked over at his partner, standing by the open driver's door, grinning at him. Didn't matter what the circumstances, the man was always looking to make jokes. Said it was the only thing kept him sane. And there was no arguing that being a cop was one easy way to get driven crazy.

'Sure did. Got a mouth on her, that lady.' Tony looked back at the Volvo. 'This car might be old, but it was in pretty damn good condition, before the incident. They must've just had it serviced, too – that air filter looks like it's brand new.'

'So this white van comes straight out of the alley, smashes into the front of the Volvo, and then this one Asian guy and one white guy get out and, in broad daylight, calmly haul this kid's ass out, put him in back and drive off.'

'Long and the short of it? Yeah.'

'What's his name?'

'The kid?' Tony flipped open his notebook. 'Stewart . . . Cameron Stewart. Friends call him Cam, apparently. He's like seventeen, only kid, father owns some hi-tech company or other, mother doesn't work.'

'You got all this from that one lady?'

'Yeah.'

'She CIA or something?'

'Retired.' Tony put his notebook away, looked at his watch and then looked over his shoulder. 'Time to get started, Mike . . . see what the parents have to say?'

'Sure . . . tell the uniforms to tape this all off, including the alley, and let's go meet the folks.'

The second hand tick-tocked across the old-fashioned Roman numeral XII and as it did so the minute hand clunked past the IV of the 'antiqued' cherrywood wall clock, oddly loud in the quiet. They'd been waiting now for almost a quarter of an hour, left to cool their heels in this room that looked like it had been ordered from some upscale catalog, delivered and then never used.

The leather furniture was so polished you'd think it'd crack if you sat on it, so neither Tony or Mike did. Instead, Tony stood looking out of the picture window at the Scene of Crime Officers crawling all over the car, while Mike paced up and down the Navajo-style rug, chewing a hangnail and muttering to himself. Somewhere in the house they could both hear voices, possibly someone crying. Not unusual, under the circumstances.

Tony got bored with staring at people actually doing something useful and wandered over to examine the group of framed photos on top of the white baby grand piano.

'This must be him.' He picked up a picture of a blond, blue-eyed kid, smiling and radiating confidence, poise and self-belief. 'Looks like a straight-A kinda guy.'

Mike stopped pacing and gestured around the room. 'What you'd expect, right? Money breeds –'

Tony never did find out what Mike thought money bred because the double doors opened and the maid who'd let them in poked her head through the gap.

'Mr. Stewart will be with you now.'

Putting the frame back on the piano, Tony turned around just as Gordon Stewart strode into the room. He looked freshly polished, iron-gray hair swept back off his high forehead, aggressively aftershaved and dressed in a charcoal suit, highly mirrored black shoes, cream silk shirt and a plain gray tie that had to have been chosen to match his hair.

'Officers, apologies for keeping you waiting, but my wife . . . she, ah, she's very emotional, as you might imagine.'

And you look like you've just walked out of Hair and Make-up on a TV set, Tony couldn't help thinking. *All set to sell something*.

'No problem, sir,' Mike nodded. 'Sorry we have to do this right now, but . . .'

'I understand, and so does my wife — shall we go through?'

Eleanor Stewart had obviously repaired whatever damage her emotions had done to her face, and was perched on a heavy brocade couch. She was all cashmere, pearls and diamonds, smoking a long, slim cigarette and with a thin, brittle smile etched on her face. Behind her and to her left, the maid stood like a statue.

'I'm sorry to have kept you waiting, gentlemen,' she leaned forward and stubbed out the cigarette, 'but it's not every day your son gets kidnapped outside your own home. Would you like some coffee?'

'No thank you, ma'am.' Mike glanced down at his watch, just to remind everyone that time was of the essence here.

'Well, if you don't mind, I will — Consuela?' The maid turned on her heels and left the room. 'Please, do sit down.'

Mike slammed the door of the car, sat back and stared at the Stewart house, built into the hillside at the end of a small cul-de-sac, with its perfectly manicured flowerbeds, trimmed hedges and 'just so' drapes in every window.

Tony turned the keys in the ignition. 'What d'you think?'

'I think I'm glad I didn't grow up in a house where every damn room could've been out of a magazine, is what I think. It was almost like we were breathing filtered air in that place, too.'

'What I mean is, why kidnap *their* son? Me, I didn't get the feeling they were *that* kind of rich. You know, they're well-off, but not like mega.' Tony left the car in neutral, pulled out his wallet and extracted the business card Gordon Stewart had given him as they left the house. 'What the hell's "Communications Infrastructure", anyway?'

'Dunno . . .' Mike turned and looked at where the wrecked Volvo had been, a dark stain on the tarmac where something had ruptured and spilt gunk on the road – all that was left now the car had been towed. 'But that's not what's bothering me.'

'So what is?'

'This is supposed to be a kidnap, right, but who makes a kidnap so public – does the whole thing in broad daylight and right outside the vic's house? It's like they were trying to guarantee maximum publicity . . . like they actually *wanted* people to see them do it.'

Chapter 2

Queen Anne Hill; Wednesday February 26th, 9.25 p.m.

Cam felt like shit. He had the mother of all headaches, every muscle and bone ached, his mouth felt like he'd recently eaten talcum powder and the last thing he remembered was some big white Ford van appearing out of nowhere and ramming into his car. The rest was a complete blank.

Now he was awake, kind of, but he'd no idea where he was or what had happened to him since the crash. What he did know for sure was that the crash had been no accident. It'd been a set-up, and this place he was in sure as hell wasn't a clinic or a hospital.

Coming to in this darkened room, Cam had been disoriented, still suffering, though he didn't know it, from the combined after-effects of a sedative injection on top of a hefty dose of chloroform. When he'd heard the door open and two people walk in, even if he'd wanted to he couldn't have moved or opened his eyes, which meant the men had assumed he was still knocked out and had talked openly in front of him like he wasn't even there.

'How long will it be before he wakes up?' one of them, the one who sounded older, more in charge, had said.

'The doc told me he'd given him enough stuff so's he'd be out for five, six hours – so any time now,' the second guy had said, sounding like he had some kind of foreign accent that Cam couldn't pin down: American, but not quite.

'He is okay, isn't he, still alive?'

Cam had felt a hand grip his wrist, then fingers take his pulse. 'Heart's beating steady like a drum – you want to check?'

'No . . . just so long as he doesn't croak on us – and make sure the door's secured, someone outside all the time from now on, okay? I didn't go to all this trouble to have him lifted and flown up here for a screw-up now.'

'Why'd we have to do it, lift the kid so out in the open? Was there some way that this would give Stewart the message it was you?'

'He'll know it's me, and I wanted it like that so the cops would get involved, put more pressure on him to make the right decision.' The older man had laughed, a humorless, derisive snort. 'He'll be kicking himself he wasn't more careful with his most valuable asset.'

'You been in touch with him yet?'

'Look, I'll do my job, you make sure you do yours, okay?' the older man had said as he walked out the room.

The second man had stayed where he was for a minute or so. Cam could hear his breathing, controlled, almost like a machine, and assumed he was just standing there, looking at him, which made him feel really spooked. Then he had heard a hard slap-slap-slap sound, a moment later realizing it must've been the man punching his own palm.

'Asshole!' The word had been almost spat out in an acid

hiss and Cam had flinched, half opening his eyes to see the back of the man as he had stormed out of the room, slamming the door behind him.

He had heard footsteps stomping away, stop and come back. Then came the sound of a key being jammed in a lock and turned, securing the door like the older man, the boss, had ordered.

Someone definitely wasn't happy.

Cam sat up on the bed, leaning back against the wall. His eyes had adjusted to the darkness and, helped by the light spilling under the door, he was now able to make out rough details of the room he was in. There wasn't much to see: apart from the bed, he could make out a small desk and chair, some kind of built-in closet, a couple of pictures on the wall and, he assumed, windows behind the drawn drapes.

There was a lamp on the desk. It was a few feet away, nearer than the light switch by the door. Soon, he was sure, he'd feel okay enough to stand up, walk over and turn it on. That would be an achievement.

He had no idea what time it was, or what day, as they'd taken his watch and there was no clock in the room. He couldn't see any light coming from behind the drapes, so it was night, probably, but which night? And where?

Not to mention the real biggie: why him?

Why had *he* been kidnapped, drugged and 'flown up' to somewhere? What made him worth all the effort? He knew he came from a reasonably privileged background, though nothing outrageous by southern Californian standards and certainly not what he'd consider 'ransom rich', so what made him a target?

He'd never thought about kidnapping much before, the subject only ever entering his field of vision when it'd featured on some TV newscast he happened to have seen; but now that he did think about it, kidnap stories usually only made the news when there'd been a screw-up and the victim's body got dumped. Sometimes, he remembered, they were killed even though the ransom had been paid. Nice thought.

Some time later it occurred to him that maybe this was all a case of mistaken identity and they'd picked the wrong guy up off the street . . . although, he then thought, that was likely to be even more of a guarantee that he'd end up dead. Wrong guy, no value. Another nice thought.

Whichever way you looked at it, the situation was not great. And trying to work out what to do was tough when you couldn't get your head straight. Then, as the fog cleared, he suddenly recalled a snippet of conversation where his father's name had been mentioned by the two guys in the room. '*Was there some way that this would give Stewart the message it was you?*' the younger one had said.

No doubt about it, really, they'd got the right person.

He thought about getting up, but still felt very lightheaded. He'd only just got over the catastrophic viral infection that had laid him out like he'd been punched by Mike Tyson — and had completely nixed him from going on the football team tour. He'd gone from awesome running back and Most Valued Player to Pale Shadow of Former Self almost overnight, and had been sick for what seemed like forever, while all his buddies were off having a great time, not due back for another week.

The doc had said that if he hadn't been as fit as he was the effects of the virus would've been even worse, which

Cam had thought could only have meant death as he'd truly felt like he was dying. Now he just felt crap. He swung his legs off the bed and made himself stand up. This was not the time, he figured, to sit around and wait to see what happened next.

Chapter 3

Queen Anne Hill; Thursday
February 27th, 1.19 a.m.

It wasn't much of a plan, and if he was being completely honest it didn't have that much of a chance of working, but it was better than doing nothing. The whole idea sank or swam on getting whoever was on guard the other side of the door to let him out. Cam had been over the whole room and knew there was no way he could break out – the door was locked, no handle on the inside, and the windows were security barred with an expanding steel gate.

There was also a tiny webcam-style video camera up next to the ceiling in the corner over the door. He'd discovered that was what it was when, not long after he'd walked over to the window, he had heard someone saying 'He's awake!' and then, not long after, came the sound of footsteps running up the corridor. Moments later he was being looked at and inspected like some kind of pedigree dog by a short, balding man who smelled of Chinese food and had a badly pockmarked face.

A younger guy, about his height but built like the types Cam had seen outside of every club he'd ever been to, had stood blocking the open doorway. He was staring into the middle distance, looking blank, thinking he was cool; they were all the same. The small man had just carried on looking and had ignored Cam's questions when he had asked where he was and what was happening to him. When the man had finished what he'd come to do he'd just turned around and walked out, not having said a word.

Cam reckoned it was about fifteen, twenty minutes later that the guard had returned with a tray of food. As he'd walked out, Cam had managed to catch sight of his watch, a large lump of stainless steel with a chunky strap, and saw that it was about 1.50 a.m.

It was later, after he'd finished his food, that Cam worked out what he could try and do. Based on the absolute fact that staying in the room was going to get him nowhere but deeper in trouble, and breaking out was just not going to happen, the only logical alternative was to be let out. Which, on the face of it, was a highly unlikely occurrence .. . except if he wanted to go to the bathroom. They surely would let him out for that. Wouldn't they?

He decided to wait to find out. The longer he left it, he figured, the more bored and tired the guard would be – and maybe the more genuine he'd sound when he asked to be let out.

Cam left it till he felt like he was about to wet himself.

'Hey, man!' Cam rapped on the door. 'You out there, man?'
Nothing.

'I gotta go . . . you know, like *really* gotta go?' Cam thought maybe he could hear someone moving.

He waited. Still nothing.

'Can you hear me?'

'I'm not deaf.' The guard sounded like he was half asleep. 'What's your damn problem?'

'I *need* to go to the bathroom. Now.'

Pause.

'Do you know what time it is?'

'Know what? I don't. You guys took my watch – and my shoes.'

'Jeez, it's nearly four in the morning . . .'

'So? I can't wait, man, I'm desperate . . . come on, you gotta let me go.'

Cam heard the man sigh, then there was the soft clinking of keys and the sound of a lock turning.

'It's down the hall,' the guard said, pointing. 'Make it quick, and don't try anything smart. You'll just get hurt, right?'

'Right.' Cam, shoeless, padded out of the room.

'Second on the left.' The guard was directly behind him, sounding only slightly more awake. 'And leave the door open.'

So, no climbing out of a window, then. One idea down. Cam opened the door, reached around to his left, feeling for the light switch, and turned it on. A vision of gleaming white marble, chrome and glass confronted him – two sinks, a bath, a shower cubicle, and '. . . where's the toilet?'

'Behind the door . . . and like I said, leave it open.'

'Okay, okay.' Cam walked into the room, his mind racing. He had as long as it took him to take a leak to come up with something, and that was it, he'd be back in a locked room, waiting. He took his time, glancing over his shoulder as he unzipped his pants. He couldn't see the guard in any of the mirrors. Eyes darting left and right, he looked around to see if there was anything – *anything* – he could use.

Nothing. Just a toilet roll, a plastic, long-handled brush . . . maybe he could rip the seat off the john and hit the guy?

And then he saw the can of air freshener on the floor, tucked behind the metallized plastic brush-holder.

Without stopping what he was doing, Cam managed to bend over, pick it up and tuck it under his arm. The narrow can felt full. It felt somehow like a weapon. And, for the first time since he'd woken up, he felt like he had a chance.

'Jeez,' said the man, still behind the door, 'you really did need that, di'n't you.'

'No kidding.' Cam finished, zipped up and then reached over and pushed down the flush. Covered by the sound of the water, he snapped off the plastic cap and put it on top of the tank. Then, holding the can upside down in his right hand, he hoped, like he'd never hoped before, that the guard wouldn't spot it as he walked out the bathroom. He took a deep breath and made his move.

'Okay, back in your kennel, guy.' The guard slipped in behind Cam as he came out into the corridor.

Cam swung his right hand in front of him to hide the aerosol, making like he was scratching his upper arm with his left hand. And just as he reached the room he was being kept in, Cam spun around, shoved the can in the guard's face and pressed the button.

The nozzle was no more than an inch, two inches max, away from the man, and a dense, perfumed cloud of air freshener erupted directly into his eyes, nose and mouth. Completely taken by surprise, the guard instinctively inhaled sharply when Cam whirled around, which meant he breathed in far more of the chemical soup than he otherwise might have. That, combined with the coating his eyes got, meant he could neither see nor breathe. To put the cherry on the cake, as the guard gagged and frantically wiped at his burning eyes, Cam kicked him between the legs. Solid.

Standing, watching the writhing heap on the ground, Cam couldn't believe what he'd just done. He suddenly realized there was a pounding drumbeat in his ears and that he was taking short, sharp breaths through his nose, the cloying smell of air freshener stinging his nostrils. He'd stopped spraying when the man had hit the floor, but was still gripping the can in his hand, like it was frozen there.

With the massive burst of adrenaline that had just been delivered into his system beginning to kick in, Cam was in full 'fight or flight' mode and jumpy as a flea-ridden cat. Pacing up and down, the rational part of his brain made him stop and think, made him carefully take stock of where he was, take in the empty corridor, the desk the guard had been sitting at – the one with the small black and white TV with the grainy picture of the bedroom on it – and made him wonder what the hell he was going to do next.

Okay. Where was he at?

He was free, kind of, or at least out of the room for the moment. But he was still trapped inside the house. It looked like the security system in the place wasn't that sophisticated, like the camera wasn't hooked up to screens anywhere else, or someone would've seen what had just gone down and he'd have had company. Cam shot a glance at the guard, not really taking in that he'd stopped moving.

Right, first things first – get him out of sight.

Bending down to grab the man under his arms and pull him into the bedroom, Cam finally noticed he didn't seem to be breathing. He got down closer, any moment expecting the man to have been playing possum and lunge at him,

23

but he didn't. Instead, almost masked by the air freshener, he smelled slightly of vomit. Cam fumbled at the man's wrist, trying to find a pulse, but no matter how hard he tried, he couldn't.

He was dead.

Flat on his back gone.

Cam rocked on his heels, stunned. He'd just meant to put the guy out of action temporarily, not deep six him. That hadn't been in the plan, killing anyone, even though the thought had occurred to him that his captors might end up getting rid of *him* for good.

He stood up, chewing his lip, his mind a blur, unable to hold onto a thought long enough to take it onto the next stage. Okay, okay, what to do . . . maybe what *not* to do, cos it didn't seem like there was much point in moving the man now. It wasn't like he was going to raise the alarm or anything. Cam looked down at the body and saw a stain spreading out from the man's crotch. Wonderful.

He was about to go – better to be anywhere than right there, right then – when he noticed there was a cell phone in a black leather pouch attached to the man's belt. He knelt down and looked at the screen. Locked. Damn. Then he saw the dull glint of the wrist watch, a Tag, as it turned out; felt like a real one, too. Really useful, and working. Flicking open the clasp, Cam took it off and pocketed it. Feeling like a total thieving bastard, he pulled the man's sneakers off as well.

His feet felt truly weird in the Nikes. They fit, kind of, but even though they were pretty clean he just didn't like the idea of wearing somebody else's shoes. Especially a dead man's shoes. He knew, though, that there was no way he'd get very far in his socks, so he had no choice.

Pushing away the horrific fact that he'd actually killed someone – he kept telling himself to deal with it later, much later – Cam took a moment to properly figure what to do now. He knew he'd been incredibly lucky so far, and that his luck could run out at any time, so what he really had to do was keep on moving and find a way out. And the only way would appear to be down.

He crept along the thickly carpeted corridor, past the bathroom, to where it turned left. He peered around the corner and saw a wide, balustraded landing with a very grand central staircase leading down to a parquet-floored hall and the double front door. This was no backwoods shack but one big, fancy house he was in.

The lights were on everywhere, but, as far as he could tell, there was no one around. The place was quiet – he found himself thinking 'quiet as a grave' and wished he hadn't, considering what was just up the corridor behind him. Could he just make a dash for it? The jumpy, itchy side of him screamed 'YES!', but a small, calm voice whispered, 'No, take it slow, man, take it slow . . .' He hovered at the edge of the landing, feeling intensely vulnerable and wishing there was some shadow he could hide in while he worked on his next move.

He dug the Tag out of his pocket. It was just after 4.30. He slipped the watch on his wrist and secured the clasp, the metal cool against his skin, the strap just a little too loose. This must be the house at its most asleep, Cam reasoned, and the chances were that even those supposed to be awake would be more than likely dozing. It sounded like a convincing argument, particularly as there was no one else with him to shoot it down, but he knew the longer he did nothing the less persuasive it would become.

Shaking his head, wishing, wishing, wishing there was something even slightly less risky he could think of doing, Cam made a dash for the staircase. It was the longest half minute of his life.

5 seconds – panic . . . stop halfway across the landing and nearly go back, positive he can hear voices . . . it's nothing . . . move on

10 seconds – reach the staircase, crouch, listen, look, move down a couple of stairs . . . they creak . . . stop again

22 seconds – ten more stairs and he's on the parquet . . . soles of the sneakers squeaking like mice as he walks

28 seconds – hand on the door knob, pushing down . . . open the door v-e-r-y slowly . . . no alarms go off, no lights that weren't on go on, but a cold, wet wind comes in . . . out of the corner of his eye he sees a leather jacket draped over a nearby chair . . . reach over, pick it up, exit

35 seconds – quietly close the door behind him.

And wherever he was, Cam knew it sure as hell wasn't anywhere even remotely near San Diego.

Chapter 4

Crockett, Queen Anne Hill; Thursday February 27th, 4.35 a.m.

It was freezing. Winter in San Diego was never this cold and this wet. When Cam had been kidnapped – only yesterday, he had to keep reminding himself – it had been warm, warm enough for him to have only needed a T-shirt and jeans. If the coat he was now wearing hadn't been left by the door, he'd have been in real trouble. No . . . actually, just worse trouble.

He was stuck outside the house now, no time for second thoughts, no going back. It was raining, he had no money, no idea where he was – for all he knew this wasn't even America – and nowhere to run to. Plus he'd just killed a man. Stone dead. Was it murder, manslaughter, self-defense? He didn't have the time to waste figuring that one out – he had to get as far away from this place as he could before anyone realized what he'd done.

Shivering, Cam turned up the jacket's collar, walked across the veranda and down the steps that lead to the brick-paved front path. As soon as he moved out from under cover of the roof, two motion-activated spotlights kicked in and flooded the pathway with a cold, white light. It was like a flashbulb going off and freezing the picture. Cam froze, too, then he became aware of the rain and he began to walk as fast as he could without looking like he was running away from anything. Keep calm, keep calm, keep calm . . .

Fine drizzle beaded on the leather coat, streaming off in tiny rivulets, and he could feel cold water running down the back of his neck, but that was the last thing on his mind. He was obsessing about the possibility of someone in the house seeing the lights go on, he was thinking about the front door opening and people, probably with guns, running after him. He was thinking about getting a bullet in the back of his head and all the lights just going out, forever, and he was trying to figure what the *hell* his next move was.

Then he realized he'd reached the street and nothing had happened.

To his left the road ran downhill, making a sharp right after twenty, thirty yards; down there he could see city lights twinkling in the darkness. Looking to his right he could see the street leading straight uphill and it seemed to him as if the sky was just marginally less black up that way.

Which direction to take? Down into the gloom, or up into what looked like it might be the coming dawn? Pulling the jacket tight around him and hunching his shoulders, Cam stepped onto the tarmac sidewalk and started walking up the hill. It seemed a more positive action, like he'd be achieving something when he got to the top. And every small victory counted.

The coat was heavy, cut in a mid-length style with angled side pockets. His hands getting cold and wet, Cam stuck them into the pockets and held the jacket closed that way.

While there was nothing except an opened pack of tissues in the right pocket, Cam could feel that there was a heavy object down in the left-hand side one. He closed his fingers around something cold and metallic and he slowly pulled out a small handgun. Stopping, he looked at it, lying in the palm of his hand. So it hadn't been total paranoia, thinking men with guns might come after him.

The street lighting was minimal, just one or two of the houses he passed had a light on and the only sound was the low patter of the rain falling through the leafless branches of the trees lining the street. He threw the gun into the thick shrubbery lining the sidewalk and moved on.

Cam felt abandoned, kind of shipwrecked and adrift at the same time, and his mind was in complete turmoil and panic. Under any other circumstances, he thought, a person who'd just escaped from being kidnapped would be looking for the nearest phone or patrol car or trying to flag down a car to at least tell *someone* what had happened and start the journey home. But this person had killed to get away, which sort of radically changed the rules. Changed everything, in every way. I mean, were you allowed to kill a man if you thought he might be going to kill you?

As he reached the top of the street, which the sign said was called Crockett, he saw a car driving along the cross street toward him, a small Japanese sub-compact, its wipers shushing backward and forward. Cam caught sight of the driver, softly illuminated by the dash lights. He was an unhappy-looking middle-aged man hunched over the wheel, and he shot him a glance as he drove by. Cam turned and watched the car go past. For a split second he had the unnerving feeling that it was going to stop and the guy would then get out and ask him what he was doing. It didn't, and Cam turned back and started walking in the opposite direction.

It was a while later, after he'd wandered aimlessly for quite a way, that he even bothered to look at any street signs. When he did he found he was somewhere called Queen Anne Avenue. Okay, that was a start. Then, as he went past a car parked in the street, he noticed it was brand new and still had its dealer plates on, from some dealership in a place called Factoria, wherever that was. More information was good, though. The next car he saw had Washington plates. State, not DC. And so had the next three cars. Chances were, then, that he was somewhere in Washington, which would explain the weather. And meant he was almost in Canada, which was a hell of a long way from home.

Actually, he realized, it did make him feel a little better, a little more grounded, knowing vaguely where he was: another small victory. He bent down and picked a three-foot long stick up off the ground, waving it in front of him and making light-saber noises. The stick promptly broke in half.

Officers Pete DeWinter and Martyn Miller were halfway through the graveyard shift and they were bored. Mid-week – Wednesday night, Thursday morning – and in a nice part of town, nothing much usually happened and, true to form, nothing much had.

They'd had a call, a couple of hours in, that someone in a house on West Prospect thought they'd seen a person – 'of youthful appearance, wearing a black coat and jeans' – attempting to burglarize a neighboring house, but they'd investigated and found nothing.

'Probably they saw a damn racoon,' Martyn had commented, 'you know, on account of the cute bandit mask?'

'Yeah,' Pete grinned, 'or maybe the carney's in town and some monkey's escaped.'

Residents of the more up-scale parts of town, where 'armed response' notices could be seen in many of the front yards, were prone to seeing things and imagining the worst. Although, it had to be said, the worst did occasionally happen, which was why you couldn't be too careful. And this was why, as they swung right off 3rd, back onto West Prospect for another go-round, Officer Miller had slowed the cruiser and cut the lights when he saw an individual walking along the sidewalk some way up ahead.

'Black coat, blue jeans, Pete.' He glanced across at his partner.

'Although he looks nothing like a racoon.'

'True, but he could be wearing a mask.'

'You read way too many comics, Mart.'

'They satisfy *all* my literary needs.'

'The same, when it comes to your diet, could be said for pizza, my friend.' Pete reached over for the mike. 'Want me to call this in . . . I mean, are we checking this guy out?'

'Yeah, I think we should.'

Pete was just about to contact their control when the figure turned left off Prospect. 'Is he carrying something? Did you see like a knife in his right hand?'

'Maybe.'

'Want video, Mart?'

'Sure, let's tape it . . .'

Cam was aware that a car had turned into the street behind him, come to a halt and switched its lights off. Aware also that no one had got out yet. Could almost feel eyes burning into the back of his head.

There was a street coming up on the left, 5th Avenue according to the sign. He hadn't been intending to go down there, but now thought it might be a bright idea if he did. As he turned the corner he tried to look at the car without seeming like that was what he was doing. A street lamp silhouetted the telltale light bar on its roof. Cops.

Instinct took over, pushing logic roughly out of the way. Without thinking any further than that he was responsible for there being a dead man in a house not far away, Cam started running, forgetting he was holding the stick in his hand like a relay baton. Forgetting he was a kidnap victim.

Officer Martyn Miller flicked the lights back on, threw the cruiser into 'Drive' and eased down the accelerator.

'Call it in, Pete,' he gripped the wheel as the car began to pick up speed, 'in pursuit of possible burglary suspect who's now going south on . . . what's that street?'

'Looks like he's taken the 5th, Mart.'

'Much good may it do him . . .'

Cam ran as fast as someone else's shoes and a heavy leather coat would let him, which – as he was a pretty damn quick running back – meant speedy. At the bottom of 5th the road turned right and he skidded around the corner like he was in a scene from some old black and white comedy, sneakers slipping on the wet sidewalk.

Regaining his grip, he powered off down the street, almost missing a small road to his right. Taking that would get him out of sight quicker than anything else he could do, so he leaped over the curb and went for it. Like a rabbit with a dog on its tail, he was taking every opportunity to zigzag his way out of trouble, so he took the next left, pelted down it, turned right at the intersection at the bottom and stopped.

His heart was going like a train and he was so hot he thought steam was probably coming off him. He undid the coat, flapping it to cool himself down, while he took stock of the situation, noticing he was now on a street called Olympic Place. How appropriate.

The sky had lightened a bit over to his right and, on the opposite side of the road, he saw some woods.

The cruiser turned into 5th Avenue and there was no sign of their possible suspect.

Pete leaned forward. 'Where the hell'd he go?'

'Must've been going some to've got himself around that corner.' Martyn floored the accelerator, the rear wheels slipping and the cruiser fishtailing slightly until he got it back under control.

'Easy, tiger.' Pete grabbed the door handle as the car slid around the sharp righthander at the bottom of 5th, narrowly missing a parked vehicle, and before he knew it they were at the intersection with 3rd and there was still no sign of their man.

'Was there a turn back there?' Martyn looked over his shoulder.

'Think so.'

'He probably took that.' Martyn hauled on the steering wheel and gunned the engine. 'Might get him coming out on Kinnear or Olympic.'

The cruiser slowed as they came to Kinnear. Nothing.

'D'you want me to call for some back-up?'

'Man, if he's not around the next corner, he's got away,'

Martyn indicated and turned onto Olympic, 'and we'll just have to wait and see if he pops up again.'

'That him up there?'

'Could be. Hit the spotlight, Pete.'

A beam shot through the early-morning gloom and picked up the figure in a black coat and jeans crossing in the road. The man – he looked like quite a young guy – stopped, stared at them as they came toward him and then made a run for it again. Darting between a couple of parked cars, he disappeared into a stand of trees on the other side of the road.

'Shit!' Martyn slammed the flat palm of his hand on the steering wheel. 'We'll never find the bastard in there.'

'Pull up. He dropped something in the road.'

Martyn slowed to a halt and Pete got out, bending down to pick up the object the suspect had dropped. 'It's a stick, Mart, maybe he was out with his dog . . .'

Hidden behind a tree, some twenty yards into the wooded area, Cam watched the cruiser roll to a halt and the cop in the passenger seat get out and bend down. He saw him stand up, holding the stick he'd dropped as he ran across the road, and say something to his partner. Moments later they were driving off and Cam realized he was shivering so bad his teeth were chattering. He should get moving again.

Chapter 5

Elliott Ave.; Thursday
February 27th, 5.47 a.m.

Making his way through the woods Cam began to realize he'd been incredibly stupid, the way he'd reacted to the cops. I mean, they couldn't possibly have known what had happened in that house back there . . . how could they? The guys who'd kidnapped him were hardly going to have called 911 when they found the body. More likely they'd be out there now looking for him, trawling the area just like the patrol car, but for some very different reasons.

Maybe he should simply have let the cruiser catch up with him and seen what happened. Maybe he should've forgotten about what he'd done and approached them first, which would not have been easy as he could still see the guard's lifeless eyes staring at him in mute accusation. But running away hadn't achieved anything, except make him look guilty of something – although if he'd told the cops he'd been kidnapped and had escaped would they have believed him? Like, how could he prove it? Jeez, he didn't even have the slightest idea where the damn house was.

Maybe, maybe. Around and around. Around and around in circles . . .

Thinking about things now, as he stumbled through the darkness, there was no question about it: he'd screwed up royally. As well as the kidnappers, he also had the cops looking for him, too.

If only he could get to a phone. Call his parents, who must be frantic . . . his father, anyway. His mother had been weird with him recently, on his case like you wouldn't believe and giving him a hard time about everything. Like it was *his* fault he'd gotten sick. She'd never been quite like other people's mothers, ever, always a little distant; but she'd never been the crabby nightmare she'd been acting like over the last few months. He'd meant to ask his dad what was going on, but there'd never seemed to be the right time. And anyway, how do you ask your dad if his wife is going through the change, or something?

There was a definite lightening in the sky when Cam finally came to the edge of the trees, the light coming from behind him now. Not dawn, but not that far away either. He glanced at the Tag he was now wearing on his wrist: almost six o'clock. He'd been out of the house about an hour and a half, but it seemed like a hell of a lot longer than that. On the up side, it had just about stopped raining, but there was still the heavy cloud cover, so low it felt like a damp blanket pressing down on his shoulders.

In front of him was a wide, six-lane highway, still slick-black from the night's rain, and the other side of it he could make out what appeared to be railyards. Which meant trains. Cam made his way out of the trees and across low scrub to a track that led down to the road. He felt dog-tired and wired at the same time, and he knew he needed some-where, preferably somewhere dry, to rest.

He stood and looked around. This was the opposite of the neighborhood he'd just been in, with lowrise factory units painted in dreary, faded colors, tacky discount stores and parking lots surrounded by chain-link fencing, topped with barbed wire, lining the street. And no phones that he could see. But the gate to one of the lots looked like it was open, the fence at its rear backing directly onto the rail-yards. All he'd have to do was get over that, find some rolling stock going south and he'd be away.

Given the choice of spending however long it took to find a working public phone – with all the chances that would give for him to be picked up by the cops or the kidnappers – and getting on a train and getting out of town, his frazzled logic circuits chose the latter.

Except life was never, ever that simple. All he'd had to do, back at the house, was get let out of the room, and look what had happened. Cam squared his shoulders and smoothed back his wet hair with both hands. Standing by the side of the road, unless he had his thumb out, was never going to get him anywhere.

The traffic was very light, so he made it across the six lanes easily and went over to the gate. Which wasn't open. It had only appeared that way from where he'd been standing, the reality being that it was securely chained and padlocked and, although there was a gap, it wasn't one that looked big enough for him to get through. Ignoring the NO TRESPASSING sign fixed to the gate, Cam checked no one was paying him any attention, then ducked down and tried anyway. No chance. Shit. He did *not* want to get seen doing this, he wanted to get into the railyards and out of sight as quickly as possible. Why the damn *hell* was he being screwed around at every turn?

Cam could feel his anger rising. He felt like kicking the gate, but knew all that was likely to do was get him noticed. He stood for a moment, assessing the width of the gap, and then realized that the coat he was wearing must make a difference, make him bulkier. He took it off, ducked down and tried again. It was a very tight fit and he was about halfway through when something caught. He felt around and found his belt buckle snagging on the steel upright.

He was getting desperate, he wanted this to be over *right now*. Sucking his stomach in and pushing hard with his fingers, Cam felt like he was pressing the buckle against his spine, but his lower half finally slipped through the gap. As he forced his chest to follow, a couple of buttons ripped off, but he'd made it. Getting up and putting his coat back on, Cam glanced around to see if anyone anywhere was taking any notice of him. Not so far as he could tell. Okay . . . everything was okay . . .

Making his way to the rear of the lot, he saw that the barbed wire down there was in a very bad condition, rusted as hell and broken in places. Some good luck at last. He really needed it because the day was breaking fast and he'd soon be left stranded in plain sight. Reaching up and grabbing the chain-link, Cam pulled as he tried to find toe-holds, the sneakers slipping and then gripping as he scrabbled up the fence and swung a leg through a gap where the barbed wire had busted.

Holding on and swaying, like you did on those ropes across rivers and ponds they always had at summer camp, he caught his breath and took what he hoped would be one last look at wherever it was he'd been. Out of the corner of his eye he saw movement over by the road and felt a surge of panic. Swinging his other leg over he dropped to the ground, landing awkwardly on his left foot and falling backward. Putting his right arm out to stop the fall, Cam felt a sharp pain in the palm of his hand. As he got up he saw he'd cut himself on some broken glass. Just great.

The cut didn't look too deep, but it was bleeding a fair amount. Handleable. Behind him Cam could hear voices; this was no time to hang around. He ran across the weed-infested gravel and darted behind the relative safety of a wall of massive corrugated-steel containers.

Out of sight he took a moment to look at his hand: a bloody mess. Remembering the pack of tissues in the jacket pocket, he got them out and used one to wipe off the worst of the blood and grit, spitting on the wound to help clean it up. As he was wadding up a couple more tissues to press down on the cut, he heard a couple of guys on the other side of the fence.

'You sure you saw something, Ray?' said one.

'Some*body*, Jimmy, I saw some*body* climb over the fence,' the second guy replied, 'and there was buttons over by the gate, off of a shirt. That's how he got in – I told Mr. Stevens that chain was too long.'

'You sure you saw someone, you call the yard security man.' The first guy coughed and then spat on the ground. 'Then you done everything you can.'

'Anyone ever tell you, Jimmy? You got the manners of a bad-mannered pig.'

'Not that I heard.'

'You must be deaf as well . . .'

Security. Not what he needed right now. He'd better find somewhere to hide and do it quick.

Making his way into the railyard, his right hand held in a

fist to keep the tissues in place, and beginning to throb, Cam searched for a ticket out of the place, keeping a watchful eye for someone who might realize he shouldn't be there. As he moved cautiously around some outbuildings and what appeared to be abandoned rolling stock, his mind raced as he tried to work out what he was going to do when he found a train that looked like it was going somewhere. I mean, which way was the right way to go?

He was tired, his hand hurt, he was hungry, cold, wet and his brain was dog chow, but he knew he had to think straight and make the right decision. He stopped for a moment, leaning back against a rusting steel signal pole to give himself time to clear his head. He wasn't stupid, he must be able to work this out with what he knew.

Okay, so what did he know? It was – he checked his watch – nearly 6.30 in the morning, he was somewhere in the Pacific Northwest and dawn had finally broken. So east must be behind him, where the sun was rising, west would then be straight in front, and, logic therefore dictated, he needed to get himself on a train going left. Or south, as it was otherwise known. Cam stood up, took a deep breath and started walking again.

He was surrounded by rolling stock, everywhere he looked just miles and miles of freight cars of all types, and somewhere in the distance he could hear the sound of big diesel engines firing up, of voices shouting and massive cast-iron links clanking together as cars began to pull away. It was like a beast waking up, and with every passing minute he felt increasingly exposed. Because the trains seemed to go on forever, with no visible gaps, the only way he could figure to move across the yards was between the cars, ducking underneath the connecting links and praying –

40

ogod-ogod-ogod – as he went that nothing moved because, if it did, there was a very good chance he was going to get crushed in the process.

How long would it take that guy – was it Ray or was it Jimmy? – to phone security, and how long would *they* take to get someone out looking? Who knew. He tried not to worry about that, and just worry about finding a train going south that he could actually get on. Desperately searching left and right, Cam saw open trailers and big, enclosed tanks, he saw grain carriers and containers. What he couldn't see was just a regular boxcar with its side door open so he could get in, like in the movies.

What he needed, he found himself thinking, was for life to be a bit more like the movies and a lot less real. Right now reality sucked, and every move he made just pushed him further away from normality, the way he used to live . . . like, what was he doing, dressed in a dead man's sneakers, wearing a stranger's coat, tired, damp and dirty, not to mention hungry, acting like a total fugitive? Nothing made sense anymore. Nothing. But, he promised himself, as soon as he was out of this place – after he'd called home – he'd go to the cops . . .

Cam was jolted out of poor-me misery mode by the sound of screeching metal as the line of trailer cars behind him began to clang and groan and slowly began to move. He swung around to take a look, stumbling slightly on the gravel, realizing, as the cars began to pick up a bit more speed, that the train was going south!

He moved back a step or two and frantically looked to see if there was a boxcar moving down the track toward him that he could get onto and hide in. Nothing.

Glancing to his right, Cam froze. Way down the front of

the train, where it curved around a bend in the track, he saw two tiny figures. Walking his way. Shit.

He had to move, fast, and that was not going to be easy. Dropping to the ground, he crawled on his hands and knees under the stationary cars on the other track and away from the southbound train. Even if there had been an open boxcar he'd missed his chance. Stuck. Nowhere to go. And dammit, on top of it, he now had the problem of what to do about the two people who may or may not have seen him.

Things were getting so risky, his chances of getting away plummeting every second he remained out in the open, but he had to keep moving until he found either a train going his way or, failing that, the last resort of somewhere to hole up for the rest of the day. These railyards could not go on forever, though, and he was going to run out of places to look. And as that thought sat gloomily on his shoulders the train in front of him lurched to his right, like it was about to move north, then stopped and slowly began to go in the opposite direction.

As far as Cam could see, the whole train was entirely made up of boxcars, and coming down the tracks was one that looked like its door was actually open. Good. But behind him he could hear what sounded like people running, like boots on gravel. Bad. Whether it was people after him or simply his overactive imagination, he just wanted to get the hell out of sight.

Running up the track, heart thumping, palms sweaty, he dropped the bloody tissue and grabbed the side of the open boxcar with both hands as it got to him, pushing off the ground with both feet. He could feel the train picking up speed . . . he could feel his grip slipping . . . he knew that if he screwed up this time it'd all be over. He'd have no energy left, and whoever was looking for him would find him laid out on the ground like some piece of garbage thrown onto the street.

That wasn't going to happen.

From somewhere, he had no idea where, he found the sheer grunt needed to haul himself into the car and out of sight. After that he had nothing left. Nothing.

Chapter 6

Queen Anne Hill; Thursday February 27th, 6.15 a.m.

'Mr. Binay?'

'Yeah, what?' Luiz Binay looked up and saw Ed Barry at the door. He put down the martial arts magazine he was reading as he ate his breakfast, kind of angry at being disturbed.

'It's Joey.'

'What about him?' Luiz looked at his watch. 'Shouldn't he have just come off his shift?'

''At's right . . . I, you know, like went to take over?'

'And?'

'He's permanently off shift. Joey.'

'Say again, Ed?'

'He's dead.'

Luiz Binay could hear Marshall Inverdale's words ringing in his ears. '*I'll do my job,*' he'd said the day before, '*just make sure you do yours . . .*' and knew he was going to take home some shit for this. 'This' being Joey, lying on the floor, choked to death on his own vomit, it looked like, and the Stewart boy nowhere to be seen. Whichever way you played the scenario back, it didn't look good.

Luiz stood up. 'This was how you found him, Ed?'

'Yeah, the door was kinda half open when I got here, Mr. Binay. Place stank of air freshener so I opened a window.' Ed lit up a cigarette and blew smoke through his nostrils. 'Ain't no expert, but this didn't just happen – he's too cold.'

'You touched him?' Luiz looked up.

'Had to check on him, right?'

'You think to check on the boy?' Luiz bent down, picked up the aerosol can lying next to Joey and shook it. Empty. 'You know, look in all the rooms, the rest of the house?'

'Done upstairs, Mr. Binay, before I came to get you. No sign.'

'Must still be here, then. The alarm didn't go off.'

'Uh . . .'

'What, Ed?'

'I, you know, checked the system on my way to get you?'

'And?'

'And downstairs was turned off, Mr. Binay. Upstairs on, downstairs front off.'

'Downstairs front . . .' A grin slowly broke across Luiz's face. Maybe this was going to work out better than he'd thought. 'You're *absolutely* sure, Ed?'

'Yup.'

'Okay.' Luiz walked over and closed the window. 'Ed, I want you to do a thorough check downstairs anyway, just in case, and then go wake up Mr. Inverdale and say I need to see him urgently. Don't tell him anything.'

'What if he asks why?'

'Say you don't know.'

Luiz was sitting in the chair by the small desk, the aerosol can next to his elbow, when Marshall Inverdale walked in, smoothing what was left of his thinning hair across his scalp, looking like he'd just been woken up and was less than happy about the situation.

'This'd better be good, Lu—' Almost tripping over Joey's body stopped Inverdale's tirade before it had time to get properly going.

'Oh, it's very good, Mr. Inverdale.'

'What the hell's going on? What's happened to Joey . . .' The color drained from Inverdale's pockmarked face as he looked around the bedroom. 'Where's . . .'

'He's gone.'

'Gone? How?'

'Far as I can tell, after he'd nixed Joey here with a damn can of *air* freshener,' Luiz pointed at the body with the toe of his black leather Reeboks, 'he walked straight out the front door.'

'He did what? How's that possible?' Inverdale's eyes narrowed. 'The security around here's down to you, Luiz. How the *hell* was he able to that?'

'Because someone asked for the front alarm to be turned off as they were going to be out late . . . and then, apparently, they forgot they said they'd turn it on when they came back.' Luiz made a thing of pushing back his sleeve and glancing down at his watch, not wanting Inverdale to see how hard he was trying not to smile. 'That appears to be how he was able to do it, Mr. Inverdale.'

Silence. The kind when you can almost hear someone's brain working because their mouth is wide open.

'And you know you have that habit of leaving your coat on the chair by the front door? Like when you come in?' Luiz didn't wait for an answer. 'Well, it's gone, too. Unless you didn't leave it there and it's in your room.'

At that moment Ed appeared behind Inverdale, shrugging and shaking his head. No sign of the boy.

Inverdale glanced over his shoulder, aware there was someone behind him. 'I, uh ... I was *sure* I activated the front alarm when I came in . . .'

The man was almost whispering, while his body language insisted the exact opposite of what he was saying was true. Luiz knew he had him in a vice and what he must not do was overplay his hand. If he did he'd lose any advantage he now had.

'Ed.' Luiz stood up, calm, in control. 'Take the Lexus and have a good look around the neighborhood, okay?'

'Okay, Mr. Binay.' Ed disappeared out of the doorway and a moment later came back into view. 'Was that the black leather coat he'd have taken, Mr. Inverdale?'

Inverdale nodded, lighting up a cigarette and waving the smoke out of his eyes. 'It would be, yes.'

Ed disappeared again only to reappear once more. 'Forgot to say, almost forgot to tell you ... there was an item – only a short one – about the boy being lifted. It was on the TV in the kitchen, on Fox News.'

'Picture?'

'Yeah, there was.'

'Okay, Ed. Be careful out there.'

The room fell silent again, only this time there was a tension in the air that crackled like static on a nylon blanket. Inverdale was in the difficult position of being the boss who'd screwed up and then found there was no one else to shift the blame onto. And Luiz could tell he didn't like it one little bit.

'You okay with that, Mr. Inverdale?'

'With what?'

'Ed going out. I should maybe have asked you before sending him.'

'No . . . no, that's fine . . .' Inverdale couldn't work out if Luiz was taking the rise or not. He also couldn't believe the boy had gone. He'd only called Stewart yesterday, as soon as the plane had landed, to tell him what the deal was going to be – basically, that he knew exactly what Stewart was doing, and it was completely fine with him. All he wanted was the electronic transfer of a *lot* of cash to a certain Cayman Islands account to keep quiet about it, plus a continuing interest in Stewart's business. Or the boy was hamburger patty. Your basic shakedown, with a few extra frills. Simple, no-nonsense, businesslike. Except now his leverage had done a disappearing act.

'And Joey?'

Inverdale focussed back on Luiz, frowning. 'What about him? Nothing we can do for him now.'

'You cool with me sticking him in that big freezer out back?' Luiz asked. 'You know, until I can figure where's best to dump him?'

'Whatever you think.' Inverdale turned to go.

'We'll find him.'

'The boy?'

'Yeah.'

'Before he gets to the cops? You really think so, Luiz?'

'I think we got a chance. He'll be freaked, you know, after killing someone? He's not gonna know what to do or where to go. Looks like he's taken Joey's shoes and watch and your coat, but he won't have any money. He's gonna be wandering the streets, Mr. Inverdale, and he can't have gotten far.'

'I hope you're right. I certainly hope you're right.' Inverdale left the room. There was no way, no way at all that he was going to tell Luiz Binay that he'd left his money clip in the jacket. And that it had $250 in it.

Chapter 7

Police HQ, San Diego, CA; Thursday February 27th, 7.09 a.m.

Mike Henrikson was already at his desk when Tony Matric arrived, and looked like he'd been there for some time. Mike wasn't that sad cop cliché of a divorced loner with no life except the job, but he could, in Tony's opinion, afford to loosen up a tad. Like, if a shift was supposed to start at 7.00 a.m. that was, approximately, when you needed to get in.

'How's it going, Mike?' Tony sat down, took the lid off his coffee and blew on a drink he knew was going to be way too hot to even think about drinking for at least five minutes.

'No new developments, no message from the kidnappers, no phone calls, nothing.' Mike looked pointedly at his watch. 'We made the news, though.'

'We did?' Tony ignored the 'you're late' gesture and took the cinnamon twist he'd bought for breakfast out of its brown paper bag and pulled a piece off.

'Yeah, just a short piece on Fox.'

'Well, it did happen late, and the local channels were always going to be more interested in that fire at the dockyard. There were actual *bodies* there, Mike – no contest.'

'So cynical so young.'

Tony blew on the coffee again, taking no notice of the comment. 'Anything back from the labs?'

'Preliminary report on the Volvo,' Mike picked a manila envelope up off his desk, 'but I really don't think there's much more to find out.'

Tony got up, took the proffered envelope and opened its flattened metal clasp. He stood by Mike's desk reading the single sheet of paper it contained. 'They were wearing gloves . . .'

'Well, at least it looks like we're dealing with professionals.'

'And the kid's a doper.'

'They found the *remains* of a joint in the ashtray, is all. Could've been anyone's, and it's not a sign of major drug use. Anyway, I don't think this has *anything* to do with drugs. That's not the feeling I get.'

'What feeling do you get then, Mike?' Tony slid the report back in the envelope and put it down on the desk. 'You still think there's something weird about the kidnap? Like you said last night?'

'Don't you?'

'I never had any involvement with a kidnap before, but, yeah, I been thinking about what you said and it sure *looks* like what they wanted to happen happened.'

'Which is?'

'Someone was gonna notice what they were up to and call the cops, right?'

'Exactly. And that is *not* your standard MO for a kidnapper, who usually does not want to be seen committing the crime and also doesn't want us involved.' Mike picked up the envelope and put it in one of his plastic file trays. 'That's normally part of the deal.'

'Okay, so if they meant for us to get involved, what does *that* mean? Got any ideas?'

'Yeah. I think whoever did it doesn't *care* that we know, they just wanted to shove the message in Mr. Stewart's face. Someone wants him to do something, we just got to find out what and why – which we'll do by taking a much closer look at Mr. and Mrs. Gordon Stewart.'

'You didn't like them, did you, Mike.'

'Who, the parents? Not much . . .'

'Wasn't the best of circumstances we met them under.'

'Did they strike you as particularly distraught?'

'I've seen better performances, but I guess shock kind of affects everyone differently.'

'Yeah, Tony, but it usually *affects* them. Mrs. Stewart was more worried about her make-up and getting the maid to make a freaking cup of coffee.'

Tony went back to his desk. 'There has to be some reason why they were targeted, but like I said to you in the car, they just don't look like they're in that kind of big money league, right?'

'Right.'

'So, we going to take one person each to do some digging on?' Tony's phone rang before Mike could answer. Tony picked it up. 'Hold on, Sarge, let me ask him – Mike, it's the front desk, there's reporters and cameras downstairs. Want to go talk to them or get 'em sent away?'

'Let's go down and speak to the gentlemen of the press and media.' Mike hoisted himself up. 'It's always a good idea to keep them on our side. You want to be the front man, seeing as how you're always telling me you're so goddam photogenic?'

'Just so I can be the one looking like a fool because we've got nothing to give 'em? I don't think so, Mike.'

'What d'you know, you really aren't as stupid as people've been telling me . . .'

Chapter 8

Hayesville–Salem, OR; Thursday February 27th, 11.39 a.m.

Cam slowly picked himself up and watched the freight train go rumbling by. Like some giant ancient creature, a never-ending metal snake on wheels that squealed and grumbled over the rails, it carried on its way without him. He stood, slightly dazed, and watched it go. Even though the train had looked like it was traveling slowly enough to make for an easy jump it had still hurt like a bastard when he'd hit the stony ground and rolled down a slight incline, and now he'd added a couple of new aches to his still-throbbing hand. The cut had stopped bleeding, and his palm was now crusted with dried blood mixed with garbage from the floor of the boxcar. He'd clean it up as soon as he found a restroom. Dusting himself down with his good hand, Cam looked at the Tag. The one, a small whisper reminded him, that he'd taken off the guy he'd killed. It didn't seem possible, but he'd been asleep for over four hours.

Even though he didn't know exactly where he was right now, he did know where he'd come from. As the train had headed south out of the railyards, right there on the skyline he'd seen the unmistakable silhouette of the Space Needle. Seattle.

Why he'd been brought all the way up there – out of state and almost out of the country – Cam had no idea. But he'd figured, as soon as the train had gotten some way out of the city, he'd get off, get to a phone and call home. He'd tell his father everything – absolutely everything – and hope he would know what to do about it.

It was a good plan, except that he'd been so exhausted by lack of sleep, so stressed by the events surrounding his escape, that even a gnawing hunger couldn't keep him awake. He'd closed his eyes and the next thing he knew it was almost midday and Seattle and the Space Needle were long gone.

Cam walked across scrubland toward a road on which he could see the occasional pickup and car moving. If he was lucky the train had continued on its southward journey and he was four hours closer to home, hopefully somewhere in Oregon and not whatever was east of Seattle. Dakota? Montana? Who knew, geography was the kind of subject where he'd have to go straight to the phone-a-friend option.

Finally, when he got to the dusty edge of what turned out to be a two-lane blacktop, there wasn't a vehicle in sight and Cam began to wonder if he'd made the right decision to bail on the train. It had seemed like a good idea at the time, more proactive than sitting on his backside doing sweet nothing, with his rationale to himself being that, once off the train, he'd at least have a better chance of finding a phone.

A phone. All he needed was one damn phone booth and a collect call to La Jolla and his troubles would begin to be over. It really should be that simple. The thought that he could be minutes away from lifting a receiver and talking to his parents almost made him forget the aches as he limped toward the crossroads he could see ahead of him. Nearing the intersection, he saw a road sign indicating that if he went right he was just a mile and a quarter from Interstate 5. That went all the way to San Diego! Cam picked up speed, energized by the thought that this could all be over soon.

Five minutes later he turned off the sidewalk and made his way across the half-empty asphalt parking lot, toward the double glass doors of the coffee shop that was part of an Amoco gas station. In the distance he could just make out the Interstate. And cutting through the sharp, oily tang of gasoline, he could smell bacon and sausage. His stomach churned and growled. He'd never been so hungry.

Approaching the doors, Cam caught sight of his reflection in the dusty glass. He looked so bad, like the kind of person who'd be asked to leave if they walked into a cafe back home, and he stopped for a moment, wiping his hands on the back of his jeans and then attempting to tidy his hair. Like that would make all the difference.

Taking a deep breath he walked to the doors. He was about to pull the right one open when a flickering light inside the coffee shop made him look up. Which was when he noticed the crappy old TV on a wall bracket above the counter. The crappy old TV with his face on it.

Cam let the door go, turned right around and walked back down toward the road. He suddenly didn't feel hungry anymore, he felt sick. That had to have been a newscast, which must mean, somehow, they knew he'd killed that guy back in Seattle. Didn't it? Like, what else *could* it mean? The less freaked side of his brain said it could just as well be a story about his kidnapping. Paranoia completely trashed the idea of finding out if it was true. As he sloped away from the coffee shop, frantically looking around for another place that might have a phone, Cam noticed a very new-looking, bright red Dodge Ram 2500 Quad pull over from the pumps and park up. California plates. Four doors, short back, very nice.

A guy got out on the driver's side and slammed the door like he was pissed about something. Pale and punk thin, he had shaggy, dark brown hair and the kind of face that looked like it spent more time saying no than yes. A girl opened the passenger door and got out. Sweet. She had bangs and reddish-brown, shoulder-length hair, blood-red nails, lots of rings and bangles, and was wearing a tight, green camouflage T-shirt and plaid pants cut just below the knee. She was looking at the guy, eyebrows raised, in a 'Who's rattled *your* cage?' kind of way.

'What is your *problem*, Jax?'

The guy stopped and turned around. 'You, Tee. You've been picking holes since we left.'

'I don't *think* so, you just take everything I say like it's a criticism.' She closed the truck door and pulled a pair of wraparound sunglasses down off the top of her head. 'You gonna lock it?'

The guy jabbed a fistful of keys at the Dodge and the locks chunked shut. 'Okay, you wanna get some lunch or what?'

Without waiting for the girl to answer, Mr. Sweetness-and-Light walked off toward the coffee shop, head down, looking like he'd sucked on a lemon. The girl followed him, coolly looking Cam over as she went past, although he couldn't actually see her eyes through the lightly mirrored lenses.

'How long till we get back, Jaxon?'

'I already told you. We should be in LA early tomorrow morning, like, you know, around 1.30? That okay?'

The coffee shop door closed and Cam didn't hear her reply.

He looked over at the red Dodge pickup. It was going to LA. His uncle was in LA. He could try asking for a lift, but he had a fair idea what the guy's answer would be. Glancing behind him, Cam walked over to the truck.

Chapter 9

Weed, CA, I-5 exit; Thursday
February 27th, 4.44 p.m.

It had been a wild guess, really taking a chance, but Cam hadn't had much choice. He either got in back of the pickup or he wandered around looking for a phone, in full view of anyone who might've seen the news report about him. So he'd bet that neither the driver, nor his passenger, would bother to look behind in the empty load bay before they drove off, and he'd been right.

One glance at the Dodge Ram and Cam had known it was a total pose-mobile. From the near-pristine state of the back he'd reckoned it was unlikely to have ever carried anything other than a light load of groceries, and they had more than likely sat up front on the rear passenger seat. The truck had been parked next to a dirty white Toyota van, which meant that when Cam had ducked in between them he was pretty much hidden from the view of anyone in the coffee shop or passing in the street. He did a couple of fast prairie dogs to check if anyone was looking his way, and then upped and rolled himself over the side and lay still, right up against the cab wall, and waited.

*   *   *

Four of the longest, most uncomfortable hours of Cam's life later, the pickup pulled off the Interstate and came to a stop. In the relative silence, with only the hum of traffic in the background, Cam could hear the muffled voices of the driver and his passenger, still bickering at each other.

He poked his head up and saw they were in a gas station. By now he had a hunger that felt like his stomach was eating itself and he was just so completely desperate to get some food he didn't care what happened to him anymore.

Sitting up he rapped on the rear window with his knuckle.

The girl – what had the guy called her . . . Tee? – turned around, did a double take and then just sat looking at him, mouth half open. The driver – Cam remembered the girl calling him Jax or something – glanced at what she was looking at, frowned when he saw Cam and then flung open his door. He came around to the back jabbing his finger like it was a pistol, held sideways, like in the movies.

'Who th'*hell* are you? What're you doin' in my truck?'

'I needed a ride, man . . .' Cam moved further away from the stabbing fist.

'You ever think of, like *askin'*?'

'Yeah, but –'

'But *nothin'*, guy . . . now get out.' The fist jerked backward over his shoulder.

Just what was it with this guy? Cam wondered. Didn't he *ever* lighten up? Getting up, he heard the girl open her door and exit out the other side of the cab. He glanced over his shoulder and saw she was standing, head on one side, looking up at him through her sunglasses.

'I saw him before, Jaxon, like at the gas station? Just before we got on the freeway?'

'You been in back all the time?' Jaxon angrily pointed a

pistol finger again.

'Well he couldn't've gotten in anywhere else, Jax. This is the first time we've stopped.'

The finger moved to point at the girl – 'Quit it, Tee!' – and came back up to Cam. 'Are you making tracks, like I said, or what?'

'Look, I needed a ride, man . . . you were my only way out of there.' Cam leaned one hand down on the truck side, stepped his left leg up and jumped onto the ground, landing a couple of feet from Tee.

'If you've scratched the paint . . .' Jaxon came hurtling around to face Cam and Tee.

'It's a *truck*, Jax . . . it's *supposed* to get roughed up, right?' Tee moved around behind Cam and stood between him and Jaxon. 'I know it's new, but get over it.' She turned and looked at Cam. 'Are you, like running away?'

'Kind of . . .'

'Cool, what from?'

'Who cares, Tee.' Jaxon grabbed Tee's arm and pulled her as he walked away. 'Let's go.'

Tee yanked her arm away and stayed where she was, ignoring Jaxon. 'Are you in trouble, like with the cops?'

Cam didn't know what to do or what to say, but he realized he had to tell these people something or they'd just leave him, stuck in whatever godforsaken place they were in.

'Look . . .' he stared at Tee's mirrored lenses, seeing only his own distorted reflection, '. . . I'm in a world of trouble, okay? And I've *got* to get back to San Diego, but I got no money, I haven't eaten since almost two days ago and I'm sorry if I've pissed you guys off, but you were my only chance . . .'

Jaxon was still hanging around, unable to be as totally uninterested as he wanted to appear. 'Why should we care?'

Tee shot him a thin-lipped glance. 'What's your name?'

'Cam. Cam Stewart.'

'What happened, Cam?'

Cam was about to say something when he was hit by a stomach cramp and grimaced.

'You okay?' Tee frowned at him.

'Nothing some food wouldn't cure.'

'Let's eat, then.'

'I'm flat broke,' Cam shrugged. 'I got nothing but what I'm standing up in, and most of that's not mine.'

'I think we can spot you a burger and fries . . .'

They sat in a booth over in the corner of the small burger bar next to the gas station in a small dot on the map called Weed; Cam on one side, Tee and Jaxon on the other. Jaxon was looking at him like he smelled. Which, probably, he did. And not for the first time Cam wondered what the hell a cool girl like Tee was doing with a spoiled-brat guy like him.

The thought remained with him as he watched them watching him stuffing a greasy double cheeseburger and fries into his mouth as fast as he could. Food had never, not *ever*, tasted as good as this. His hand felt better, too, now that it'd been washed and had a blue Band-Aid on it that the waitress had been kind enough to give him.

Tee had told him to eat and then talk, and he'd taken her at her word. This also gave him time to think what to do, what to tell them. Could he tell them *everything*? Would that make Jaxon more or less willing than he already was to take him to LA?

Thing was, if he made up a story that wasn't convincing, and they figured he was lying, he'd be screwed; and if he told them the whole truth, or at least enough of it to actually be convincing, they might call 911 at the first opportunity. Maybe, he thought, it'd be best to stop short of admitting to murder, or manslaughter or whatever it was that he'd done back there in Seattle.

'So,' Jaxon swept some spilt salt off the Formica tabletop, 'what's the story, morning glory?'

Cam sat back, glancing from Jaxon to Tee and back, and took a deep breath. 'I was kidnapped, like back in San Diego? They, uh, they must've drugged me, cos the next thing I knew, after my ass was hauled out my car right in front of my house, I was waking up locked in some bedroom. Which, it turns out, was in Seattle.'

'Your old man rich or something?' asked Jaxon.

'Rich? Not really . . . he does okay, but he's not some multi-millionaire or anything.'

'What's he do?' Tee looked up from cleaning her sunglasses, and Cam noticed she had blue, blue eyes.

'My dad? He runs a business communications thing called Contxt, cell phones and stuff.'

'So why kidnap *you*, guy?' Jaxon, pointing the finger again.

Cam remembered the voice he'd heard in the bedroom back in Seattle, could hear the man saying: '*Have you been in touch with Stewart yet?*', which made it sound like they, whoever they were, knew his father. But what could his father be involved in that was worth kidnapping for?

'Why *you*, guy?' Jaxon repeated, reaching over and prodding Cam this time.

'I dunno . . . how the hell would *I* know? I just got lifted off the damn street.'

'You sure you didn't run away from home, then run out of cash?'

'Leave it out, Jax. Just because you fabricate all the time doesn't mean everyone else does.' Tee picked out all the brown sugar sachets from the bowl and lined them up neatly. 'How'd you escape?'

'I sprayed an aerosol can right in some guy's face . . .' Cam paused.

'And?' Jaxon shrugged.

'And what?'

'And that's how you got away, a quick *ph-ssst!* of deodorant and you walk out?'

'It was air freshener. Just about a whole can.'

'Cool, a *whole* can.' Jaxon kind of smiled. 'Whyn't you go straight to the cops when you got out? Why're you hiding like some crim when you're like the *victim*?'

Cam had come across people like Jaxon before, sly guys who liked to pull wings off flies, stick pins into small animals . . . guys who delighted in pain and destruction. He knew Jaxon was pushing him, needling him, trying to get a reaction out of him. He could feel himself tensing. He wasn't hungry anymore, but he ached and he was antsy and he wanted to get the hell home.

'I killed him . . . I'm a victim *and* a criminal. Okay?'

'Killed who?' Tee frowned.

'The guy guarding the room I was being kept in. He was gagging, he couldn't see and I just kept spraying until he collapsed. I think he must've chucked up . . . I took his sneakers and this watch,' Cam held out his left wrist, 'and I went.'

'You took the guy's *sneakers*?' Jaxon looked weirdly shocked, like taking someone's shoes was somehow worse than killing them. 'Why?'

'I didn't have any.'

'Are you sure he was dead?' Tee looked straight at him, slightly quizzical, as she began sorting the pink sachets. 'Like did you check?'

'Why didn't you have any shoes?'

Tee glanced to her left. 'Jesus, Jax, will you quit with the damn shoes? It's not important . . .'

'I did check, and I couldn't feel a pulse . . . He was dead.'

'Awesome. But I don't see why you didn't go to the cops.'

It sounded like a much more reasonable doubt when Tee said it, and Cam looked away for a moment, thinking about how he'd felt when he'd seen the black-and-white in the street: scared, guilty, hyped. 'I was freaked . . . I just ran, I had to get away. That's all I could think about.'

'How'd you end up in Hayesville, of all places?'

'I jumped a train.'

'Killer hobo,' Jax sniggered.

Tee ignored him. 'You call anyone yet?'

'*Shit* . . .' Cam had been so hungry he'd completely forgotten about ringing home. He got up and looked around for a phone. 'Gotta call my dad! They took my cell and I –'

'Over in the corner, by the washrooms,' Jaxon nodded, looking behind Cam.

'You can use my cell . . .' Tee started to rummage in her bag.

'It's okay.' Cam got up and began walking off toward the payphone. Stopping, he patted his pockets and turned back. 'No money . . .'

'Make it collect, stupid.' Jaxon shook his head.

As Cam made his way over to the phone he was sure he heard Tee call Jaxon an asshole. On the nail there, girl, he thought as he picked up the chipped, slightly oily receiver. Right on the nail.

Five minutes later Cam slid back into the booth and slumped against the cracked red vinyl. He could feel the tension, the pressure that had built up to the point where he felt like he'd tear himself apart, gradually fading and being replaced by coma-like exhaustion.

'What he say, your dad?'

Cam sat up, pushed his hair back and took a deep breath, feeling like he hadn't had enough oxygen for days. 'He couldn't believe it was me . . . wanted to know where I was, how I'd got here and stuff, was I okay . . . he said he'd call the cops, like let them know I was free, and to get myself down to my cousin's place in West Hollywood,' he looked over at Jaxon, 'if a lift's still okay . . . cos my dad said he'd send a car to pick me up there.'

'Whereabouts you wanna go?' Jaxon, being halfway friendly.

'Just off Santa Monica, south of Melrose.'

'It's on our way, right?' Tee shot a glance at Jaxon and then looked back at Cam. 'Jaxon's place is on the PCH, almost opposite Wilshire.'

'Cool.'

'You know it?' Jaxon waved at the waitress for the check.

Cam nodded. 'I spent a lot a time fooling around on the pier and the beach with my cousin, like when we've visited them.'

'It's my dad's place, but it's just me and Tee, and sometimes my brother, now that my dad got hitched again last year.'

Cam didn't know quite what to do with Jaxon 2.1, the new

improved version. What the hell could Tee have said to him? The bill came and Cam watched Jaxon pay, embarrassed that someone else was having to pick up his tab.

'When this is all over, I'll come back to LA and take you guys out, right?'

'Whatever, man.' Jaxon wasn't looking at him, stuffing bills into his jeans pocket. 'This isn't a problem, like it's good to do the Samaritan thing once in a while, right, Tee?'

'Right, Jax.'

'I'm gonna take a leak. See you out by the car?'

'Gimme the keys, then.' Jaxon twisted around on his heel as he left the table and lobbed the keys back at Tee, who plucked them out of midair like a true pro. She sat waiting till he was out of earshot and then got up. 'He's not a bad person, most of the time . . . you just caught him on one of his dickhead days.'

'What did you say to him?'

'I told him to quit being such a hardass, like even if you weren't telling the truth – which I happen to think you are – all you needed was a damn lift, and what harm would that do? And like wouldn't *he* want people to give *him* a break if the tables were turned? Honest to God, he's like a kid sometimes, Jaxon. He gets jealous and needs bringing back down to earth.'

Chapter 10

Santa Monica Blvd. & Robertson, LA; Friday February 28th, 12.34 a.m.

Six hours later they came down Santa Clarita and drove on into San Fernando. Ordinarily, Jaxon would have taken 405 down to Santa Monica, but, still in nice mode, he'd agreed with Tee that they could drop Cam off right near Dorrington if they went on, took the Hollywood Freeway and came off at Highland.

An hour or so on, Jaxon pulled up by the curb, just north of Doheny, and put the shift into neutral. Tee looked over at the back seat where Cam was shrugging on the leather coat he'd taken from the house in Seattle.

'You cool with this? Being dropped here?'

'This is great, guys . . . it's only like a couple of blocks over. I'll be fine now.' Cam reached across and lightly touched Jaxon's shoulder. 'Thanks, man . . .'

'No problem.' Jaxon turned, nodded and gave a half smile as Cam opened the door and stepped onto the sidewalk. He felt wiped, but so close to a home he knew, to family who cared, that the tiredness didn't matter.

Tee lowered her window. 'Well, it's been interesting, gotta say that, real interesting . . . never expected this trip would get us involved with a kidnappee. So, look after yourself, Cam, it's a wicked world out there!'

Jaxon threw the gear into first, dropped the clutch and the truck squealed off into the night, Tee waving out of her window for a second or two. Cam stood, watching the truck blend into the traffic, the sharp smell of freshly-laid rubber pricking his nostrils, and thought how totally weird life could get . . . that you could meet people, spend time with them, travel hundreds of miles together, sharing thoughts, ideas and stuff, and then they were gone and you'd likely never see them ever again.

He looked around, searching for the nearest way across the boulevard, and wondered if anyone would be up at his uncle's house at – he glanced at the Tag – nearly twenty of one. Cam had told his dad it'd be late when he arrived – he hoped he wouldn't have to wake anybody when he got there.

Walking to the nearest set of lights, he stood and waited for them to change so he could cross. As he waited, something glinted in the periphery of his vision and he glanced down. In the gutter, half hidden by general road detritus, he focussed on a handful of change that must have fallen out of someone's pocket. His dad always picked up coins he found in the street, said they were lucky, and force of habit made Cam bend down and do the same.

The DON'T WALK sign turned to WALK as he collected the six or seven coins and he waited till he was the other side to count what he'd gotten. Eighty-nine cents in change. Cam blew most of the dust off, put the money in the coin pocket of his jeans and set off to walk the two blocks down Doheny to the Dorrington turn, oddly happy that he wasn't totally broke anymore. Maybe his dad was right, he thought

69

– maybe it was a good sign.

As he walked he thought about the journey from the aptly named Weed down to LA. A lot of the time had been spent listening to music – the Dodge Ram, naturally, had an awesome sound system and Jaxon had an equally cool selection of CDs, both purchased and custom-burned – but they had talked, too. In fact, once he had got started, Jaxon was pretty free with the information.

Coming from a typical media family, Jaxon Colby's father was something big and sexy and unspecified in the movie business, his mother a delinquent PR queen. They'd divorced thirteen years ago, when he was nine and his brother, Sy, was eleven, and his dad had since been married twice, the latest go-round being to a woman twenty years his junior, or what Jaxon called a trophy wife.

A couple of months after their divorce, Jaxon's mother had realized she was a lesbian and gone to live in Monterey, leaving the boys with their father and a series of Hispanic maids. Which meant, Jaxon said, that he and Sy both spoke fluent Spanish and were pretty up to speed on the geography of Central America.

It didn't sound anything like the stable, run-on-rails kind of life Cam had had. His parents, who'd known each other since their sophomore year, had started dating in college and got married soon after graduation, were the other end of the family spectrum from Jaxon's. His mother had never, so far as he knew, worked, and hadn't ever, in his presence at least, uttered the word lesbian. He too had grown up with live-in help around the house, but it was the kind of help that he'd mostly had little to do with, the kind of help that called his dad 'Sir' and his mother 'Ma'am' and stayed in their quarters until called upon to be of service. Some he got on with, like the woman, Consuela, who was there now; others he'd hardly said one word to the whole time they'd been in the house.

Thinking about it, his own life had always been far more defined by what he did outside of his house and his family – the sports, school, his longstanding friendship with Kenny and Ted, the clubs they belonged to – than it was by his relationship with his parents. His father was a driven, busy, busy man who always managed to find time for him when he needed it, and his mother . . . well, he thought, he'd always assumed she cared, because that's what mothers did.

Tee, whose name was actually Taylor Philips, had, Cam now realized, given out few personal details about herself. It was Jaxon who had told him how long they'd been together – six months, give or take – that they'd met at a club somewhere in Westwood, and the fact that Tee, unlike him, was not a born and bred Angelino. All she'd really mentioned about herself was that she'd grown up in the Valley – Reseda, he thought she'd said – and that she was between jobs, a comment that'd made Jaxon snigger and Tee punch his arm in response, admitting, okay, so she hadn't actually worked much since moving in with him.

Although Jaxon had, over the journey, become a lot friendlier than he'd been when Cam first met him, he was still someone whom Cam wouldn't naturally have spent much time with under more normal circumstances. Tee, on the other hand, was a different matter. He found her totally fascinating – sharp, funny, good company, great looking – though he'd been very aware that she'd told him Jaxon was the jealous type, so he thought it was probably best not to be over-friendly. And he still couldn't work out why she was with the guy. Unless it was the money . . . and the wheels, the house on the beach and all the other stuff a rich daddy's money could buy. But could she really be that shallow?

Part of him, the part that had chosen to kind of forget they probably would never meet again, really hoped not.

Cam was suddenly aware that he'd been walking for some time on autopilot. He looked up and saw a road sign some way down the street and realized it said the next left was Rosewood and that meant he'd gone way past his turning.

He began walking back down the street, still thinking about Tee, about why would a girl like that ever choose to go out with a guy who drove a beat-up old Volvo? *Used* to drive, he reminded himself, as the image of a white van flashed in his head . . . he could hear the sound of tearing metal as it smashed into him, the sound of splintering plastic and glass, the sudden explosion of an airbag right in front of his face. It was only a couple of days ago, but it seemed like years. Cam reached Dorrington and turned right.

His uncle's house was halfway up the street on the left-hand side, and he could feel a sense of relief flooding through him as he walked over the other side of the road and began looking for the grey slatted gates and fence that fronted the property. He was just approaching some house's fancy stone gateway, complete with integral video entry, when its IR sensor switched on a halogen spotlight and almost blinded him. Holding his arm up in front of his face, Cam exited the cone of acid white light and carried on walking.

'There he is!' The voice, coming from somewhere up ahead, sounded very excited.

There's who? thought Cam, fuzzy white blobs still burned into his retina so he couldn't see properly. Then car headlights switched on and he heard an engine being cranked up and turning over.

'It's him!'

Instinct overrode everything. Cam didn't stop to think why him, he just ran for his life.

Chapter 11

Dorrington Ave., LA; Friday February 28th, 1.34 a.m.

Behind him, too close for comfort, Cam could hear voices shouting, hear the wheels of the vehicle spinning like crazy, trying to get some grip and take off after him. Who the hell these guys were he had no idea, nor what the hell they were doing waiting for him outside his uncle's house. Were they cops? The kidnappers? But this was not the time to stop and figure things out.

As he ran, arms pumping, legs a blur, he had a kind of weird déjà vu thing happening. This was just like back in Seattle, with the cop car after him; only now it was warm and dry. Skidding around the corner onto Almont, Cam hared down the street, aware that this time the big difference was that this car was a heck of a lot closer.

Up ahead he could see lights coming down the street toward him, fast, and seconds after the car went past there was a screech of brakes, blaring horns and raised voices. Cam risked a glance over his shoulder and saw that his pursuers were momentarily blocked from following him by the other car. Looked like his dad knew a thing or two as it seemed like picking up those coins had turned out to be lucky after all.

He knew he had to use these vital seconds gained from the screw-up down the street, but how? Basically, he had to get off the street, that much was obvious. The longer he stayed visible, the more likely they'd catch him, whoever they were. He slowed down. Across the road, behind a low picket fence, there was a mid-sized, Spanish-style house, one car out front, no lights showing, with a pathway leading down the side, presumably to the back yard. A pathway that was partially overgrown by bushes. Hoping no one involved with chasing him could make out what he was doing too well, Cam bent low and scooted over to the other side of the street.

Art Kellaway Jr. was shitfaced. But what the hell, there was nobody to give him a hard time for it and he might very well just stay that way for the next four days. *They* wouldn't be home till next damn Tuesday, Terri and the girls, so what did he care? 'Cept maybe he'd better sober up Sunday night on account of he did have to go to work Monday. He'd make a note, stick it on the fridge to remind himself.

Art didn't like being left on his own, but he liked visiting his in-laws even less, the stuck-up bastards. They'd never liked him. Thought he was a blue-collar redneck, even though he was a junior veep with a nationally advertised brokerage company. So he voted Republican, was a fully paid-up member of the NRA and had a pro-life bumper sticker – so what? The bumper sticker was just a wind-up joke anyway, and screw 'em if they couldn't take a joke . . .

Art popped another can of beer and took a bite out of the stuffed-crust double-hot pepperoni that had recently been delivered by some obvious illegal (damned if *he* was gonna cook himself one damned thing this weekend, and that included nuking what had been left in the freezer for him). Wiping his hands on his jeans, Art picked up his Glock 21 and sighted it at the picture in the big silver frame that dominated the collection on top of the piano. Walter and Jo-Ann Frieslander. Boy, didn't *they* look smug.

'Pow!' Art's right hand leaped up in the air as he faked the .45's recoil. And it was genuinely fake as, truth be known, Art had never actually fired the gun. One day, he was always promising himself, he'd get around to joining a club. Meantime he'd make do with imagining the crapped-up mess he'd've made of the hateful picture of his in-laws if he really had fired (he could see them now, sitting around the dining table in their big Studio City condo with *his* family, looking so damn superior).

Art reached over and took the fully loaded clip out of the lockable metal box where he kept the gun, pushed it into the grip and put a bullet in the barrel. I mean, why not? No kids around or anything.

That was when he heard the racket half a dozen aluminum recliners make when someone knocks them over and freaks out your stupid cat.

Art, all 5'11", 230lbs of him, was up out of his chair like someone had stapled his ass, which would have been an impressive sight, if anyone had been there to see it. And it was all the more impressive as, during this process, he'd disengaged the Glock's trigger safety mechanism and fired the pistol, and now Art didn't have to imagine the crapped-up mess a bullet would make of his in-laws' picture. Or the hole a .45 calibre bullet made in his wall.

Ignoring for a moment exactly how he was going to explain all this to Terri, Art shook his head in a vain attempt to get rid of a substantial beer buzz and the loud ringing he now had in his ears and made straight for the patio doors. As he opened them, letting the fresh night air in and the smell of cordite out, the solar-powered yard lamps he'd bought the previous week turned on and he saw a figure in a black jacket running away from him toward the back fence. Through *his* yard! Art was gonna protect his damn property, see if he wasn't . . .

The trouble with dark, overgrown pathways was, while no one could see you, you couldn't see a thing either. In the relative quiet, Cam had to admit that aluminum yard furniture cascading to the ground, followed by a screeching cat, made a hell of a noise. No point in creeping about now, so he disentangled himself and legged it for the rear of the yard, only to set off a series of antiqued, motion-activated, lantern-style lights.

Behind him he heard what sounded like doors sliding open and then there was a hysterically loud explosion and the light a couple of yards in front of him disintegrated into a million pieces. Gunfire? Had his pursuers caught up already? A slurred voice was yelling something he couldn't understand and, at the same time as he heard the bark of the gun going off again, what felt like a red-hot poker whacked his left upper arm. Christ . . . he'd been hit!

Although his arm was hurting like shit, Cam kept running as a third and then a fourth shot were fired and must've gone wild. In front of him he could see, in the yellow glow of the lanterns, the end of the yard coming up. Instead of being able to take his time and quietly negotiate getting over the fast approaching six-foot-plus fence, he was going to have to do it as fast as he could.

Cam sped up, and when he was three or four feet from

the fence he leaped and made a grab for the top, gasping from the stab of pain in his arm but not letting go. Scrabbling with his feet as he hauled himself up, he swung a leg over and rolled, it seemed like in slo-mo, until he felt it was okay to let go and drop to the ground on the other side. The landing sent a burning jolt up his arm and he realized he could feel something warm and sticky running down his left arm. He glanced down and saw a dark stain as blood trickled onto the pale flesh of the palm of his hand. Not good. He stood, panting, waiting till he got his breath back, and wondering if the shooting was going to start again . . . listening for the sound of someone coming down the yard. Listening hard. Nothing.

He wasn't being followed – he'd just had the misfortune to disturb some whacked-out gun nut who, thankfully, couldn't shoot too straight.

Art stood a little unsteadily on the patio, a hand over one eye as he tried to focus on his back yard. With both eyes open, as he'd discovered firing the Glock, things tended to double up. He couldn't see any sign of the intruder and, frankly, he was too tired to give a shit right now. Right now what he felt like he really deserved was another beer to celebrate the successful defense of his property and the christening of his gun.

Back inside the house Art discovered the phone was ringing, or rather the base unit was, and for the life of him he couldn't figure out where he'd put the handset, so he left it and went off to the refrigerator.

Chapter 12

Almont Drive, LA; Friday February 28th, 2.01 a.m.

Cam reached over and felt his upper arm, finding two ragged holes in the smooth black leather. He had to get somewhere quiet, with more light, and take a closer look at the damage which, if he was lucky, wouldn't be as bad as it felt.

He crept out of the bushes and scanned the property he now found himself in, wondering what could possibly happen to him here. Rabid guard dogs? The place looked quiet enough, no one out looking to see what all the noise had been about, although there was a light on in one of the downstairs rooms. Cam knew staying put was not an option, and he'd have to risk it and just get out of this place as fast as he could.

Keeping to the edge of the yard, he walked quickly toward the side of the house furthest away from the lighted window, making the shadows without incident. Another ten, twelve feet and he came to a substantial metal grille spanning the gap between the house and the boundary wall. Topped with spikes, there was no gate in it and he wasn't even going to think about trying to climb over. Which meant he had to go around to the other side of the house and hope to hell it wasn't the same around there.

Cam stood, drenched in sweat and frustration, pissed, angry and in pain. All he wanted to do was go home – why couldn't he just go home? He felt like screaming, bellowing his bitterness and resentment at the night, like kicking something to get his own back. Instead, he peered around the corner of the house and ran as quietly as he could to the opposite corner. Somewhere in the distance he could hear police sirens and wondered if they had anything to do with the recent outbreak of hostilities he'd caused.

There was also a grille down the other side, but this one had a gate in it. Padlocked, dammit. Instead of panicking, Cam kept it together and began to search as carefully and quietly as he could, hoping, hoping, hoping that the guy in this house was like his dad and had left the key somewhere 'safe'.

It was under the fifth plant pot he tried.

Walking down the street, attempting to look inconspicuous but also like he belonged there, Cam tried to figure out what had happened at his uncle's house. A nagging thought kept on coming back to him: who else but his father had known he was going to be arriving at the house on Dorrington?

It didn't make sense. Why would his dad rat him out? But then . . . what if those people had been sent *by* his dad? On the phone he'd only said he'd arrange to get him picked up, he hadn't specified when. Cam had just assumed it would be the next day – it had never occurred to him anyone would be waiting for him when he arrived. He stopped walking. Should he go back? What if his first reaction had been right and those people were still there and they *weren't* from his father? In the end caution and paranoia won out and he carried on toward the brighter lights of Santa Monica Boulevard. He'd find another pay phone and call home and check stuff out first.

Before that, though, he had to deal with his arm. The wound was still bleeding, while the pain had subsided slightly into a dull but throbbing ache. He wouldn't be able to do much, but anything was better than nothing. Nearing the main street, he saw a small parking lot with a couple of dumpsters in it and he went behind them. Seconds later a black four-door sedan with two men in it glided by, turning left on Santa Monica. He didn't see them, they didn't see him.

Kneeling down, Cam gingerly took off the leather coat, examining the bullet holes: one small and fairly neat, the other bigger and more ragged. Entry and exit. The thought flicked across his mind, like what kind of damage would've been done had the bullet hit his actual body? Putting the coat down on the tarmac he undid his shirt and half took it off. In the chill night air his skin goosebumped as he looked at the bloody gouge the bullet had ploughed through his deltoid muscle, a few inches below the shoulder joint. Looked like it'd taken out the cent-sized immunization scar he'd had and given him an altogether much bigger one.

He removed his shirt completely and ripped the left arm off, wiping as much blood as he could from his hand with the sleeve and then using it as a bandage, binding it around the wound as tight as was possible with one hand. Cam then put the one-armed shirt back on, followed by the jacket, and stood up. He felt dizzy, steadying himself against one of the dumpsters for a moment. He wasn't going to be playing football for quite some more time to come, the state he was getting into, but he couldn't stand around whining to himself about that. What he had to do now was to find a phone.

The first one he came to had been vandalized to extinction, but the next was in reasonable working order and he dialed the operator to make his second collect call home. But no one was there. Nobody to accept the charge. So he couldn't even leave a message.

Cam put the handset down, turned and leaned back against the phone. What the hell now? He was totally stymied, no one to talk to. All his friends – all the friends whose numbers he knew off by heart – were away, off playing football and having a great time. Anyway, circumstances like these there weren't *that* many you *could* call . . . for him it would be Kenny or Ted, the tightest buddies you could ever have and the two guys who'd always be there for him. Except now they weren't.

As there was no way for him to get in touch with them, and nowhere for him to go, that left him stranded in West Hollywood with – he dug the coins out of his jeans – 89 cents to his name. Shit. What were his parents doing not being at home? He was about to pick up the receiver again and ask to be put through to his dad's cell when he remembered that both his parents had had their numbers changed recently and he hadn't memorized them. Shit, again.

He'd been staring into the middle distance for he didn't know how long when his eye caught and held an old red pickup turning onto the street some way down. It made him stand up straight, suddenly alert. He did know someone, two people . . . Jaxon and Tee. True, he didn't know their phone number or address or anything relevant like that, but he could hear Tee's voice in his head – '*Jaxon's place is on the PCH, almost opposite Wilshire*' – and figured it would be the only place on that part of the Pacific Coast Highway with a brand new, bright red Dodge Ram parked outside.

All he had to do was get there.

Except the chump change he was carrying was not going to get him very far. Could he hitch? Right . . . this time of night someone sane and trustworthy was going to stop and pick *him* up, the way he looked. So *not* going to happen. Cam didn't know how many miles it was down to the beach, probably five or six, maybe more, but he did know that he was in no state to walk it. No way. He was just about to reconsider the whole hitching thing when he saw something coming up the street: a bus.

What a novel idea.

A moment like this was like having privilege stuck right in your face, being made to realize just what a lucky bastard you'd been all your life, really without ever knowing it or properly appreciating it. Thing was, he'd never been on a bus, except a school bus, in his whole life, didn't know what they cost to use, how to read a schedule, nothing. But it looked like now was the time to find out.

The bus roared past and he just caught that it was a No. 4, 2nd and Santa Monica to Venice and Broadway, going north. So he had to find a stop on the other side of the street and hope something was still going back down his way at this time of night.

Quite how Jaxon was going to react to him knocking on his door, Cam didn't want to speculate, but he'd run out of options and had exactly nowhere else to go, nobody else to turn to. Like he'd seen the bums do in downtown back home, Cam pressed the button on the phone to see if any-one had left any change in it, and when nothing came out he turned and walked down to the nearest set of lights. Fixed in his mind was that this *had* to be his last task, he had no more energy, could no more run than fly and need-ed this insanity to stop. Really.

As he stood by a set of traffic lights, waiting for a green, a couple of blocks back up a black four-door sedan stopped at the junction with Santa Monica. The driver looked both ways, then turned to his passenger, who shrugged.

'If he's bright enough to've got away, he's not going to be walking around out in plain sight where we can see him, right?' The driver, who wasn't really asking a question, mere-ly stating what he considered to be the obvious, put the car in reverse. 'This is a waste of time. I'm going to swing back past the house on Dorrington one more time and then call it a day.'

'You're the boss, Mr. Gartner.'

'Out here I am, Matheson.'

Chapter 13

Dorrington Ave., LA; Friday February 28th, 2.29 a.m.

'Mr. Stewart? Yeah, it's Tom Gartner here. No, no we haven't got him . . .' Tom Gartner powered up the sedan's window and adjusted the heating. LA sure was colder than San Diego. 'Yes, Mr. Stewart, that's right . . . yes, he was here. When? About an hour and a half ago . . . what happened? He ran, sir, upped and ran away . . . Yes, we *were* in the car and he *was* on foot, but we got blocked by another vehicle and he got away.'

Gartner sat still, nodding his head as he listened to the angry voice buzzing like a hornet in his ear. He reached up and adjusted the volume on his wireless earpiece, glancing out at Matheson who'd vacated the car to have a smoke. Quite why they couldn't have waited until tomorrow to come to LA to pick up the kid, Mr. Stewart had not seen fit to explain, but something told Gartner he wasn't in possession of all the facts.

'Yes sir.' The rant had stopped, for the moment. 'I know it seems incredible that we don't have Cameron with us and are not on our way home, but something spooked him and he ran. Like I said.'

Gartner had earlier made an executive decision not to tell his boss the real reason his beloved boy had high-tailed it off down the street. Like the fact it was all down to that dickhead Matheson totally screwing things up that the kid had run. And fact was, Matheson had screwed up twice in one day. First, running a red and getting a ticket, and second, getting *way* too excited and yelling out 'There he is!', instead of waiting quietly for the kid to walk right up to them. If he had his way, and he believed he would, the facts would remain a secret, a piece of 'what goes on tour, stays on tour' information. Gartner had already made that abundantly clear to Matheson.

'Yes sir, we have searched thoroughly, as thoroughly as we can under the circumstances . . . It's dark, sir, that's what I meant by "circumstances" . . . Yes, we will be resuming at daybreak, but I don't hold out much hope. I think our best bet is to wait until he contacts you again, sir.'

The hornet started up again in Gartner's ear and he winced. Resting his arm on the leather-covered center console, he played with the car's motorized rear-view mirror controls set into a panel in the door, wondering what the hell he was doing. He had been hired to stop industrial espionage and protect intellectual property, not chase after runaway kids, but if you got paid what he got paid, when the boss said jump, you asked 'How high, sir?' And then, finally, when the rant died down, he got some more information.

'Okay, sir, I'm glad you told me that. We'll maintain a very low profile now we know there could be other people out here looking for him . . . Of course I understand how important it is to get him back – has this Mr. Inverdale called you again? No? Okay, let me know if he does.' Gartner allowed himself a thin smile: he felt a lot better now. 'So where was he? . . . Seattle, okay . . . D'you know how he escaped? . . . Fine, and how did he get to LA? . . . Okay, right, have you told the police? . . . No, no, and I don't think you should, not until we've had a chance to debrief him first . . . Yes, Mr. Stewart, rest assured I'll keep in touch.'

Gartner picked the phone up off the dash where he'd put it, ended the call and then took the earpiece out and put it in his pocket. Well, well, well. He checked out the window again and saw Matheson finishing his cigarette. So this kidnap thing wasn't just some prank, like he'd thought. He knew a lot more about Mr. Stewart's business than Mr. Stewart would probably think was appropriate – being called Head of Security was just another way of saying you had a license to be very nosy – but he didn't know anything about any Marshall Inverdale. Or why he was trying a crude shakedown on his boss. If he'd been brought up to speed earlier he wouldn't have taken some lightweight like Matheson along for the ride.

And the fact that the boy had managed to get away and get down to LA was a surprise. He'd only met the kid once – well, not even met, seen with his father out on the street one time – but he'd just assumed he was some soft rich boy. Obviously wrong there.

Why he'd run, Gartner couldn't say for sure, but guessed he'd probably thought the welcoming committee was Inverdale's people, come to take him back to Seattle. The boy had been lucky to get away, lucky that car had blocked them long enough for him to get off the street. The only thing that worried Gartner was the shooting they'd heard not long after the kid had disappeared. He hoped to hell Cameron Stewart had nothing to do with it, but as he hadn't spotted any ambulance activity he thought this was unlikely. The last thing he wanted was to bring the boy back to San Diego in a box. Not good for future employment prospects.

In a suite in a downtown San Diego office building Alfredo Perro maneuvered his cursor over to activate a drop-down menu, clicked on the 'Save' option and swiveled his chair away from the screen in front of him, taking off his headphones as he did so.

'The boy's in LA,' he said to the woman who was sitting the other side of the room, engrossed in some serious nail care.

'What?'

'I said he's in LA . . . the Stewart boy.'

'LA? How the hell'd he get there?' Sheila Ikeburo frowned and put down a wooden nail file.

'Train and pickup truck, apparently.'

'They got him back, then.'

'Nope, he's still on the loose.' Alfredo nodded back at the screen behind him. 'Stewart's pick-up team screwed up instead. From what I can gather, the boy's already been in touch, like before we got a tap on the line? We should've been quicker off the mark. I told Inverdale.'

'You still surprised when he doesn't listen?' Sheila got up, yawned and stretched. 'Want me to call him now? I guess he'll want to know . . .'

'Yeah, call him . . . why should we be the only ones awake.'

'You gonna email him the sound file?'

'Yup.' Alfredo turned back toward the screen. 'He seems like more trouble than he's worth, that kid . . .'

Chapter 14

Santa Monica Blvd., LA; Friday February 28th, 3.15 a.m.

He still had change, a whole fourteen cents left after paying for his ticket, and the bus had been right on time – no traffic to hold it up. Cam sat halfway back, close to the exit doors and nowhere near the two other people on the bus, both of whom looked about as happy as he must do to be there. The driver, who was wearing shades, had looked over the top of them at him when he'd got on, a look that said, loud and clear: 'You piece of street shit, come messing up my bus', and, staring at his reflection in the window, Cam couldn't really blame him. He looked like he'd been recently dug up.

The bus seemed almost to fly down the street, unobstructed apart from an occasional red light. Road signs flashed by – Beverly Boulevard, Wilshire, Rodeo, Avenue of the Stars – and then they were driving through Century City, over Westwood and on past Sepulveda, which was where Cam fell asleep as if he'd been hit with a brick. He woke up when the bus jolted to a halt, throwing him forward in his seat, its air brakes hissing like a bunch of rabid cats. He sat up, completely disoriented.

'End of the line, buster.' The driver hit a button and the doors next to Cam sighed open, sounding as tired as he felt.

'This Ocean?' Cam rubbed his face with both hands, feeling the rough beard growth, and the movement sent a stab of pain through his arm.

'Ocean and Arizona, just like every damn time.'

'Thanks.' Cam stumbled out of the bus and down onto the sidewalk. It took him a moment to get his bearings and then he crossed the road and walked toward Ocean Avenue. The Pacific Coast Highway wasn't far away, Jaxon's house, too. All he had to do was get there. Under normal circumstances it wouldn't be a lot to ask your body to do, but right then all he was fit for was to drop.

Finally making it to Ocean Ave., Cam then traipsed, without really thinking about why he was doing it, over to a crossing. There was no traffic to speak of — he could have walked on a red — but he waited anyway for the green light and shuffled across to the other side. There, in the grim shadows, he could just make out huddled, ragged groups of people, small fires burning, piles of bags, supermarket carts loaded with who knew what, muttered conversations, cackling laughter, a whole community who'd hit rock bottom and stayed there for the company.

Cam walked over to the barrier wall that was the only thing between him and a precipitous drop to the PCH. He leaned against it and stared down at the houses that bordered the beach and looked out at the ocean, the other side of the eight lanes. Wilshire Blvd. was to his right, he was pretty sure, and he looked up that way, eyes straining to see a red pickup. Nothing. His heart sank, because if the stupid thing was parked up in a garage there was no way he'd ever figure out which house was the right one.

And then he saw the sudden flare of a spotlight turning on some way down the PCH and, in the newlycreated pool of light, he saw a flash of red. A Dodge Ram, for sure. It was there. All he had to do now was get across the highway and some of his troubles would probably be over.

Cam turned to go along to the walkway he knew was down toward the pier and found his path blocked by someone in a wheelchair: big torso, powerful shoulders, thin, stick-like legs, a mean look on his face and wearing a badge that said, HI – MY NAME'S STANLEY!

'Doing a little night-time sightseeing, guy?'

Cam glanced to his left, checking whether this character had any back-up. 'No.'

'Must be just visiting friends, then . . . that it? Looking for some action, right? I got action, up, down, sideways . . . what you looking for?'

'Nothing, man, really.'

'Everybody looking for something, that the way it is, guy . . .' The man had skittery, half-closed yellow eyes, and his hands, which looked like they were bandaged, never stopped moving as he twitched the wheels left and right, back and forward, left and right.

'I gotta go, man.' Cam stepped left to go around the man, who instantly moved his chair to block him again.

'What if I say I kinda don't *want* you to go . . . know what I mean?'

Something inside Cam snapped. 'Look, *Stanley* . . .' He paused, rubbed his hand across his face and then jabbed it at the man. 'You know, the past couple of days? I've been kidnapped, I jumped trains, took rides in the back of trucks . . . I've been chased, I've been shot at and right now? Right now I got all of fourteen cents in my pocket. You want it? You can have it.' Cam threw the coins at the man in the wheelchair, who ducked, the change scattering on the path behind him. 'All *I* want is that I get to be left alone, so get the fuck out my way, okay?'

Cam, who felt brittle as glass, noticed figures moving out of the shadows, streetlight glinting off something small and sharp that one of them was holding.

'You got problems, Stan?'

Stan glanced over his shoulder. 'Not like this dude, man . . . he in a world of pain.' He looked back at Cam. 'I strongly suspect you don't belong down here, you *way* outta your territory . . . don't know why, but I believe it sounds like maybe I should cut you a break this once. Where you headed?'

'Other side of the PCH?'

'The bridge?'

'Yeah, the bridge.'

'I'll walk you down.'

'Why?'

'Could just let you deal with whoever else is out hunting tonight, but don't have to make a shit day any worse than it already is now, do I . . .'

Fifteen minutes later, Cam stood outside the house looking from the red pickup to the front door. Ten, twelve steps and he could be ringing the doorbell. He started walking, then hesitated, not quite past caring what the reaction would be to him waking the two of them up at four in the morning. The adrenaline from the confrontation with Hi – My Name's Stanley! was long gone and he had less than no energy left. Maybe he should just curl up outside and wait for morning.

But his arm hurt, he was cold and he was hungry, so what the hell, ring the bell.

He pressed the button and held it for a ten count, then pressed it some more and waited. And waited. And then he heard the whirring of an electric motor above him and he looked up to see a motorized vid-cam pointing straight at him. He waved, attempting a smile, which he felt sure made him look anything but friendly.

There was a click next to him. 'Cam? That you?' It was Tee. She sounded groggy.

'What's left of me, yeah.'

'Why're you here? What happened?' Cam could hear another voice, kind of growling in the background. Jaxon was awake, too.

'I been, like, shot.'

'*Shot?*' Tee's shout made the speaker crackle. 'Wait there, I'll be down.'

Cam leaned back against the house, feeling like he was about to collapse. Above him he heard the camera motor whir again and then the speaker clicked.

'You're a b-a-a-a-d penny, man . . . and you look like shit.'

'Sorry, Jaxon.' Cam looked up at the glinting lens pointing at him. 'I had nowhere else to go, man.'

The front door opened and Tee was there, a Chinese silk dressing-gown wrapped around her, beckoning Cam in. 'Ignore him, he doesn't do early.' She stood looking at him for a moment, shaking her head. 'We better get you fixed up. Were you, like, serious about getting shot, or did you just mean shot *at*?'

Cam didn't say a word – he didn't have the energy to go into the whole thing right now. He simply pointed to the holes in the jacket and held up his left hand, stained with dried blood.

'Shit . . .'

'Right.' Cam could feel himself swaying.

'Come on, we'll go to the kitchen. You can sit down and I'll get you something.'

Cam followed Tee down a short passage and into a hallway with a staircase leading up to the second floor. Sitting on the first landing, dressed in red boxers and a gray T-shirt, Jaxon lit a cigarette and got up. 'Don't bleed on anything expensive, okay?'

Tee carried on walking. 'Like I said, ignore . . .'

The kitchen was all limed oak, stainless steel and white marble tiles, straight out of an up-scale homes magazine feature, except for all the dirty dishes in the double sink and take-out boxes on the central worktop unit.

Tee led him over to a low-backed stool. 'You can bleed all you want in here, so take the jacket off and let me have a look.'

'You can handle this stuff?'

'Biology major, cut up live frogs and watched their little hearts beat . . . I'm sure your shoulder isn't going to be that gross. Wanna coffee? Sandwich? Left-over Chinese?'

'All of the above . . . I haven't eaten since wherever it was we last ate.'

Cam undid the jacket and started the delicate job of taking it off without causing himself too much pain. By the time he'd finished and hung the scarred, dusty item of clothing on the stool – a far cry from the designer garment he'd taken from the hallway of the house in Seattle – Tee was putting a tray in front of him. A steaming French press full of fresh coffee, a mug and a couple of sachets of sugar sat next to what looked like a stacked ham and salad on wheat, with mayo and pickle, plus a take-out box with some Singapore noodles in it.

Tee shrugged. 'You said you were hungry.' She peered at his bandaged left arm. 'I'll get some stuff and deal with that. Don't go anywhere.'

Cam watched her pad barefoot out of the kitchen, then he turned back and picked up one half of the sandwich. By the time Tee came back, carrying a green plastic box, he'd finished everything.

Pouring water into a bowl from the kettle she'd boiled to make coffee, Tee damped the bloody shirtsleeve Cam had wrapped around the wound and began cutting it away with a pair of nail scissors.

'The bleeding's stopped and it looks like it's started to scab,' Tee cautiously pulled at the ragged bandage, 'so this might hurt when I pull it away, Cam.'

'It already does . . .'

The warm water loosened the material and Tee was able to remove it fairly easily. They both looked at what was underneath.

'Boy, has that taken a chunk out . . . looks a total mess.'

Cam winced as he turned his arm. 'Could've been a whole lot worse, could've actually been hit somewhere major . . .'

'I'll clean this up best I can, then you're going to bed and tomorrow someone who knows what they're doing is taking over. I've reached the limit of my medical skills.'

'I can't go to a doctor or a hospital or anything – that would mean the cops and I just want to get home.'

'Calm down, guy, I'm not calling the cops. Trust me.'

Easy for her to say, so much harder for him to do, but Cam had finally run out of options, so he nodded and sat

back. He watched Tee bathe the wound with a stinging antibacterial wash, dry it and smear on some antiseptic cream,
her fingers cool on his damaged skin. Carefully taping a cotton pad over the injury, she stood back to admire her
handiwork.

'You can sleep in the spare room. I've already made the
bed up.'

'I . . . you know, like, thanks. Thanks for everything.'

'Hey, no problem . . . you turned a dull day into a diary
day, so the thanks are on you.'

Chapter 15

La Jolla, San Diego; Friday February 28th, 9.14 a.m.

The atmosphere in the room was, at best, what you could call icy. Gordon Stewart, pacing the deep-pile carpet, looked tired but immaculate, tense but groomed; Mrs. Stewart appeared to have smelled something old and very dead and sat in a way that said, loud and extremely clear, 'I bite if spoken to.' Tom Gartner had picked up that message the moment he'd walked in. He was quite sure he could deal with Mr. Stewart, who was pretty much all exhaust noise and no acceleration, but his wife was always an entirely different proposition. He might well be Head of Security at Contxt, but she had the knack of making you feel like you were ten years old and waiting outside the Principal's office.

Mr. Stewart stopped pacing. 'So . . . that's it, no sightings of him. Cameron's just disappeared?'

'Los Angeles is a big city, sir. He could be anywhere.'

'Anywhere? He had *no* money, he told me he hadn't got a dime! How's he gonna *get* somewhere with no money?'

'We don't know that the people who gave him a lift didn't give him some, sir. You know, just in case? People do that kind of thing.'

'Why are we wasting time speculating, Gordon?' Mrs. Stewart wasn't looking at anyone in particular as she spoke. '*I* want to hear what Mr. Gartner thinks we should do next.'

Tom Gartner was used to the spotlight being turned on him and having to keep it all together, and he was not going to let an arctic bitch like Eleanor Stewart phase him. Instead, to give her some of her own medicine, he waited a beat longer than he knew she was expecting him to take to reply . . . and started speaking as she was about to make some obviously sarcastic comment. 'We lie low, Mrs. Stewart, and we wait and see. Or at least that's what we've got to look like we're doing.'

'And just exactly what *are* we going to be doing, Mr. Gartner? While we look like we're doing nothing?'

'We are actually out there now. We're already on the case, ma'am . . .' Another long beat, just to wind her up. 'I figure Cameron ran because he was spooked by something, may even have spotted us and thought we were this man Inverdale's people – but as you so rightly say, ma'am, there's little or no point in speculating. What we do know is that Cameron has few resources or contacts – you know, like maybe he has the address of the guys who brought him to LA – so I doubt he's gotten far from West Hollywood and he definitely has limited options open to him –'

'Cut to the chase, Mr. Gartner.'

'He'll either call collect again, or go back to his uncle's, Mrs. Stewart.' Gartner carried on, wishing he had a clue what was *really* going on here, because he could guarantee there was a lot more that he wasn't being told. 'Whichever, we're still out looking for him, and I've sent two more teams up to LA. Lo-pro though.'

'Lo-pro?'

'Jargon, excuse me. Low profile, ma'am, because of the likelihood of this Inverdale having men there in LA as well.' Gartner nodded toward Mr. Stewart, now standing behind his wife, indicating where that piece of information had come from. 'And also, we haven't so far said anything to the cops about him being free. I'm not 100 percent happy with that, but as it's the way you want to play things I think we can all agree that we want him back here and debriefed before we do, right?'

'Sure, sure . . .' Mr. Stewart, snapping his fingers nervously, started walking up and down the room again. 'What I want to know is *why* we haven't heard anything else from Inverdale. No further contact, nothing. I know you know I haven't told you everything, but believe me when I tell you it's better that way, Gartner. Suffice to say that there are reasons why Inverdale wants the cops involved, and equally valid ones why I don't.'

'Clearly, dear, but we are only likely to have problems with the police if we act in any way other than how we're supposed to – right, Mr. Gartner?'

Gordon Stewart looked from his wife to Gartner and back, with a face that mimed '*What?*'

'Concerned, distraught, baffled, "why us?" parents, like the ones you see pleading on the news,' Eleanor Stewart explained. 'Which is, of course, what we are. Except without the TV, I am *not* going to do that.'

Gartner stayed silent. Concerned, distraught and baffled? Three adjectives he'd never think of using to describe his boss's wife. Stuck-up, controlling and heartless, now *there* was an accurate description . . .

'And what about not having, you know, a ransom note or something?' Mr. Stewart was beginning to pace again.

'Without *some* kind of contact we can tell the police about, this doesn't look very much like your regular kidnapping.'

'Well, it isn't your *regular* kidnapping, is it, Gordon.' Mrs. Stewart got up and walked over to an antique blond wood armoire which, when she opened the doors, revealed itself to be a very modern computer workstation-cum-home office. She pulled out a drawer, picked up a white envelope that Gartner could see had been opened and held it out toward her husband. 'Here's the ransom note we got this morning.'

'What? You didn't – when did this arrive?' Gordon Stewart, looking totally shocked, reached out to take the envelope. 'What's Inverdale up to?'

'Nothing.'

'Nothing?'

Gartner felt like he was at the country club watching his employers playing word tennis.

'It's not *from* Inverdale.'

'Not? Then who . . . who else could it possibly be from, Eleanor?'

'It's a fake.'

'Fake? What the hell d'you mean, *fake*?'

'Fake, as in bogus, sham, phony.' Eleanor Stewart carefully took a sheet of paper out of the envelope. 'I made it last night . . . I think it's rather good.'

'You?'

'Yes, me. I realized the lack of some kind of contact was going to look suspicious, and I also knew there was no way we'd get anything from that louse Inverdale, so I "got in contact" myself. It's kind of generic, but I figured it was better not to try and get too clever.'

'Mr. Stewart, sir, could you take the letter from your wife and put it on the coffee table so I can see it?' Gartner nodded at his boss, who took the letter and made to actually hand it over to him. 'No sir, on the table.'

'Why?'

'Because he doesn't want his fingerprints on it.'

'Exactly, ma'am.' Gartner bent over to look at the single sheet of 80 gram, standard issue bond paper, the kind found in every copy shop. 'If this was real, I would want as few people as possible to touch it. They, the police, would expect you and your wife to have done, but I should know better.'

'What does it say?' asked Gordon Stewart.

Gartner quickly scanned the five lines of typing at the top of the paper. '*We have your son*,' he read out loud, '*and it is going to cost you one and a half million to get him back alive . . .*'

'Why 1.5 million bucks, Eleanor?'

'I thought that didn't sound too fantastic. What do you think, Mr. Gartner?'

Gartner was about to respond when he felt his cell phone start to vibrate and he took it out of his jacket pocket, flipped it and looked at the screen before answering. 'Excuse me . . . Yes? Outside now? Okay.'

'A problem, Mr. Gartner? You look concerned.'

'That was Matheson, in the car, Mrs. Stewart . . . it seems the police are here.'

'Nice to see our tax dollars at work so early.'

In the distance they could all hear the door chimes and Gartner knew that it would only be a minute or so before the maid came to tell them who had arrived. He walked straight over to a side table, picked up the phone and dialed a number.

'Hello? Yes, you can help me – could I be put through to

Detective Henrikson? My name? Thomas Gartner, I work for Mr. and Mrs. Stewart . . . the La Jolla kidnapping? Right, well, we have received a letter . . . Yes, okay, I can wait.' Gartner hit the mute button and looked over at his puzzled employer. 'The first thing I would do is call, sir. I have to act like I don't already know the cops are here.' He pressed the mute button again. 'Yes? Oh, I see, they're on their way over right now? Okay, thanks for your help.'

As he put the phone down there was tap on the double doors into the room.

'Come!' Mrs. Stewart swiveled around to look at the maid. 'Yes?'

'It's the police, ma'am. The same two detectives. They say they have a few more questions.'

'Show them into the other room, Consuela. Then get me some tea before you bring them in here.'

'Ok . . . good.' Gartner rubbed his hands together. 'This isn't perfect, but I'm sure we can make it hang together. What's the story – when did you "get" the letter, Mrs. Stewart?'

'Consuela brought me the mail at around 8.30, but I didn't look at it until just after 9.00 which is when I found the letter. It obviously hadn't been mailed and just had Gordon's name printed on the front of the envelope, so I called you both in here, where we opened it.'

'I was here for an early morning meeting, because you, sir,' Gartner looked at Gordon Stewart, 'can't come to the office for obvious reasons, and as soon as we realized what we had I called Henrikson. The only hole in the story is how it got in your mail.'

Mrs. Stewart's smile didn't reach her eyes. 'We have to give the police *something* to figure out, Mr. Gartner.'

'Let's just hope they don't get it right, ma'am . . .'

The office suite smelled stale. You couldn't open a damn window and the AC had been off all night. They'd heard it kick back in at around 8.30, though it hadn't made much difference yet. Alfredo Perro pulled the headphones down off his ears. His mouth felt like it had been coated with wool and if he had a toothbrush he'd go and clean his teeth, but he didn't so he popped another piece of gum instead. He looked over at Sheila Ikeburo. 'D'you think he meant they'd had a *ransom* note?'

'How do I know?' Sheila looked distracted. 'Are you *sure* I can't have just one cigarette?'

'I told you before, you'll set the smoke alarms off.'

'Man, I hate California sometimes.'

'Just quit smoking . . .' Alfredo watched Sheila get up and go and look out of the window.

'It sounded like – what was his name? Gartner?' Sheila looked around and Alfredo nodded. 'It certainly *sounded* like Gartner meant a ransom note, but who the hell it's from I have *no* idea. I knew we should've bugged the damn house . . .'

'You want to talk to Inverdale?'

'No, I did it last time. I'm going out for a cigarette.'

Chapter 16

Santa Monica Beach; Friday February 28th, 11.23 a.m.

Cam woke up with basically no idea where he was, a feeling intensified by the fact that everything felt oddly different . . . strange pillow, sheet and blankets instead of a quilt, the unmistakable aroma of what some soap-powder chemist thought mountain air smelled like. Definitely not home territory. And he ached. All over, but especially his arm.

With the pain came the memories of how he'd got where he was, and he slowly sat up to take a look around Jaxon's spare room. Light spilled through the Venetian blinds in bright slices, heralding yet another fine LA day. He got out of bed to take a look at it. The room faced the flat expanse of empty, dun-colored beach and he could see the pier way to his left. Some kind of raking machine had been over the sand, but there was hardly anyone but two or three joggers out there to enjoy the effect.

He was still peering through the gap he'd lifted in the blinds when there was a light tap on the bedroom door. Cam, buck naked, looked around for something to put on, but the pile of clothes he'd left on the floor after taking a quick wash in the en-suite bathroom wasn't there anymore.

He didn't quite leap back under the covers, but almost.

'Yeah?'

'You awake?' Tee's voice sounded muffled through the solid wood door.

'Just came to . . .'

'I washed and dried your clothes, I'll leave 'em outside. Come get some breakfast or whatever when you're ready, okay?'

'Right . . . thanks . . .'

'Oh, and I threw out the remains of your shirt . . . left you something else.'

'You did? Right . . .'

Half an hour later, properly showered and dressed in clean, 'mountain fresh' clothes, Cam walked into the kitchen ready for food. No one was there, but, out on the deck he hadn't realized was there the night before, he could see Tee, Jaxon and another guy sitting at a wooden table. He went over and slid the glass door open, stepping out into the sunshine. Three heads turned toward him.

'Nice shirt, man.'

'Can it, Jaxon.' Tee shook her head. 'I had to toss Cam's and you *never* wear the thing. I found it on the floor at the back of your closet.'

'Look, I appreciate everything you guys've done, and I wouldn't've come here if I didn't have to, but I was desperate.' Cam started to back toward the kitchen door. 'I'm outta here. In fact if I could just make *one* collect call I'll go now.'

'Sit down, Cam, and shut up, Jaxon.' Tee pushed her chair back and got up from the table. 'Cam, this is Deacon.'

'Hi.' Cam nodded at the newcomer and sat down across from him.

'He's gonna look at your arm.'

'He is?'

'Sure.' Jaxon grinned. 'He's gonna give you a coupla shots, check your teeth, give you a worming tablet and you'll be good to go!'

'Ignore him – you two want to come inside now, or, like, do it later?'

Deacon shrugged. 'Now's good for me.' He looked over at Cam. 'You?'

'Yeah, why not.'

'I'll make coffee, then.'

Tee went inside, which left three uneasy guys wondering what the hell to do next, and no one seemingly prepared to make the first move.

Eventually Cam broke the silence. 'You, like, a doctor then, Deacon?'

'Trainee *doggy* doctor, man!' Jaxon got up from the table and made for the door. 'Only way he knows to take your temperature is sticking the thermometer up your ass.'

Cam watched him go, amazed at the sheer couldn't-give-a-shit attitude of the guy. 'Is he always so charming?'

Deacon looked down at his hands and then over his shoulder at the beach. 'He can be such a major jerk sometimes, you know?'

'Yeah, I figured . . . and I only met him yesterday.'

'Oh, you could never accuse Jaxon of hiding his true nature.'

'You're Tee's friend, then.'

'Oh yeah, known her since forever . . . she's always made like, you know, *unique* choices when it comes to boyfriends. She's cool, though.'

'Why . . .' Cam looked back into the kitchen.

'Why Jaxon? Who knows, except Tee has always treated her relationships like projects. She told me once they've *got* to have an edge to be interesting. Maybe there are hidden depths to Jaxon you only get to see when you actually *live* with him. Nice house to do the research in, though.'

Cam fell silent, not wanting to follow where that comment was going. 'What did Jaxon mean?'

'Mean?' Deacon frowned.

'The trainee thing.'

'Oh, that . . . I'm at Cal Poly in Pomona, training to be a veterinary surgeon. Third year.'

'You're a *vet*?'

'Tee said it was nothing *illegal*, but that you just needed a dressing changing, right? I can do that, no problem.' Deacon smiled, like he got requests to do this kind of stuff all the time.

'*Vets* can treat people?'

'I'm not going to *treat* you, I'm gonna change a dressing. What happened to you anyway?'

Cam considered making up some story, telling this guy Deacon he was fine and that he was sorry Tee had bothered him. But his arm still ached and he knew it would be a good idea for *someone*, even a damn vet, to look at it. He took a deep breath. 'It's a long story, but the reason why you're here is because someone shot at me last night and I got hit.'

'Which explains why you don't want to go to a regular physician.' Deacon stood up and walked around the table toward the kitchen. 'Come on, let's go take a look. But you realize I can't give you any medication, like if anything's wrong you really *have* to go to the hospital or something.'

'What could be wrong?'

'You've been shot, man!' Deacon's voice rose. 'You have a wound, wounds can go septic, you can get awesomely sick, okay?'

'Sorry . . .'

'No problem.'

Cam stayed sitting at the table. 'Why are you doing this for me, Deacon?'

'Cos Tee asked me, and she never abuses the privilege of friendship.' Deacon looked into the kitchen where Tee was standing at a worktop with her back to them. 'Was it ever your lucky day when you met her, man . . .'

Cam sat at the table in the dining area, which Tee, rather ominously, had covered with a plastic cloth. On the cloth was a small, unzipped, but not open, leather case which Deacon had put there. He was over by the sink washing his hands in some stuff he'd brought with him and Tee was boiling some water on the stove. Jaxon, from the sound of it, was somewhere upstairs playing Green Day at maximum volume.

'Take your shirt off, would you, Cam?' Deacon came over to the table, drying his hands on some paper towel. 'Don't want to mess up another one.'

'You expecting mess?'

'Best be prepared. Tee, when the water's boiled, could you pour about a pint in a bowl and bring it over with some more paper towels please, and an empty bowl?' Deacon sat down next to Cam, smiling. 'You have *no* idea how great it is to have a patient who actually can understand what I'm saying to them.'

'Third year's pretty advanced, right?'

'Advanced enough to remove a bandage, so don't worry.'

Deacon proceeded to snap on a pair of surgical gloves and nudged the leather case with his elbow. 'Open that, would you.'

Cam flipped the case apart to reveal a gleaming array of stainless steel implements, a pack of cotton balls and a couple of small plastic bottles. Deacon picked up a pair of angled scissors and started cutting the adhesive tape holding down the thick cotton pad Tee had put over the wound. Cam involuntarily tensed his arm.

'Relax . . .' Deacon put the scissors down and began lifting the pad, which didn't want to move. In the background Cam could hear the water start to boil. 'Even though Tee put cream on, it's stuck a bit, so I'm gonna have to try soaking it off, okay?'

'Whatever you have to do,' Cam nodded. 'You're the vet . . .'

Tee put a Pyrex bowl full of steaming water on the table, half a dozen or so sheets of paper towel next to it and sat down to watch. 'Light okay here?'

'D'you have a lamp you could bring over?'

'Sure.'

As Cam watched Tee go off to look for an extra light, he felt hot water on his arm and looked down to see Deacon teasing the bottom layers of the cotton pad away from his skin with a wet Q-tip. The whole job took almost five minutes, during which Tee came back, plugged in a heavy, chromed desk lamp and switched it on. In the hot pool of light the livid wound managed to look both worse than he'd imagined and yet also more unreal than it had the night before. The pain wasn't imaginary, though.

'That was no pea-shooter you were hit by . . .' Deacon whistled through his teeth. 'Half an inch the wrong way, guy, and you'd have been looking at major trauma.'

Cam peered down at his upper arm. 'So it's not that bad, then?'

'Appears to be scabbing over quite nicely, but I'm going to sluice it out with a strong antibacterial, check it out and then wrap it up again.' Deacon picked up one of the plastic bottles and poured a measured amount into the water. The room filled with the sharp smell of hospital. 'When you get to wherever you're going . . .'

'San Diego. La Jolla, actually.'

'Very nice, but when you get there, see a *real* doctor, okay?' Deacon pulled off some of the cotton he'd brought with him, soaked it and began washing out the bloody gash, holding a hot, wet swab against the wound, throwing it in the empty bowl and then repeating the process until he was satisfied it was as clean as he could get it.

Tee got up. 'I'm gonna make some brunch – how does eggs Benedict with a side of links sound?'

'Add a cup of coffee,' Deacon didn't look up as he spoke, 'and it sounds perfect.'

'Great, thanks.' Cam smiled at Tee, then noticed Deacon was leaning in toward his arm and squinting as he dabbed with a fresh piece of cotton. 'What do you see?'

'Don't know – Tee, does this place have a magnifying glass or something anywhere?'

'I think I've seen one in a drawer in the den. Want me to go see if I can find it?'

'Please . . .' Deacon threw the swab into the bowl and sat back. 'Weird.'

'What is?'

'Well, there *appears* to be something in your arm, and I know what *I* think it looks like.'

'So what is it?' Cam twisted his arm around as far as he

could to get a better look.

'Wait a second, wait a second!' Deacon held Cam's arm. 'Stay still for a moment – Tee? *Tee?*'

As he called she walked back into the room holding a brass-bound, four-inch diameter magnifying glass and handed it to Deacon. 'This do?'

'Terrific.' Deacon picked up a pair of tweezers and concentrated on Cam's arm again. 'This, as they say, is going to hurt you . . .' he swiftly reached in with the tweezers and pulled something out that, from the jab of pain, didn't want to come out, '. . . more than it hurts me.'

'What the f—'

'Got the little bastard! Tee, could I have like a side plate?'

Gripped in between the tweezers, Cam could see Deacon had extracted something about the size of a rice grain from his arm. 'What the hell is that?'

'You, my friend, had a chip on your shoulder . . .'

'He did what?' Tee put a side plate next to Deacon and leaned over, moving the magnifying glass in Deacon's hand so she could see better. 'You saying this is like one of those ID things?'

'Exactly like. In fact I'm absolutely positive it's an RFID – a radio frequency identification device.'

'You mean like they put in pedigree mutts?'

The three of them turned around to see Jaxon standing in the doorway, the music still thumping away upstairs at a physical level, which was why no one had heard him come down.

'Your parents need to keep tabs on you or something?' Jaxon walked through to the kitchen, grinning. 'You've like been leading a dog's life and you didn't even know it, man!'

111

Chapter 17

Police HQ, San Diego; Friday February 28th, 12.05 p.m.

Tony Matric sat with his feet up on his desk, staring out the window. Mike Henrikson was off berating some luckless clerk because the photocopier had jammed again and kind of *welded* some paper to the rollers. Or at least that's what it had looked like when they'd opened up the front to try and fix the damn thing. Which left him wondering about the morning they'd just had – another brittle interview with the Stewarts which got nowhere, and the only move forward being the ransom note.

   He leaned over and picked up a photocopy of it off his desk, the last one to make it out of the machine before it ground to a halt, and looked at the words printed at the top of the sheet of paper:

> We have your son, and it is going to cost you one and a half million to get him back alive. Instructions, which must be followed to the letter, will arrive shortly. Any funny business and I promise the boy will *not* make it.

The actual letter was off being tested to pieces by forensics, not that Tony thought they'd get much. He'd given it a cursory once-over and reckoned it was consumer-quality inkjet output on a standard bond paper – which, unless they could find the actual printer, wasn't going to get them very far – and he could almost guarantee there'd be no fingerprints apart from the parents' and possibly the Gartner character's.

Tony put the photocopy down, picked up his notepad and then dug into his jacket pocket, fumbling for a business card he'd put there. A couple of seconds later he managed to retrieve the $3^1/_4$ x 2 inch piece of expensive pasteboard. The reverse was printed in color to look like a computer circuit board and, cleverly picked out like they were part of the circuit, were the words SYSTEMS DESIGN, MANUFACTURE, MANAGEMENT and INSTALLATION. The front was plain white and gave company and personal details in a clean, ultra-modern typeface and design. Thomas Gartner, so the card declared, was VP for Personnel & Security at Contxt Inc., and Contxt were in the business of communications infrastructure. Which, he now knew, because he'd asked, basically meant they were in the cell phone business, designing, manufacturing, managing and installing the stuff that bounced the calls around. Well, someone had to do it.

He put the card down and flipped open his notebook to where he'd taken down the plate details of the black sedan parked outside the Stewart house. The one with the driver who had got on his cell the moment he'd spotted their unmarked car. Picking up the phone Tony dialed a number, gave the plate to the voice at the other end to have it checked out, down to its tire tread. He was just about to call Records when Mike came back in, followed by some guy with a lot of ballpoint pens in his shirt pocket.

'Fix the damn thing, Rich, or I swear I'll toss it down the elevator shaft.'

'Sure, Mike . . . you do that.'

Tony put the receiver down. 'You know *everyone* in this place, Mike?'

'I know everyone who counts . . . You had anymore thoughts about that note?'

'Educated, precise, no-nonsense, very unemotional.' Mike looked unsure, so Tony counted the points out again. 'Look . . . educated, as in no spelling mistakes – so probably an older person – and knows how to use a word processor; precise and no-nonsense, as in no wasted words, and that death-threat finale is so kind of matter of fact, sounds like a school report, right?'

'Well, at least there's been contact. Any idea when we'll get something back from forensics?'

'They said ASAP, but that's no guarantee.' Tony reached to pick up the phone again, then stopped. 'Hey, there's something's been lo-grade bugging me ever since we went there today.'

'What's that?'

'Tom Gartner, the security guy.'

'What about him?'

'I was just about to call Records,' Tony tapped a pencil on his desk, 'cos I got this *real* strong feeling I've seen him before and I can't figure out from where.'

'You mean like a perp?'

'No, from the job, us. Could even have been from way back when I was in uniform, I don't know. He didn't ring any bells with you?'

'No, nothing at all. Just annoyed me.' Mike went over to

his desk and began sorting through paperwork that had piled up during their time out of the office. The second envelope he opened contained the results of a search he'd had done into Gordon Stewart's business operations and he sat back to read it with interest. Some minutes later he glanced up and saw Tony chewing on a pencil like it was a stogie and smiling like a cat. 'You win the lottery or something?'

'I wish . . . No, just called Records and I was right.'

'Right?'

'Gartner *was* a cop, down in Chula Vista. *That's* where I came across him, about ten, twelve years ago.'

'And?'

'And apparently he kind of had to go.' Tony looked at a note he'd made. 'Says here it was suggested he tender his resignation before any official action had to be taken.'

'What had he done?'

'Not enough evidence to actually prosecute, but suspected of, to quote the guy in Records, "an unhealthy association with known criminals",' Tony shook his head, 'and now he's a veep at some company and in charge of security. D'you think he got the job on the principle that it takes a thief to catch a thief?'

'I think we should ask him. I think we should sit Mr. Gartner down and have a good, long talk with him.'

'What came in the envelope, Mike?'

Mike held up the sheaf of papers. 'Stewart's business life in copious detail – a net which also seems to have brought in stuff about *Mrs.* Stewart.'

'Let me guess – does some kind of charity work, or maybe has an interest in a small shop on Silverado selling chic imported knick-knacks.'

'Au contraire, Tony.' Mike stabbed a finger at the top sheet. 'Says here she's a trustee of something called the Doctor Corporation, which is some kind of healthcare outfit and has offices on 4th and Broadway, no less.'

'Didn't realize Stewart had two businesses.'

'He doesn't – he's not listed as having anything to do with Doctor Corp.'

'He isn't?' Tony looked surprised. 'Oh . . . Well, d'you think this has *anything* to do with the kidnapping?'

'I haven't got a goddam clue, but this itch I told you I got that says something doesn't fit? Well it just will *not* go away.' Mike got up, walked over to Tony's desk and picked up the photocopy of the letter. 'And I don't like this, either.'

'Why?'

'It's everything it should be and nothing it shouldn't – like it's from a manual on how to write ransom notes – and we have *no* idea how it got into the house.'

'But now we have a note, everything goes up a notch, right?' Tony looked around the room. 'I mean . . . we get more feet on the street, yeah?'

'Seeing the Chief . . .' Mike looked at his watch, '. . . in half an hour. But they never asked once, did they?'

'Who?'

'The Stewarts, Tony. They *never* asked about how many people were working the case . . . why?'

'They trust us?'

'Yeah right . . .' Mike's phone began to ring and he reached over to pick it up. 'I don't think so, and I sure as hell don't trust them – Henrikson . . .'

116

Chapter 18

Police HQ, Seattle; Friday February 28th, 12.05 p.m.

Officer Martyn Miller was at a loose end. Pete DeWinter, his partner, was late in because of some unspecified domestic upheaval at home, and he was just hanging around, kicking his heels, waiting, bored. The squad room was quiet, hardly anyone to talk to, and everyone who was there seemingly heads-down busy. So, what to do with himself? As Martyn looked idly around the room his eye caught the flicker of a computer screen over to his right. It was the dedicated intranet machine, and there was no one using it.

He put the lid on his paper cup of take-out black coffee, walked over and sat in front of a computer that looked like no one gave a shit about it, which was basically true – it belonged to nobody and was abused by everyone. The screen was finger-marked to hell, the light grey plastic casing covered in years of grime and bits of adhesive tape, and all the most popular letters on the keyboard were all but worn off. Martyn picked up the mouse, which felt kind of sticky, and ran the cursor over to 'NEW SEARCH'. May as well use his time to see what was going on in other places.

First he checked out Portland PD, jumping onto

Sacramento, San Francisco, hopping down the coast to Los Angeles and then, some twenty minutes meandering later, he found himself looking at stuff out of San Diego, stuff that included information posted about a kidnapping in broad daylight. With a picture of the vic, looked like a kid, late teens.

Martyn sat forward and squinted at the screen. It was so damn dirty he couldn't see the head and shoulders shot properly, so he reached over and wiped it with his thumb to make the picture clearer, a move that had completely the opposite effect. He turned and looked around the room.

'Anyone got something to clean this screen?'

No one looked up, but a toilet roll came sailing over toward him and a voice yelled, 'Ass-wipes do ya?'

Martyn, who still played baseball occasionally, reached up and caught the roll, yelled his thanks back and tore off half a dozen sheets. Now he needed some water, but he really didn't want to have to go all the way down to the end of the corridor to the water cooler to get it. He shrugged. Lukewarm black coffee would just have to do. Prizing the plastic lid off, Martyn dipped the wad of paper into the coffee, squeezed and then wiped just the bit of the screen over the face. He sat back, frowning and scratching his chin, which achieved nothing positive except to remind him he needed to buy some new razor blades.

This face was ringing bells like a pinball machine, but, for the life of him, Martyn could *not* think where he'd seen it before. He looked at the screen and concentrated hard, as if staring the face out was going help put a name to it.

'You okay, Mart?'

Martyn looked left then right and found his partner standing near him, a puzzled expression on his face. 'Yeah,

yeah. . . I'm fine, Pete.' He beckoned. 'C'mere and look at this . . . who the *heck* is this guy? I recognize the face but I don't know why.'

Pete came over and bent down to take a closer look at the image on the screen. 'Why's just that spot cleaned up?'

'Forget the damn screen, look at the picture!'

'Okay, okay . . .' Pete stared for a second or two, then stood up and walked away.

'Where you going?'

'Check something.'

'What?'

Pete looked back, still walking. 'The videos.'

'What videos, man?' Martyn got up and followed him as he walked out of the squad room.

'We still got the same cassette in from the other night, right . . . you haven't changed it?' Pete took a left and went down a short flight of stairs that would take them out into the parking lot.

'You mean in the car, our patrol car? Yeah.'

'"Yeah", you've changed it, or "yeah", it's the same cassette, Mart?'

'It's the same, why?'

'You remember the other night, up on Olympic? That guy we lost when he ran off into the woods? Dropped a stick we thought was a knife or something, remember?'

Martyn slowed down as they went out through the door and into the lot. He hadn't taken his jacket with him and the damp cold made him shiver involuntarily. 'You think that was the same guy from San Diego?'

'Yeah, looks just like him.'

'So he escaped?'

119

Pete stopped by their patrol car and unlocked it. 'Must have.'

'What's a kid looks like he's Ivy League material doing running *away* from us if he's gotten free from the people holding him?'

'Search me . . .' Pete took out the video cassette and locked the vehicle again. 'Shall we check and see if I'm right?'

The image quality was not terrific, and the footage that'd been shot as they'd chased the shadowy figure in the black-and-white was useless. But, as the car turned onto Olympic and Pete had hit the spotlight, things got better.

'Freeze it now, Pete.' Martyn pointed at the screen. 'No, rewind a second or two . . . a *second*, Pete . . . right, hold it there.'

The screen froze, leaving them with a stark, grainy mono picture that caught the subject, mouth open and looking right at the camera lens. Even with the harsh lighting bleaching out much of the detail, there was little doubt that the person they'd chased in the early hours of the day before in Seattle was the same person who'd been kid-napped right off the street in some upscale part of San Diego. No doubt at all.

'So,' Martyn stood up and stretched, 'the kid gets lifted . . .' he picked up a scratch pad from the table on which he'd made some notes, 'at around four in the afternoon on the 26th in this La Jolla place, right? And what, fourteen hours later?' Pete nodded. 'Fourteen hours later we catch him on video acting suspicious around Queen Anne Hill, two states and a good couple of thousand miles north.'

'That is what it looks like, Mart.' Pete chewed his lip.

'Doesn't make much sense though, does it? Like you said, why was he running away from us? You'd think he'd be *happy* to see the cops.'

'Something's screwy, right?'

Pete nodded. 'What're we going to do?'

'Go see the Captain and . . .' Martyn glanced down at his pad again, '. . . get him to call this guy Mike Henrikson, find out what he has to say . . .'

Chapter 19

Police HQ, San Diego; Friday February 28th, 12.47 p.m.

Mike Henrikson put the phone down and looked over at Tony. 'Did you get any of that?'

'Kind of gathered someone's saying our boy's been seen in Seattle, that right?'

'Yeah. On the street, clear sighting early yesterday morning, fourteen hours after he got taken.' Mike stood up. 'And he ran *away* from the cops.'

'It was cops who spotted him?'

'Absolutely. That was some Captain up in Seattle, he just had the information brought to him by a couple of his guys.' Mike looked at something he'd written on a pad. 'Officer Martyn Miller and his partner Pete De Winter were on patrol, had had a report to look out for some burglary suspect and when they saw what turns out to be Cameron Stewart, he took off. Ended up disappearing into some woods, apparently, and that would've been it if Miller hadn't happened to see our posting and his partner recognized the picture.'

'Good memory.'

'They'd been running tape in their vehicle.'

Tony nodded. 'So why hasn't the kid called his parents?'

Mike sat on the edge of his desk. 'Who says he hasn't, Tony?'

'But the note . . .'

'I *said* I didn't think it looked good, didn't I? If that kid's out, he has to have been in touch with his parents, guaranteed. And that means the parents are lying through their perfect teeth.'

'Lying *and* faking evidence.' Tony picked up a pencil and began chewing the end. 'But *why*? What the hell are they trying to hide?'

'Dunno, but at least we now know they're trying to hide something. It's not a suspicion anymore, not just me having a problem with their stuck-up attitudes.'

'Are we going back? Confront them with the facts?'

'What facts? All we can say – and we can only assert this, not prove it – is that their son is no longer a captive. We can figure he *must* have called them, but again, no proof. So I think we go for their phone records, pull all of them, cell phones, landlines, everything. And go for a tap as well.'

Right then Tony's phone rang; he took the pencil out of his mouth and leaned forward to pick it up. 'Matric . . . Yeah, okay, let me get a pad.' Tony scanned his desk and ended up grabbing the nearest sheet of paper. 'Fire away . . .'

Mike watched him scribble down some quick notes and then end with a very dynamic period that had a circle around it. 'That the information about the car?'

'Yup.' Tony looked up. 'Not a lot though – it's registered to Contxt Inc., no surprises there, and nothing else of any real interest. It picked up a traffic violation – ran a red – yesterday, up in LA. Driver gave his name as Simon Matheson.'

'You think he could be the guy was in the car outside the Stewarts', the one who got on his cell the moment he saw us?'

'Possible. Maybe he's Gartner's driver.'

'What time was the ticket?'

Tony referred back to his notes. '11.46 p.m., on Sunset.'

'I wonder if he was driving Gartner then, and if he was, what the head of personnel and security could've been doing up there at that time of the night?'

'We gonna bring him in and find out?'

'Why the hell not.'

Marshall Inverdale lit his tenth, or maybe it was his eleventh, cigarette of the day. He'd lost count and was not about to check the ashtray to find out. He was tired, having been woken early by the call from San Diego about the boy being in Los Angeles, and he hadn't been able to get back to sleep. The second call a couple of hours ago, about the ransom note, had really screwed the whole day – like, hello, *what* ransom note?

A ransom note was never part of the plan, as this was more of a business deal than a regular kidnap. So, as *he* wasn't responsible for sending it, did this mean there was someone else out there trying to muscle in? If there was, it changed the picture somewhat . . . someone else who knew what the Stewarts were up to and wanted some action kind of complicated matters.

What he'd supposed would be a simple little job had turned into a waking nightmare. By now the boy *should* have been tucked up safe across the border. Instead he was somewhere – who knew where – in the vast urban sprawl of LA, and there was the very dead body of one of his erstwhile employees, stored at −3° in the freezer and waiting to be disposed of. Great.

Both he and Luiz Binay had misread the kid, or maybe simply not figured exactly how far desperation could drive someone. Experience had taught him it wasn't easy to kill a man – not in terms of pulling the trigger, or whatever, so much as afterwards, in your head. You needed a certain frame of mind to be able to deal with taking a life, and then living with the memory. Inverdale wondered how Cameron Stewart would cope with that.

He didn't wonder for long, as he had his own problems to handle. He was having to figure out how to deal with people – people who he goaded on an almost daily basis with the axiom 'failure is not an option' – who were becoming aware that he'd neglected to succeed. If there was one thing Inverdale hated it was being made to look like a total incompetent. He was relying on this operation to give him a hefty pay-out, and staring at the reality of being back at square one did not make him feel particularly happy.

The fact was, though, he wasn't completely in deep shit. There was still a chance of getting the boy back, and no reason to pull the plug on the operation just yet. Outside, Inverdale could see Luiz, along with Ed, moving boxes into the Chevy van as there was no point in being in Seattle anymore. He'd have to watch Luiz, who he knew would suspect, correctly, that he'd been fairly economical with the truth when it'd come to explaining how the boy had got out the house. It was never a good idea to have a subordinate who had something on you, not good at all, and it was a situation that would have to be monitored very closely.

Having already organized the jet out at Sea-Tac, he emailed San Diego to tell Alfredo Perro and Sheila Ikeburo, the two people he'd hired to look after the operation down there, that he and the others would be arriving later in the day and to make sure everything was ready. Now all he had to do was pack up his stuff and make sure everything was wiped down. He sat at the desk, logging off and closing down his small titanium i-Book.

Checking the room one more time he packed the computer into its bag and picked up his coat. His other jacket, the nice Italian leather one, was somewhere in LA, and Inverdale exited the room speculating idly what had happened to his gun. And how much was left of his $250.

Like a lot of born dirt-poor, self-made men, Marshall Inverdale was often careless with his own personal money and invariably penny-pinching in his dealings with other people: he'd earned it and he'd goddam spend it exactly how he liked. His investment in what he thought of as the Stewart Project had been quite considerable, so far, and because the kid had gone AWOL it was going to cost considerably more before he got anywhere near his anticipated return. But he would get his money. He always did.

Chapter 20

Santa Monica Beach; Friday February 28th, 2.16 p.m.

Deacon finished cleaning up Cam's wound and carefully re-bandaging it. All the poking around had made it start to bleed again and it still hurt like hell.

'Would you mind if I took this?' Deacon pointed at the tiny RFID capsule that had been in Cam's arm.

'No . . . but why?'

'I want to see if I can scan the thing and get the information off of it.'

'What information?'

'Jaxon was right. This is the kind of thing animals, primo dogs and cats, get tagged with. All you need to do is scan them, which activates a tiny transmitter in the tag and it like broadcasts the information it's holding.'

'I was *tagged*?'

'Kind of looks like it.'

'Why?'

'Couldn't say, guy, but,' Deacon picked up the capsule and wrapped it in a piece of cotton, 'once I've scanned it we could maybe find out who did it.'

Cam didn't say anything. He was thinking back, trying to

remember anything that would give him a clue to what this thing was doing in him.

'You okay?'

Cam looked up. 'Yeah . . . just, you know, trying to get my head around this stuff.'

Deacon put the ball of cotton in the leather instrument case, zipped it shut and stood up. 'I'll come by later, okay?'

'Sure.' Sitting at the table, Cam watched Deacon go. He was on his own again, like he had been for the last couple of days, with just what was going on inside his head. The house was silent now, no longer pulsing to the thunderous bass line produced by what had to be an awesome sound system. He figured Tee and Jaxon were somewhere upstairs, he didn't know exactly where. Or doing exactly what.

Which was the thought that did it.

Cam felt the house close in around him and knew he had to get out for a while – walk around, think things through, try to put some distance between him and what was going on so's he might have a better chance of understanding what it all meant. And try not to think about what Tee and Jaxon might or might not be doing. He went out onto the deck and took a look around. It was warm in the sunshine and down the beach, to his left, the Santa Monica Pier looked like as good a place as any to lose himself for an hour or so.

He thought about going back inside to leave a note, but figured no one was going to worry too much about where he was, so why bother. Opening the gate at the side of the deck, Cam went down the flight of wooden steps and set off across the beach, feeling better with every step in the sand – even with the nagging reminder in his head that he still hadn't called home. He knew it wasn't just because he didn't even want to make a collect call without asking Jaxon if it was okay – no point in giving the guy ammunition – it was really because he was scared what he'd find out when he did call.

He knew his fears weren't wholly logical, but then not a lot that had happened to him over the last few days was, especially finding this weird RFID thing in his arm. But how screwed-up did you have to be to start suspecting your parents of being involved in any of what was going on?

'Why are you so down on the guy, Jax?'

'Why are you so, like, sweet on him?'

'I am not!'

'You so are, making him breakfast, getting Deacon over to put a Band-Aid on his scratch.' Jaxon leaned back in the black leather armchair and stared up at the ceiling. 'You two, you're like new best buddies.'

Tee was wandering around the room, her body language saying that she really didn't care what Jaxon thought, her eyes telling a whole other, different story. She was fit to spit, but Jaxon wouldn't know till it happened.

'You've got no reason to be jealous.' Tee stopped by the CD tower and made like she was looking at stuff.

'You think I'm jealous?'

'I don't *think* anything . . .' Tee moved on and stopped again when she came to the window that had the cool ocean view, her back to Jaxon. Out on the sand, walking away from the house, she saw someone: tall, blond hair, shirt, jeans. Could be anyone, except for that shirt. She wondered where Cam was going. 'He's gonna be gone soon.' She turned to look at Jaxon. 'Go out for a ride, he'll probably have left by the time you get back.'

'Right, I go for a ride so you can –'

'Can what?' Tee's voice had an edge, like a fresh Gillette right out of the pack.

Jaxon sat up. 'Just kidding around –'

'So grow up.' Tee glanced over her shoulder; the blond figure was already more than halfway to the pier. 'I need some air. See you later.'

Without waiting to hear his reply, Tee walked out the room, leaving Jaxon to try and work out how he'd lost the argument when he was so goddam sure he had the strongest hand. Where the hell had he gone wrong?

He left it till he heard the front door closing – telling himself that he wasn't scared of Tee, only that he knew from experience that it would be better to give her space – and then he went downstairs to find he was in an empty house. Where was the damn house guest? They couldn't've gone out together, could they?

Wondering where the hell that left him, Jaxon's angry gaze fell on Cam's black leather coat, still hanging on the back of a stool in the kitchen area where he'd put it the night before.

Up on the pier, standing out over the water and looking back at land, gave everything a different perspective. Cam stood, leaning on the metal guard rail, and tried to work out whether this difference would help him understand what was happening to him.

Getting kidnapped was a very physical kind of experience, like being ripped out of your life, violently removed from everything and everyone you knew. It had also had more of a mental effect, kind of focussing his thoughts on the fact that he was probably going to die. Escaping had pushed him to the edge, made him go beyond any limits he'd thought he had. It was, he realized, all about not thinking too much about what you were doing, or you might not do it.

And then there was killing someone.

Snuffing out a human life, even if it was the life of a person who might be going to kill you, was heavy shit. It basically made him a murderer. Even if no one ever found out what he'd done, he'd still be one in his head. And if he was caught, maybe some slick lawyer would be able to plead something like aggravated manslaughter . . . justifiable homicide? Was there something called that? If there was, did it make what he'd done okay, you know, ethically?

He'd been taken to church every Sunday and taught all about Jesus and everything, but in his house it was something you did because it was expected of you. You did this stuff because you had to be seen to do it, not because you took it remotely seriously. He'd been pretty young when he'd realized that truth. Going to church one day a week and mouthing a load of words, singing a few songs, didn't actually mean a thing. Didn't mean you believed in God. But some of it stuck, like 'Thou shalt not kill', and not just because it was against the law – smoking dope was against the law, but that didn't make it so wrong, not like taking a life.

Cam really didn't know how he felt about the fact that he'd left a man dead on the floor in that house back up in Seattle. Glad to be alive, was one way to put it, which kind of justified what he'd done. If he never had to answer for his crime, maybe, given time, he'd be able to bury it and forget he'd ever done it. Maybe. Right now he felt overpoweringly happy to be living, and at the same time, guilty as hell.

Guilty, confused and growing angrier as he began to think about the tag Tee's friend Deacon had found. What had he called it? Radio frequency something . . . whatever, what it came down to was that someone had put the thing in his arm and he now had a sneaking suspicion when and where, which was another reason why he hadn't called home. Because it was when he was twelve, could be thirteen, but no later, when his mother had taken him for what she'd said was an inoculation. Not to their regular doctor's office, but to some other place — he couldn't recall where, as he'd probably had his head in a comic book the whole journey there. He remembered the actual incident because the doctor had numbed his arm first, which even then he'd thought was odd, and then injected him, twice, and it had hurt like shit afterward.

If he was right, what was his mother doing, taking him somewhere and having that done to him? Did his dad know? The two people he loved and trusted the most in the world, and he was standing on the Santa Monica Pier, unable to make up his mind if he should pick up the phone and tell them where he was. First he turns up at his uncle's house, somewhere only his dad knew he'd be going to, and finds a reception committee waiting to grab him, and then Deacon discovers that thing he figured only his mother could've been responsible for having put there.

Cam's head felt like it was about to explode. He turned away from the ocean, thinking that a beer or something was called for, and found himself staring straight at Tee.

'Not about to jump, are you?'

'What?'

'You look kinda suicidal, man.' Tee frowned. 'What's up, Cam?'

'How'd you know where I was?'

'Saw you from the house.'

'Does Jaxon know you're here?'

'What if he does or he doesn't?'

Cam looked away, feeling the tension knot in his shoulders and his neck. 'Because I got enough shit to deal with without stirring up anymore, okay?'

'Forget about Jax. You want to chill for a while?'

'Iced tea?'

'Why not . . .'

Chapter 21

Santa Monica Beach; Friday February 28th, 4.20 p.m.

They'd passed on the honky-tonk place on the pier, which advertised that you could 'dance, eat and drink' there, and had moved on down to the promenade and the Carousel Cafe. At the home of the frostee and frozen yogurt you could sit out in the sun, and Tee claimed the burgers were also better there.

They didn't end up eating anything, just talking and talking over a series of iced teas and coffees. It didn't solve anything, but talking about the stuff messing up his head helped Cam sort it out. Just saying to someone else that you didn't trust your parents – hearing the words spoken out loud – and gauging their reaction gave the thoughts more reality.

'It's okay, Cam.'

'What is?'

'Thinking bad stuff about your folks ... they're just people, like everyone else. Not so special.'

'You believe that?'

'Sometimes.'

'I don't have a brother or a sister, you know.'

'So?'

'So I never had anyone to talk to about my parents.'

'What about your friends?'

Cam thought about the things he and Kenny and Ted talked about and it was mostly football, girls, cars and girls. Parents? Never. 'We just talk about stuff, you know?'

'Guys, huh? So in touch with their emotions.'

As they left the cafe, Tee put a penny in the machine outside, cranked the handle and gave Cam the resulting souvenir. What had been a coin was now a stretched and flattened oval that read 'I love you!' above two hearts pierced by the same arrow. Cam didn't know what to do except mumble his thanks, put the keepsake in his jeans pocket and wonder what the hell it meant. If anything.

It was well after five when they walked back into the kitchen to find Jaxon chasing his fifth Corona with a couple of fingers of bourbon. All five beer bottles were next to him on the table, along with the JD, and he'd reached that stage of drinking where deliberation kicked in and you do everything in kind of slow motion because you don't want to screw up.

'See . . . I *tole* you, didn't I? What'd I tell you, huh? Best buddies . . .'

'We bumped into each other, Jaxon.' Tee avoided looking directly at Jaxon or Cam and went over to the fridge to take a look inside. 'We just hung out down by the pier and shot the breeze . . . Wanna sandwich, anyone? I'm starved.'

'So what stories's he been telling you, Tee?'

'Stories?'

Jaxon picked up a half-empty Corona. 'Yeah, stories . . .' He took a swig and used the bottle to point at Cam. 'He's

135

fuller of the damn things than Dr. Seuss . . .'

Cam could feel himself going red as he stood, thumb hooked on his coin pocket and touching Tee's recent gift. 'What're you talking about, man?'

'I'm *talking* about like everything you say, Mr. Kidnapped, I-killed-a-guy-up-in-Seattle Man . . . I believe you to be a damn liar, man, I think you live in cloud-whatever-land.'

'Cuckoo, it's cloud *cuckoo* land.' Tee shook her head and went back to looking through the fridge.

'Whatever . . .'

'You calling me a liar?'

'Think I must be, guy . . . what you gonna do about it, Mr. I'm-stone-broke?'

'Will you cut the Mister shit . . .'

Jaxon sat back, made a whole performance of lighting a cigarette and then threw a silver-colored money clip, inlaid with some kind of blue stone, onto the table. It held a thin fold of bills and Jaxon smiled a mildly shit-faced smile, nodding at Tee. 'Waddaya think of *that*?'

'What am I supposed to think, Jaxon?'

'You're *supposed* to think, "What is this doing in the dude's jacket when he's *supposed* to be flat broke", right?'

'You went through his stuff?'

'Yeah, so?'

Tee slammed the fridge door shut so hard it bounced back open again. 'First,' she stared at Jaxon, 'you don't go poking your damn nose into other people's stuff, that is just so not what you do, and second,' Tee turned to look at Cam, cold, eyebrow raised, 'what d'you have to say about the money, Cam? Have you been on some kind of fantasy trip and decided it would be fun to take us along for the ride?'

'I don't know anything about any money, Tee. D'you think I'd've starved myself, jumped trains and snuck into the back of trucks if I wasn't broke? Anyway, like I said, that's not my jacket. I took it from the house up in Seattle and the only thing I found in it was a gun, which I threw away.' Cam glanced at the table, the money clip glinting in the white light from the overhead lamp, and then looked back at Tee. 'You really think I made this all up? The kidnap and everything? What kind of sick bastard d'you think I am?'

Tee picked up the clip, turning it over in her hands, feeling its weight and examining the inlaid decoration. 'Nice, but I don't think New Mexico turquoise and silver is quite your style, Cam . . .' She pulled the bills out and counted them. 'Two hundred and fifty bucks in fifties, not bad for walking around money . . . Where'd you find it, Jax?'

'In the damn coat, like I told you.'

'Where in the coat?'

'Some inside pocket.'

Tee saw the battered leather jacket, still on the back of the stool where Cam had originally hung it. She put the money clip down and picked up the jacket, looking carefully at the interior.

'You think *I'm* lying?' Jaxon sat up, pointing at himself with the hand holding the lit cigarette, scattering ash on the table.

'No, Jaxon, I just want to see where it was.' Tee finished with the left-hand side of the jacket and switched over to the right, stopping for a second and peering at the seam where the silk lining was sewed onto the stiff leather. 'Well, look at that . . .'

Cam walked over. 'What is it?'

Folding back a quarter inch strip of lining, Tee revealed a

thin nylon zipper about three inches long. 'Looks like a kind of secret pocket – this where you found the money, Jaxon?'

'Coulda been . . . maybe.'

Tee pulled the zipper down and felt inside and outside the hidden pocket. 'Leather lined, too . . . kind of not surprising you didn't know it was there.'

'Look, I, uh . . . I'm very kind of grateful for everything you guys've done,' Cam reached out to take the coat from Tee, 'but I think it's probably about time I went.'

'And go where, do what?' Tee held onto the coat.

'Take what I owe you guys out of that money,' Cam nodded at the clip, 'and I'll go find a motel or something.'

'Not an option.' Tee pulled the coat back and hung it on the stool. 'We need to find out what's going on with you, man.'

Jaxon slammed the almost empty bottle on the table top. 'What's with this "we" stuff? I can't believe this bullshit!'

'What's not to believe?'

'Oh, just *everything* . . .' Jaxon got up quickly, swayed like he was suddenly hit by a strong wind and sat down again. 'I need a drink.'

'What you need is some food to soak up all that juice, something like spaghetti and meat sauce, which I shall now make – and, as Jax is in no state to be trusted with a knife, you,' Tee pointed at Cam, 'are on onion duty.'

Tony Matric hated it when important stuff turned up close to the end of his shift. It meant you were kind of duty bound to deal with it and, while the Stewart case no longer looked like it was a kidnapping anymore, it was still a priority.

In front of him were the Stewart phone logs. All of them. Tony shrugged, wondering how he'd got stuck with the nitpicking, brain-numbing job of trawling through yards of paperwork and all Mike had to do was sit in some booth listening to a few messages. All partners were equal, but some, it seemed, were more equal than others.

An hour later, some time around half past six, Tony had just completed his check when Mike walked back into the office.

'You still here? Thought you'd be long gone.'

'The phone logs came in and I figured it'd be best to go through them and clear that job out of the way. You get anything off of the Stewarts' message service?'

'Nada,' Mike shook his head. 'You?'

'One thing.'

'What?'

'A call from some flyspeck called Weed.' Tony got up and went over to the map of California and pointed to a red pin he'd stuck in it, up near the Oregon border. 'Came in at just after five in the afternoon yesterday, collect call.'

'You think it was the boy?'

'I'd put money on it.'

'And I think I'd join you.' Mike went over and sat at his desk. 'Find anything else?'

'Nothing much, but I'm still waiting for the cell phone records. They won't come in till Monday now.'

'Tomorrow we bring Gartner in.' Mike grinned. 'I think we've got enough to sweat him, see if he calls for a lawyer or whatever . . . I'm looking forward to that.'

'You think he'll give anything up?'

'He's an ex-cop, Tony, he knows all the tricks, what we can and can't do . . . we're just going to have to play it by ear with him, see where we can lead him.'

'And the parents?'

'Depends on what we get out of Gartner. All we have on them right now is still circumstantial.'

Tony got up and stretched. 'What d'you say to a beer when we've finished?'

'I say "two beers".'

'Why didn't I think of that?'

'Which reminds me, did you remember to send that picture of Cameron Stewart up to LA like I asked?'

Tony flipped a lazy salute. 'Yessir!'

'Good, good . . . and I've just had another idea.'

'Tell all.'

'Pizza.'

Tony looked dumbstruck. 'Genius . . . let's go.'

Chapter 22

Santa Monica Beach; Friday February 28th, 8.16 p.m.

Jaxon had just about made it through the meal without falling off his chair. But, as Cam and Tee were clearing the table, he crashed out, face down in what was left of his plate of spaghetti and meat sauce and they had to take him upstairs. It was no easy job; asleep, he was a dead weight they had to haul like a sack, but when he'd sort of woken, halfway up the stairs, insisting he wanted to go back down again, it took a lot of persuading to stop him.

They'd eventually left him, sprawled on the massive double bed in the master bedroom, cleaned up, fully clothed and covered with a light blanket. He was, they both agreed, going to be a bear in the morning but, added Tee, why change the habit of a lifetime.

'So why d'you stay?' Cam hadn't meant to ask, but the question, which had been hovering at the back of his mind like a nervous child, just kind of escaped.

They were in the lounge, Tee flicking through an extensive collection of DVDs, Cam watching her, not what she was doing. The house was quiet and, in the bigger silence that blossomed after he'd asked his question, through the open window Cam could hear the ocean, breathing like an old man.

'There's a question . . .' Tee shot a glance at Cam and looked away. 'Why?'

'Forget I asked . . . none of my damn business.'

'True, but it's a fair question, and one I've wondered about. Not often, but sometimes. But, see, when I *do* ask myself that question, no one else hears and I don't have to answer. I can ignore it and it *will* go away . . . thing is . . .'

Tee went back to looking at DVD titles.

'Thing is what?'

'You ever see that movie *Theorem*, by what's his name . . . Pasolini? A real art house number. A friend of mine had a copy on tape and I obsessed over it for a couple of months and fell in love with Terence Stamp, who I gotta say, you look a little like. You seen it?'

'No.'

'He plays this guy who kind of just turns up and seduces this whole family, everyone from the maid to the father, and then just leaves and nothing's ever the same.' Tee came and sat at the opposite end of the sofa, left leg curled up under her. 'And you're kind of left thinking "is he just an innocent catalyst or is he God or something" . . . and I feel kind of like I'm in some sort of a reprise.'

'S'cuse me?'

'In my own version.'

'Your own version of what?' Cam felt hot, sweaty, but didn't want to think about why.

'The movie, *Theorem* . . . and you're the mysterious stranger who just drops into our lives out of nowhere. But I don't think you're God or anything, just that I feel like it's time I answered those questions I've been neglecting to face up to, like why the hell *am* I with Jaxon.'

Cam nodded and Tee lifted her right leg, reached over and nudged him with her toe, leaving her bare foot against his leg. 'Are you blushing?'

'Me?'

'Do you have a girlfriend?'

Did he have a girlfriend? What? This wasn't a conversation, it was a random Q&A that seemed designed to embarrass him. He coughed and looked away. 'Not right now, no.' The truth? He was actually between, having dumped Carole-Anne Statler, who was nice but too nice, and about to make a play for this total cheerleading babe called Deena Provine. But the last thing he was going to do right now was go into that kind of detail. For reasons he felt were probably far too obvious, he wanted Tee to like him, not think he was some asshole jock.

'You must be in between, right?'

Cam nodded.

'Are you the dumper or the dumpee?'

'Dumper,' he answered, before he'd even thought whether he should or not. 'But –'

'No explanations needed, I'm just curious about who you are.' Tee leaned forward. 'So why did you dump her?'

Cam felt like he needed distance and fresh air. He got up and went over to the open window. 'Is this some kind of game?'

Tee sat back and watched him, smiling. 'Could be . . . you asked me why I stay, I'm asking you why you went.'

'I asked you, but you didn't answer.' Cam pushed the window further open and felt a cooling breeze.

'True, and the answer is, I don't really know why I stay. What d'you think, Cam? Is it because this is such a buff

143

joint?' Tee spread her arms wide and looked around the room. 'Or d'you think I really *lurve* him, despite the fact he can be such a green-eyed jealous jerk? Or maybe it's because I feel sorry for him, poor, confused little rich kid, and I want to bring out the *nice* Jaxon that's hidden under the arrogant, self-centered exterior . . . which d'you think it is?'

'Dunno, don't know you – or him – well enough to say.'

Tee stood up and walked over and stood next to him by the window. The wide darkwood sill came up to chest height and she put both elbows in front of her, folded her arms and leaned on it, looking out into the darkness at the ocean. 'Why do any of us stay anywhere, right? I know this isn't gonna be forever – like *marry* Jaxon? I don't think so – and I know I'll be moving on. I just don't know when, to where and with whom, so I'm staying here until I do. It's as good a place as any, and a lot better than some.'

If having Tee with him on the sofa had been difficult, standing right beside her was a lot tougher. Cam could smell her – a light, sweet, complex fragrance, warm from her body. He was so close he could make out every eyelash, the haphazard pattern of tiny freckles on her face, the finely detailed lines on her lips, all picked out in the yellow uplight from the lamps on the deck below. Looking at her profile – where else *was* there to look? – he watched her blink, watched her nostrils flare as she took a deeper breath of the salt air and all he really wanted to do was reach out and touch her.

Instead, it was Tee who turned to look at him, leaned over and stroked his cheek with the back of her hand. 'Strange road we travel, Visitor.'

'Visitor?'

Rather then answering, Tee gently pulled Cam into her and kissed him.

It wasn't anything he could fight. As he felt her touch him, stroke his back, run her fingers up his neck to hold his head and push his lips harder onto hers, the last couple of days of pain and fear and loneliness melted away as if none of it had ever taken place. All that mattered was happening right there. It was an intense focus that blotted out the rest of the world – it was all now, no past, no future, just this absolute second of experience.

And then the door buzzer went.

Loud. Insistent. Reality biting back.

Cam felt like the electric impulse that had activated the unit had been fed through his spine. He and Tee broke apart, but still held onto each other, both turning to look at the source of the interruption – a video entryphone over by the stairs. The screen was lit up and on it they could see a face looking right at them from across the room.

'Deacon,' said Tee, taking a deep breath. 'Damn his inappropriate timing.'

Even though, logically, Cam knew Deacon couldn't see them, he felt observed. Caught out. Guilty. 'Better let him in, right?'

'God, I suppose so.'

'He did say he might come by later.'

'Always a man of his word.' Tee glanced at the videophone, then leaned over and traced the outline of Cam's lips with her tongue. 'Like I said, a strange road . . .'

Cam watched her go over to press the button to let Deacon in. 'Why, um . . . why'd you call me a visitor?'

'I didn't call you *a* visitor, I called you Visitor.'

'And?'

'And,' Tee buzzed Deacon in without talking to him, 'that's Terence Stamp's character in the movie . . .'

Deacon sat on one side of the dining table, Cam and Tee, well apart, on the other. In the kitchen a Mr. Coffee wheezed and gurgled its way to a fresh jug of organic Colombian mountain blend.

'Did I, you know, by chance *interrupt* anything?' Deacon looked with studied innocence from Tee to Cam.

'Just the search for something decent to watch on TV.' The coffee machine hissed and bubbled to its climactic finish and Tee got up. 'You know what the DVD collection's like here, all not-so-special effects and hardly any storyline. You want sugar and milk, Deacon?'

'Half-and-half, if you've got it.'

'Did you, you know, find anything out about the chip?' Cam smiled, leaning forward; friendly, open, innocent of whatever Deacon might be thinking he was guilty of.

'Where did you say Jaxon was?'

'Upstairs.' Cam nodded out of the room.

'He got completely loaded and passed out in his food.' Tee brought back three mugs and put them on the table. 'We had to put him to bed.'

'Lucky boy, having such good friends to look after him.' Deacon smiled at Cam, who felt himself redden.

'Quit trying to make something out of nothing, man . . .' Tee pushed a mug over to him. 'What've you got?'

Chapter 23

Santa Monica Beach; Friday February 28th, 11.03 p.m.

'I had to wait for the right moment to have a look at the chip.' Deacon took a small plastic box out of his pocket, put it down in the middle of the table and tapped it with his finger. 'These babies are normally scanned when they're like *inside* something, you know, subcutaneous. Anyway, I finally managed it.'

'So what did it say, man.' Tee snapped her fingers a couple of times. 'What was in it?'

Cam, looking sideways at the plastic box, was by turns anxious to find out which secrets the chip had given up and equally scared what he might discover about himself. He looked up to find Deacon staring back at him. 'What?'

'Don't worry, Cam. Like I said, I got everything off it, but I've no idea what any of it means.' Deacon reached into the inside pocket of his windbreaker and brought out a sheet of paper, unfolding it and spreading it out in front of him.

On it Cam could see just one line of printed letters and numbers. He turned the paper around to look at it properly. '05291985c – 03111986b: CAS/ETS: 7/25/Gen1:©D®Cp1999: 0016192831983. What the hell does all that mean?'

'Couldn't tell you, pal. Much a mystery to me as it seems to be to you.'

'You got *no* ideas, Deacon?' Tee turned the sheet of paper her way and peered at it. 'This is unlike you . . . not been taking the brain supplements lately?' Tee smiled at Cam and pointed at Deacon. 'The oh-so-logical scientist here takes these New Age tabs in the *weird* belief they'll make him *even* more intelligent.'

'Gingko is not New Age, Tee, and I take them to aid memory function, not intelligence.'

'Whatever . . .' Tee looked back at the numbers and letters. 'What's normally on these things, you know, when they're like in a dog or something?'

'Some kind of code that identifies the individual animal, and a way of contacting the owner, like an email address or a website.'

'Code numbers is all I can see.' Tee got up and walked into the kitchen area with the paper.

Cam leaned back in his chair to see where she was going. 'What're you doing?'

'There's a whiteboard here, one of those wipe-clean things you're supposed to use to leave notes to each other in this jam-packed busy world we live in? I'm going to write the stuff on it big, so we can stand back and really look at it.'

Deacon got up and took his jacket off, hanging it carefully on the back of his chair. 'You been on some kind of management training course, Tee?'

'Just think better on my feet . . . on the move, know what I mean?'

Deacon grinned at Cam. 'It's a classic control strategy. When you stand up, you dominate . . .'

'Beat it, Deacon.'

Cam walked into the kitchen to find that Tee had written the information onto the board in letters about three inches high. There were five lines, breaking after each colon, so it appeared:

05291985c – 03111986b
CAS/ETS
7/25/Gen1
©D®Cp1999
0016192831983

'Still means sweet nothing to me,' Deacon shrugged. 'Cam?'

Cam was standing, staring intently at the whiteboard, puzzled.

'Have you got something, Cam?' Tee cocked her head to one side.

'That top line . . .'

'What about it?'

'The second batch of numbers, after the dash?'

'What about them?'

Cam took the marker off Tee, walked over to the board and drew forward slashes after the second and fourth numbers, then turned to look at Tee and Deacon. 'That's my birthday, Tee.'

'No shit? We're both Pisces.'

'Such a terrific validation of the whole astrology scam,' Deacon rolled his eyes, 'what with you two being such similar characters and all . . .'

Tee ignored him and began counting on her fingers, swore and started counting again, whispering something under her breath.

'You want a calculator?' Deacon pointed back at the table. 'I got one on my cell . . .'

Tee didn't answer. Instead, walking over to Cam and taking the marker, she drew two more slashes after the second and fourth digits of the first group of numbers.

'And that means what?' asked Deacon.

'It's nine months, give or take, before his birth.' She nodded at Cam. 'See? It's May 29th, 1985, with a "c" after it, to March 11th, 1986, with a "b". Conceived and born.'

'Very specific, wouldn't you say?' Deacon hitched himself up and sat on the counter top.

'Specific?'

'It's not my area of expertise, but, while we all of us know the exact day we were born . . .' Deacon paused and put his hands out, palms up.

'No one can be *absolutely* sure when the deed was done, right?'

Deacon pointed a finger at Tee. 'On the button.'

'What the hell am I doing walking around with this stuff in me, anyway?' Cam waved at the board. 'And what's the rest of it mean?'

'I hate to sound like a stuck CD, but I have no idea and,' Deacon looked at his watch and then slid off the counter, 'it's late and I gotta go, guys. You two going to keep on keeping on, or sleep on it and see what the morrow brings?'

'Meaning?' Tee's eyes narrowed, just very slightly.

'No hidden messages . . .' Deacon smiled as he walked past Tee, picked up his jacket and looked over at Cam. 'Sorry I couldn't be of more help, guy, but if you're still brainstorming this thing tomorrow and want another head, give me a call, okay?'

'Thanks, man . . . thanks for everything.'

'No es nada, compadre.' Deacon waved at Tee. 'Call me, girl, yeah?'

'Sure. You going without giving me a hug?'

'Where were my manners . . .'

'D'you think he knows? How the *hell* could he know?'

'Deacon? He has the most finely tuned, indecently accurate social radar in the known universe. Want a nightcap?' Tee held up an open bottle of Courvoisier. Cam shook his head, but Tee went ahead and poured a couple of small shots anyway. 'He knows stuff before even the people who are going to do it know. It's freaky.'

'Is he . . .'

'Gay? That he doesn't know.'

'How can he not know?'

'Some people just don't, like they're not *in* the closet and screwing everything in a skirt to prove what an hombre they are, but neither are they cruising the scene.' Tee chinked her glass against Cam's and took a sip. 'I think he probably is, but on the other hand I don't know everything about his life.'

'Aren't you, like, *curious*?'

'Not so's I have to pry. He's never said anything and neither have I. He's a smart guy, he'll figure it out, one day.'

'Will he say anything?'

'To Jaxon? I seriously doubt it . . . what's to say? And anyway, he doesn't like Jax, never has.'

What's to say? What's to *say*? Was this Tee's way of letting him know he was just somebody, some*thing* she figured she could fool around with?

'What's up?'

Cam refocussed on Tee, who was looking at him like he'd actually said out loud what he'd been thinking. 'Nothing, why?'

'Oh, I don't know. You just had a look on your face that said you were kind of pissed at something I'd said?'

'No . . .'

'Look, I didn't mean what happened . . .' she looked up at the ceiling, indicating upstairs, '. . . didn't *mean* anything, just that, like, what's he going to say, right? Deacon didn't *see* shit.'

'So . . .'

'So what?'

Cam sat back and drank too much brandy, feeling it hit his stomach and blaze. Tee was not making things any easier. He felt he was taking part in an emotional game show where audience got their yucks seeing the contestant blindsided when he least expected it. 'I'm confused.'

'I like you . . . a lot, okay? Does that help?'

Cam nodded, but didn't say anything.

'And I, ah, meant what I did.'

Cam nodded again, straight-faced. 'I'm glad.'

'Plus, if it makes you feel any better, *I'm* feeling pretty confused myself . . . this was definitely not on my To-Do list for today, you know?'

'What about Jaxon?'

'You mean "what about the future?"' Tee did that half-smile thing he recognized as a habit of hers. 'You want me to tell you what happens next? Tough. I have no idea. Except that I do know if, right now, you try and jump my bones all bets are off.'

Cam put his glass down and held both hands up, shaking his head. 'I need all the friends I can get.'

'Correct response.' Tee smiled then rolled her eyes, yawning. 'Jeez, I am *tired*, man.'

Cam got up, leaving the rest of the brandy in the glass.

'See you tomorrow, Tee. Sleep well.'

'Don't I get a hug?' Tee pushed her chair back and stood up, too.

'Are you trying to make my life difficult, or what?' Cam looked away, shaking his head.

'No . . .' Tee moved around the table and kissed him lightly on the cheek, 'just more interesting. You sleep well, too, Visitor.'

'I think I've had enough of interesting to last me a long time . . .'

Cam lay in bed unable to sleep, *way* too much going on in his head. It wasn't only Tee, although she was right at the very top of a list headed 'Stuff To Be Dealt With'. Right behind her was the shit to do with his parents and the damn chip in his arm. What was *that* all about? Why had he been taken to some doctor's office when he was thirteen or something to have that put in him? Who could possibly need to know when he'd been conceived, and whatever else the other crap Deacon had downloaded meant?

Questions, questions, questions, and none of them – including Tee – had any easy answers. He still hadn't figured out why those people had been waiting for him outside his uncle's, or, more to the point, why he'd been kidnapped in the first place. He felt lost, surrounded by facts that meant nothing, clues that went nowhere, puzzles he had no chance of solving. It all would've made his head hurt if the brandy hadn't mellowed his alpha waves to the point where sleep was the . . .

Chapter 24

Santa Monica Beach; Saturday March 1st, 9.46 a.m.

Cam had forgotten to draw the drapes the night before and woke up with bright sunlight right in his face and a low grade, minor league headache grumbling just above his eyebrows – internal weather conditions that lifted after a savage shower. He made his way, barefoot, downstairs to the kitchen, wondering what the hell the next twenty-four hours could possibly bring to top the surprises delivered the previous day.

As he came along the hallway into the dining area he heard the opening bars of a song on the stereo system. Low violins, a simple repeated piano phrase and then a plaintive voice he didn't recognize, singing about how he'd paid all his dues, picked up his shoes and got up and walked away, cos he was just a boy and didn't know how to play . . . just a boy, giving it all away. Cam stood and listened to the whole song, which went to the fade with the words 'just a boy . . .' and then an ID for a station called K-Earth 101 cut in.

Cam went on into the kitchen thinking how weird it was how the radio sometimes did that, provided the perfect soundtrack to your life, like you had Quentin Tarantino doing what he always seemed to be able to do in his movies and choosing absolutely the right song for what was happening. He'd never felt more like a boy, less able to control his life, since he was a pre-teen.

In the kitchen Tee was bending down, inspecting the progress of an English muffin under the grill, when he walked in. 'Who was singing that song, Tee?'

'That last one?' Tee straightened up, frowning. 'That was, you know, that guy from The Who, the lead singer?'

'Pete Townshend?'

'Lead *singer*, dummy . . . Roger whatsisname, Daltrey. They were my dad's favorite band.'

'Were?'

'He took them a little too seriously and died before he got old.'

'Sorry?'

'Line from one of their songs, "Hope I die before I get old" . . . he used to sing it all the time.'

'Jeez . . .'

'Yeah, but I was nine when it happened, had a long time to get used to it.'

'What happened?'

'He drank and drove, straight into an overpass on the freeway . . . shit!' Tee spun around and pulled the tray out from underneath the grill. 'Burnt . . .'

'Why don't we go out and get some breakfast . . . I got some money now, I can buy and,' Cam held his arms out, pointing at his bare feet, 'I could do with some fresh clothes too.'

'Cool! There's a great coffee shop not far from here, and a Gap over on I think 3rd Street.' Tee stopped and looked him

155

up and down. 'You just want some generic stuff, right? You don't want to go, like, *shopping* or anything?'

'As long as it's clean, I don't care . . . is, um, is Jaxon up?'

'Still sawing logs.'

'Right . . .'

'So let's git before he wakes up.'

'What's he going to do if he comes down and finds we're not here?'

'Wonder where we are and be snippy when we get back, what else?' Tee switched the toaster off. 'C'mon . . .'

It was a beautiful day. They decided to walk over to 3rd Street first, buy Cam some essentials and then go and have a late breakfast, Tee's logic dictating that the longer you left it the more you could order as reward and compensation for waiting.

Over cups of cappuccino so big you could almost have washed your hands in them, they ate a couple of giant Danishes and then Tee took out the sheet of paper Deacon had brought over the night before. Cam, who had other things on his mind to talk about, hoped his disappointment wasn't plastered on his face.

'I was looking at this stuff on the board this morning, but got nowhere else, so I thought we could have another go now – like this number.' Tee smoothed the paper out and pointed at the end of the line.

'What about it?'

'Looks like another date, right? See at the end, 1983?' Tee pointed again. 'But whichever way I try and figure the thing, I can't make any sense of the rest of it. You?'

Cam picked the sheet up and sat back, chewing on his lower lip. 'Got a pencil?'

'Maybe . . .' Tee moved stuff around in her bag, took a few things out, put some of them back, checked her cell and finally pulled out a cheap ballpoint advertising some insurance company. 'Here you go.'

'Thanks.' Cam took the pen, clicked it open and did a quick piece of addition at the bottom of the paper. 'Right . . .'

'What you got?'

'See that bit there,' he indicated the copyright mark and circled ©D®Cp1999, 'I'm positive 1999 was the year I had that chip put in me, when I was thirteen.'

'So "D" copyrighted something, and "Cp" registered it, in 1999 . . . but what?'

'Me?'

'But *why*, right? I mean you're a buff-looking guy, and all, but hardly *pedigree* material!'

Cam threw a sugar packet at her. 'Just an idea – you got a better one?'

Tee ducked out of the way, then reached over and turned Cam's left wrist toward her. 'Shit, is that one o'clock?'

'No,' Cam pulled his hand away and checked for sure, 'five after twelve.'

'Late enough, we better go.' Tee scooped the last of the foam out of her cup with her finger as she got up.

'I'll go pay . . . should I get a Danish for Jaxon?'

Tee nodded. 'And a tall skinny latte as well, if you don't mind.'

'Why should I mind?'

'You mean, like he can't help being a jerk?'

'I didn't say that.'

Jaxon was still asleep when they got back, the house quiet except for the radio station, which they'd left playing when

157

they went out. Cam disappeared into his room to put on the clothes he'd bought, while Tee went to sort out Jaxon, who, she said, needed to wake up or he'd go completely nocturnal.

Tee came back in the kitchen about five minutes later, looking annoyed. 'I've kinda had it with oldies, Cam. Could you turn the radio off?'

'Been bugging me, too – where is it?'

'In that dresser next door, open the front and you'll see it. You need a pilot's license to operate the stupid thing, which is why I mostly just leave it.'

'How is he?' Cam pointed upward with his thumb.

'I've seen worse . . . he'll be down in a minute. Where'd you put that coffee?'

'In the microwave, like you said.'

'Thanks.' Tee went over and programmed the machine to zap the take-out coffee, leaning back against the counter to look at the whiteboard after she'd pressed the 'Start' button. 'Wish I could get my head around the rest of this stuff . . .'

'What stuff? And will someone *please* change the damn radio station?'

Cam turned to see Jaxon, looking pale and kind of monochrome, standing watching them.

'Want a shot of caffeine? We brought you back a latte.' Tee indicated the humming microwave. 'Got you a Danish as well, punch those sugar levels up.'

'You already went out?' Jaxon made a thing of ignoring Cam. 'How nice . . . what else you been up to?' Before either of them could reply, the microwave dinged and Jaxon shuffled over to get his coffee, noticing the board as he pulled the door open. 'Someone got a math project?'

'Deacon came around last night. That's what he downloaded off that chip he found in Cam's arm.' Tee pushed a jar toward Jaxon. 'You want sugar?'

Jaxon shook his head. 'What's it about then, this stuff?' He blew on the coffee and took a sip.

'We've a fair idea what the top line means, *no* idea about the next two, getting somewhere with the fourth and *totally* confused about the last one.' Tee walked over to the board. 'It looks like it should be a date, but plainly isn't.'

'Date? More like a phone number with an international dialing code. Did you say there was something to eat with this coffee?'

Cam passed a plate with the Danish on it over to Jaxon, who grunted as he took it.

'Phone number?' Tee frowned. 'How'd you get that?'

'Zero-zero-one, right?' Jaxon took a bite of the Danish. 'It's the code you use to call the States, like when you're in Europe or wherever?'

'That right?' Cam looked at Tee. 'I've never been abroad, you?'

Tee shook her head.

'Coupla hayseeds . . . see, after the zero-zero-one?' Jaxon put the plate down and went over to the board. 'Next three figures are the city code – six-one-nine – the rest are, you know, the phone number. Right?'

'So, whatever six-one-nine is, that's an area code for that city?' Tee picked up the cordless from the countertop. 'What's the information number?'

'It's San Diego,' said Cam, taking a deep breath. 'Six-one-nine. It's San Diego . . .'

159

Chapter 25

Santa Monica Beach; Saturday March 1st, 1.22 p.m.

'You just gonna *stand* there?' Jaxon, leaning against a cup-board, smirking, took another bite out of his Danish.

Cam looked over at him. 'What?'

'Call the damn number, why don't you, put us out of our misery.'

'Call it?'

'Well you ain't gonna find out if it *is* a phone number by looking at it, pal.'

Cam went over to where Tee was standing, still holding the cordless handset, and she gave it to him. 'Now or never, right? Could mean absolutely nothing . . .'

'Put it on speakerphone, Tee, so we can all hear.'

Cam glanced at Tee and shrugged his agreement. She took the handset back off him, put it onto the base unit and pressed one of the buttons. A loud dial tone came out of the unit's speaker.

Jaxon grinned at Cam. 'Dial away, man.'

Cam punched in the ten-digit number and the pitch changed to a ring tone. He stood, looking at the phone, the odd way you do with inanimate objects, expecting them to actually *do* something, other than sit there in front of you.

Then the call got picked up.

'This is the automatic answering service of the Doctor Corporation of San Diego, California,' said a woman's voice. *'Our office hours are 8.30 a.m. to 5.30 p.m., Monday to Friday. If you are calling out of normal office hours, and would like to leave a message, please do so after the tone and your call will be returned as soon as possible. In an emergency, please contact your individual consultant on the cell phone number you have been provided with. Thank you for calling the Doctor Corporation.'*

Click. Beep, beep, beep . . .

'Want to leave a message?' Tee queried. Cam shook his head and she reached over and canceled the call. 'That mean a thing to you, Cam? Heard of this Doctor Corporation?'

'Nope.'

'Genius!' Jaxon finished off the last piece of the Danish and made a deal of licking each of his fingers.

'Sorry?'

'Give it up for me, man.' Jaxon grinned at Tee, pointing at himself. 'I got the goddam number for you, right? Solved your little problemo.'

'Yeah, thanks, Jaxon . . .' Cam pasted on a smile. 'That was pretty neat.'

'Damn right, bro.'

'Got any ideas about the rest of it?' Tee went over to the board and put ticks next to the top line and the one at the bottom. 'We still got three more to go.'

'Talking of gotta go,' Jaxon scratched the stubble on his face, 'it's Saturday, right? I have to be over at my dad's — who's got the time?'

Cam glanced at his wrist. 'One thirty.'

'Gonna be late.' Jaxon waved as he walked out of the kitchen. 'Thanks for brunch.'

Tee and Cam looked at each other, surprise registering on both their faces, and then, before either of them could say anything, Jaxon walked back in.

'If you've gone by the time I get back, pal, nice knowing you,' he said, turning straight around and walking out again.

Silence. Front door slamming. Muffled engine turning over. Screech of rubber. Silence again.

'That's the one thing you can guarantee, with Jaxon.' Tee shook her head and looked out the kitchen window at the beach.

'What is?'

'He never tries to pretty stuff up . . . he thinks it, he says it.'

'I suppose I'd better get my shit together and find somewhere else to crash.'

'Screw that.'

'Got the strong impression I've outstayed my welcome, Tee . . . you know, like *really* time to go?'

'He doesn't want you to go, he just doesn't *like* you.'

'And d'you have *any* idea how it feels to be somewhere where someone wants you out? Granted, the rest of my life's no breeze, but don't you think maybe I should try and sort this bit out first?'

'It's not just you . . .' Tee stayed looking through the window at the sea, '. . . do *you* have any idea how confused *I* feel? You can't just *go*!'

'That's a whole other thing,' Cam stayed where he was, not sure what would happen if he went over to Tee, 'and I can't deal with that right now. Right now I have to find out about *my* life, find out what's been happening to me – what's *going* to happen to me. There's a *dead* person up in Seattle, Tee, and I did it.'

'That was self-defense, you said.'

'Dead is dead, no way of prettying that up, either.'

'Look . . .' Tee turned around, but stayed where she was, the couple of feet between them acting like a no-man's-land safety zone. 'If I sound selfish and kind of self-obsessed, I'm sorry . . . like I know any problems I have are no way as bad as yours, but you coming here, it's made me look at what I'm doing . . .'

Cam watched her face, sad, so sad, looking like she was maybe going to cry, and he truly hoped she wouldn't because then he knew he'd have to go to her.

'*I* know I'm here much more for the place and cos it's easy, than for what I feel for Jax . . .' Tee took a deep breath, '. . . what I've *ever* felt for him, if I'm honest. So, now I've faced up to that, I have to pack up and go . . . no more living the lie. Which is good, except I have *no* idea what to do with the rest of my life, which was one of the reasons why I stayed here, cos that way I didn't have to think about it.'

'Same boat, you and me.'

'Kind of you to say so, but let's face it, my petty dilemmas are a storm in a, you know, little bone china teacup compared to what you're having to deal with.' In one seamless move, Tee plucked a chopstick out of a glass jar on the counter, pulled her hair back behind her head, tied it in a knot and stuck the chopstick through it. 'Want to go look up the Doctor Corporation on the computer?'

'Ah, sure . . . how d'you do that thing with your hair?'

'By not thinking what I'm doing.'

Jaxon had a fully accessorized high-end Mac laptop, with internet access through his cable service, set up in what he liked to call his office, looking out over the ocean on the second floor. He almost never turned the Mac off and the big plasma screen it was plugged into sprang to life the moment Tee sat down at the desk and shifted the mouse.

Cam looked around the room. 'What does he do, Jaxon? Does he work?'

'Yeah, kind of.'

'What at?'

'Oh, this and that . . . likes to say he's a producer, you know, movies and stuff? But all he's done since we've been together is a couple of music videos. Although there's sup-posed to be a script out there he's got something to do with.'

'So all this,' Cam waved at the room, 'is kept afloat by Daddy?'

'Pretty much.' Tee shrugged and looked down at the key-board. 'Let's get started – should we Google this Doctor place first or try guessing what their web address is?'

'Google, I guess.'

Tee pulled up the Google home page and typed ['The Doctor Corporation, San Diego'] into the search window and pressed return. The Mac's screen blanked as the search engine did its behind-the-scenes stuff, and then cleared to reveal its listing of possible answers. Right at the top, third entry down, was the Doctor Corporation. The web address was doctorcorp.com.

'Want to go there?'

'Sure.'

Tee clicked on the heading, the screen cleared again and then loaded up the requested home page. Right across the top, in white letters out of a blue background, was the company logo.

DOCTO® CORPORATION

'Nice graphic.' Tee pointed at the R in a circle. 'That's like the medical symbol, right? Neat, huh?'

'Kind of . . .'

Running down the right-hand side of the screen was a menu of options – 'About Us', 'Contact Us' and 'Centers of Excellence' – and the rest of the page had a photograph of a fairly nondescript high-rise office building with the words 'The Future of Medical Services' under it.

'Low key,' said Tee, clicking on 'About Us'. 'Wonder what they've got to say about themselves.'

The photograph disappeared, replaced by a short block of text.

'The Doctor Corporation was formed twenty years ago to push the boundaries of fertility research, providing leading-edge medical services and the highest levels of care available,' Tee read off the screen. 'To ensure that this aim of continual excellence is always achieved, we actively pursue a research policy that has put the Doctor Corporation at the forefront of medical innovation. Is that it?'

'Scroll down.'

Tee moved the mouse over to the right of the screen. 'There's nothing else to scroll down to, Cam.' She tapped on 'Contact Us', which brought up a new email message window in Outlook, and then tried 'Centers of Excellence', which gave two addresses, one in San Diego. Tee printed that page out.

'That solves the copyright line from the chip, then,' said Cam.

'What does?'

Cam wrote ©D®Cp1999 on a piece of scrap paper. 'It means copyright Doctor Corporation 1999, you know, like a D and an R being short for Doctor?'

'Way to go, check another line off . . . s'pose we'll have to wait till Monday to ask them what level of care dictated they had to chip you, right?'

'How d'you find out more information about a company like that?' Cam pulled up a spare chair and sat next to the table. 'I mean, if they don't seem to want to provide it themselves?'

'Hire a private dick?'

'I don't think my budget runs to that . . .'

'Okay, fall back on Plan B.'

'Which is?'

'My Plan B always seems to be "Ask Deacon".'

Chapter 26

La Jolla, San Diego; Saturday March 1st, 1.17 p.m.

Eleanor Stewart put the receiver down on the desk. 'It's Gartner.'

'Who?' Gordon Stewart, mind elsewhere, looked up from the paper he was reading.

'Thomas Gartner? Employee, Head of Security?'

'What about him?'

'He wants to talk to you.' Eleanor nodded at the desk as she walked away. 'He's waiting on the phone.'

'Has something happened?' Gordon got up from the table. 'Is there any news about Cameron?'

'He says the police had him in for questioning this morning.'

'Cameron?'

'*Gartner*. Do you want some lunch?'

'Why'n't you call me before, Tom?' Gordon Stewart was wearing a rut in the Navajo-style rug. 'What did they want, what did they ask?'

'I didn't call because,' Gartner, watching him from the sofa, counted on his fingers, 'one, nothing really happened – it seemed to be more about me than anything else – and two, I didn't think it was worth getting bothered about.'

'So what did they ask? Must've asked *something* if they took the trouble to bring you in.'

Gartner got a cigarette pack out of his jacket pocket. 'Mind if I smoke?'

'I don't . . .' Stewart watched Gartner open the pack, 'but Eleanor will probably stub it out in your eyes if you light one up.'

'Fine . . .' The pack returned to its pocket.

'So?'

'So that cop, Matric? He remembered me from when I was a uniform, made some sarcastic comments about what was a guy like me doing in a job like this.'

Stewart frowned. 'He was in Chula Vista?'

'Apparently. He was rookie, it was a long time ago and I've kind of wiped that tape.'

'The past never dies, just goes to sleep, right?'

Gartner looked blankly at his boss. 'Yeah. Anyway, Matric and his partner dicked me around about that, but I told them you knew all about my youthful indiscretions. They were on a fishing trip and they didn't have anything to give me a real hard time over, and they also knew they couldn't try anything on with me.'

Stewart glanced at his security chief. 'Was that it then, just a chat about the old days?'

'Not quite . . .' Gartner stood up. 'Can we go outside? I could really do with a smoke.'

'You can fire up the whole damn pack when we've finished – what else did they ask about?'

Gartner sat back down. 'They know we – me and Matheson – were in LA the other night, but they don't know why.'

'And how the hell they know that?'

'Matheson ran a red and we got pulled over.'

'Matheson? Stupid little –' Stewart stopped in mid-stride, like he'd walked into a glass wall. 'They checked out your *car*? Shit! Why're they investigating *us*?'

Gartner shook his head. 'I told you, it's not you, it's me they were checking on.'

'If Matheson was driving, how'd they figure you were there with him?'

'They asked.'

'They *asked*?'

'Yeah, but it's okay, I hadn't been doing anything wrong and it would've been an easy lie to get picked up on, so I thought the truth was most probably the best option.'

'They want to know why you were there?' Stewart sat down in the armchair opposite Gartner.

'Sure, and I said it was really nothing to do with them, but that if they wanted to know, I'd been up there on company business, in my company car, with my company driver. Which was all completely true.'

Stewart sat back, steepling his hands. 'You think they know?'

'Know what?'

'That the kidnap thing isn't kosher.'

'If they *knew* that we'd both be down the station house right now, sir.' Having screwed up over the cops pulling him in, something he knew Mrs. Stewart would use against him if she could, Gartner felt the control was coming back his way. 'I don't think we have anything to worry about, Mr. Stewart.'

'Oh really?'

'No. Inverdale no longer has your son – who is, if I may

169

say so, doing a very good job of not getting found by any-one – and it's true that the best option would be if we got to him first, which I think is what will happen. I don't know why he hasn't called us back yet, though I'm sure there's a reasonable explanation, but he's not going to be calling Inverdale, and even if the cops find him before we do, that's fine.'

Stewart made an 'it is?' face.

'It's fine because what can he say? You told me he doesn't know anything.'

Inverdale cracked his knuckles, making a slightly juicy pop-ping sound. Alfredo Perro, his headphones hanging around his neck, made a face, looking over at Sheila Ikeburo, who raised one eyebrow back at him.

'Why d'you think the cops pulled Gartner, Al?' Inverdale stretched and uncricked his neck. He was changing hotels, or at the very least upgrading his room to something with a more comfortable bed. Last night had been torture.

'Could be anything, boss.' Alfredo shrugged; how the hell was *he* to know why this guy had been pulled – he was just a listener. 'Any ideas, Sheila?'

Sheila looked out the window, not saying anything for a long moment. Neither she nor Alfredo had worked for Inverdale before, just knew him by reputation, which was often the case in the twilight, never-quite-legal world of sur-veillance they inhabited. He was supposed to be okay, a grifter who had hit the big time, made serious money but still liked to do business. She was surprised how unprepos-sessing he looked – short, balding, bad skin; expensive dresser, though.

'Ideas?' Sheila focussed back on the question. 'Yeah, that

having a bug in the house would've been a big help to us, right?'

'Who knew we'd ever need more than a phone tap?' Inverdale got a pack of cigarettes out, took one and lit it, blowing the smoke out through his nostrils. 'Anything else of interest, Al – like the boy has phoned and you were waiting to surprise me with the news?'

'No, but, ah . . .' Al looked up at the ceiling.

Inverdale followed his gaze. 'What?'

'Smoke alarms.'

'Are you serious?'

'Whole building, boss.'

'We have to go out on the sidewalk.' Sheila motioned at the office door with her own pack. 'It's the only exercise I get.'

Inverdale dumped his just-started cigarette in an unfinished cup of take-out coffee. 'They'll be telling us what to do in our own damn homes next.'

Al unwrapped two Twinkies he'd taken from a box on the table. 'They can do what they like as long as they don't ban these things . . . So, why've you guys come down to San Diego? I thought the boy was in LA.'

'He is, but we don't know where. In all likelihood he'll come home, and we *do* know where that is. I've got the place under observation.' Inverdale watched Al put both the Twinkies in his mouth at the same time. 'That is disgusting.'

Al chewed for a moment and swallowed. 'Smoking's disgusting. That was merely childish.'

Chapter 27

Santa Monica Beach; Saturday March 1st, 3.25 p.m.

Plan B had been put into motion and Tee had agreed they'd meet Deacon at some place he knew off Wilshire. Cam was kind of glad they were getting out of the house, where there would just have been the two of them. Dangerous chemistry. He felt the tension between them – well, there was certainly tension from where *he* was standing – and with everything else that was going on the last thing he needed was yet more emotional turmoil.

But it felt good, him and Tee walking along Ocean. Close. Then, as they crossed the street, their hands touched, so briefly you could've missed it, but neither of them did. They touched again, and this time he knew it was less by chance, more by design, and, as they touched, Tee's finger hooked his and held it. Tight. Just for a moment. And then they were back to walking side by side, leaving Cam wondering if it really had happened.

He looked at Tee, half smiling, half questioning.

'What?' She smiled back.

'Nothing . . .'

'Damn . . . I shouldn't't've done that.'

'Oh yes you should,' Cam glanced away then leaned over and kissed her, 'but, ah, I probably should not have done that.'

'Yeah, well . . .' Tee stopped walking, breathed in and exhaled slowly. 'Can we both agree to put a complete hold on things until both you and I know what the hell we're doing with our lives? Can we do that?'

Cam nodded. 'I guess.'

'Okay . . . right . . . let's go see Deacon.'

Matheson indicated right and turned the black Mercury Sable off Santa Monica, pulling into a vacant parking space. He looked over at his boss. 'You want me to do the meter, Mr. Gartner?'

'You got change?'

'How long d'you want?'

'Hour should cover it.' Tom Gartner glanced at his watch. 'All we have to do is do a trawl through the park down there with the picture of the kid. Shouldn't take long.'

Matheson unbuckled and opened the car door. 'Why d'you think he might've come here?' Matheson knew he was on a very short leash with his boss, as close as you could get to being fired without being shown the door. If he hadn't yelled out, they'd have the kid and everything would be A1. So, keep talking, keep it friendly, keep the job. It was a theory.

'The Stewart boy could be holed up with some street people.' Gartner unclicked his seatbelt. 'You know, having no money you tend to end up with others in the same place? It's a bit of a wild card, but better than just driving around.'

'Why here?'

173

'We start at the beach and work back up to West Hollywood. You never know, he could've bummed the bus fare, hitched a lift, even walked.'

'Long way to walk, sir.'

'You do what you have to, right? You got no money, you walk.'

'I just wish I hadn't –'

'Shouted out?' Gartner interrupted. 'Yeah, me too, but seeing as we can't turn the clock back, put the damn money in the meter and let's get going.'

Cam pushed the door of the cafe bar open and held it for Tee, following her in. At the back of the place he could see Deacon sitting, facing them, at a table. Not alone.

'Who's he with, Tee?'

'Like I'm psychic?'

'Just asking . . .'

Tee made her way through the tables toward Deacon, the woman he was with turning around to look as she got close. 'Hi Deke, we early?'

Deacon looked puzzled. 'No. Why?'

Tee glanced at the woman. 'We weren't expecting company.'

'Right, okay.' Deacon stood up. 'This is Sarah . . . Sarah Baldwin. Sarah, meet Tee and Cam.'

Tee went and sat next to Deacon, leaving Cam the seat by Sarah, who smiled up at him as he pulled out the chair. Cam noticed the spatter of light freckles across her olive-skin face, the lines radiating from the corners of her dark brown eyes and the ones across her forehead. An open, friendly, interesting face. Serious, he thought.

'You guys want something, coffee or whatever?' Deacon looked over at the waitress, standing by the bar.

174

'Regular coffee for me. Cam?' Tee looked at Cam, who nodded. 'A couple of regulars, thanks. So, Sarah, why're you here?'

Deacon, who was signaling for two more coffees, shook his head. 'I told you she could be direct, Sarah. She's here, Tee, because I *asked* her to be here, to help. You wanted me to help, right?'

'Yup.'

'Sarah's like a journalist –'

Cam reacted as if someone had stubbed a cigarette out on him. '*Journalist?*' He pushed his chair back, staring at Deacon. 'Why?'

'Hey, guy.' Tee reached over and gripped his arm. 'Chill.'

'My father said you should *never* trust a journalist, poking around and stuff, and like I don't *need* that right now!'

'Maybe your father thought like that because he's got something to hide, Cam.' Tee let go of his arm and sat back. 'What d'you think?'

Cam didn't know what to think. He'd grown up listening to his dad's mantra about what a load of low-lifes reporters were, but the last few days had turned everything upside down. *Did* his dad have something to hide?

'I'm not actually a journalist . . .'

They all turned to look at Sarah.

'Not right now, anyway. I'm really more of a researcher *for* journalists. Kind of. On a TV show?'

'Researcher.' Tee grinned at Cam. 'We need a researcher. Which show?'

'It's called *RealiTV* . . . cheapshit stuff, but it gets lapped up by the cable guys cos it's kind of edgy and we attract the advertisers.' Sarah glanced at Cam. 'I know what you mean about journalists, I recognize the description. It's what

I was until very recently. Did the training and all, got the job and then, a few months ago, I got laid off and I've had to take whatever comes along until I can get back in where I belong.'

Cam shifted awkwardly in his chair, moving slightly back toward the table. 'So . . . what did you do?'

'Worked on a paper doing features, and then I moved to a news station. I really like TV, I can't wait to go back to a live news desk, but there's not many openings.'

'Okay . . . sorry for losing it.' Cam shrugged.

Sarah smiled. 'That's all right.'

'What's Deacon told you?'

'Just that you want to find out about some organization, get some deep background on them.'

Cam looked over at Tee and then glanced at Deacon. He felt confused. He hadn't been expecting anyone else to be at the meet, had been freaked by finding out this woman, Sarah – who seemed like a nice enough person – was a journalist, and now he had to figure how much she really needed to know. It was obvious that having a professional researcher doing stuff would be a big help, but, but, but . . .

'Look, what it is, we need to find out as much as we can, as fast as we can, about something called the Doctor Corporation,' Tee said, walking into the conversational gap and breaking the silence. 'They're out of San Diego. Can you do anything over the weekend at all?'

'The web never sleeps . . . you got anything at all on these guys?'

Cam took a folded sheet of paper out of his jacket pocket. 'This is all we have. It's just what we found on their site.'

Sarah took the print-out, opened it up and scanned it quickly. 'Interesting logo.' She refolded the paper and put it in her bag. 'I'll get going as soon as I get home.'

Cam watched her as she stood up. 'You know I don't have much money . . . did Deacon say?'

'He did. Pay me later − if I get you something useful, okay? If I come up with nothing, you won't owe me a cent.'

Cam nodded. 'Thanks.'

'One other thing . . .' Sarah sat down again, checked her nails and looked directly at Cam.

Cam frowned. 'What?'

'There's a story here, right? I can tell there's something good. Now I *promise*, on my life, that I will not spill a bean, but if whatever this is looks like going public? I would like to be the one to break it. You let me do that and it'll be *me* owing *you*.' Sarah checked her nails again. 'Deal?'

Silence. A long, uneasy one during which Deacon rearranged stuff on the table and the coffees eventually arrived.

Tee turned to her friend. 'You trust her, Deke?'

'Sure . . .'

'Just how far?'

'Further than I can spit, okay, Tee? Trust *me* here . . . I know what's at stake and Sarah's good people.' Deacon turned to Cam. 'She won't let you down, guy.'

Cam paused for a moment, then offered his hand to Sarah. 'Okay, deal.'

Matheson hung back, watching Gartner hold out a black and white picture and a couple of dollar bills to the man on the bench. 'A deuce to look, more if you score.'

'What, like did I seen him? That kinda thing?' The man swiped the picture and the money and squinted at both before pocketing the bills and then taking a closer look at the six-by-four piece of paper. 'I see lotsa people jus' like him everyday, walk by like they shit don't smell.'

'This would've been probably at night. He wouldn't've looked quite as neat and tidy as this either, maybe wearing a leather coat. Would've also been in the last couple of days.'

The man, his unshaven face blotched and puffy, used his free hand to reach underneath his coat and scratch as he continued to look at the picture. 'Leather coat, you say?'

Gartner nodded.

'Was a boy down here recent, *he* had a leather coat. Stanley tried to move on him and got a buncha change throwed at him. Was a angry boy, I heard him shout stuff, and Stanley said he said he'd been kidnapped and –'

Gartner took the picture back. 'Where's Stanley?'

'Did I score?'

Gartner handed over a ten-spot. 'Where's Stanley?'

'He ain't here.'

'Where is he?'

'Wassa time?'

Gartner looked at his watch. 'Quarter after four.'

'He's prob'ly still out working the street. He won't be back till it's dark, less he done real well.' The man leaned forward and Gartner got a blast of *eau de hobo* which made him almost gag. 'You want me to give him a message?'

Gartner took a ballpoint out of his breast pocket and wrote something on the back of the picture, then he took a $20 bill out of his wallet and tore it in half. 'Give him this and get him to phone me. He does, he gets a nice bonus and you get the other half.'

'What if he don't phone, man?'

'Wipe your ass with it . . .'

Back in the car Gartner could still smell the guy on the bench, like the odor molecules were glued to the inside of his nose. 'You got any cigarettes, Matheson?'

Matheson watched his boss fire up and blow smoke out of his nose a couple of times and then throw the half-smoked cigarette out the open car window, wondering what the hell he was up to.

'You got any gum?'

'Sure.'

'Give me a stick. Please.'

'Sure.' Matheson reached into his pocket and handed over a pack of spearmint. 'You okay?'

'You didn't smell that guy? He's a walking WMD.'

'What do we do now?'

'We're going to get a beer and a burger and wait to see if this Stanley does the right thing.' Gartner shifted uneasily in his seat. 'You itch, or anything?'

'No, why?'

'No reason . . . let's find somewhere to eat.'

'You believe that street bum, sir?'

'What's to believe? He didn't know what I was looking for. He gave up that information about the guy saying he'd been kidnapped with no help from me. That was genuine. The man we have to be careful with is Stanley . . .'

'Because he knows he has stuff we want?'

Gartner nodded as Matheson started the car. 'And that makes it a seller's market.'

Chapter 28

Santa Monica Beach; Saturday March 1st, 7.03 p.m.

Dusty was a whiner and Stanley surely hated whiners. He hadn't got a lot of time for Dusty anyway, the guy smelling to hell and back on a good day, so let's not mention about when it got hot. But today he was really going for it, waving this torn piece of green paper – which, on closer inspection, turned out to actually be half a $20 bill, exactly like he claimed it was – and insisting that there was money in this thing for Stanley too. All he had to do, Dusty insisted, was make a call to the guy with the other half of the $20 and they'd both get paid.

Well, Stanley had been alive long enough to know that nothing, not nothing, was ever that simple. Not ever.

'How you know he was no cop, man?' Stanley twitched his wheelchair back, forward, left, right.

'No badge, man, neither him or the sidekick. You ask any-body.' Dusty waved in the general direction of everywhere. 'He using bucks for a badge, man.'

'Why you say this person got so interested in me?'

'He showing around some picture of some college boy, but saying he don't look like that no more, but could be wearing a leather coat, and *I* say that boy, all the time complaining and shouting at you about being kidnapped an' all, *he* had a leather coat. That's all, man. True.'

'What picture?'

Dusty rummaged around in the layers under his coat, which Stanley thought was just him scratching until his hand came out clutching a folded piece of paper. 'This here . . . got a number on the back, the man wrote it and then give it me, said for you to call.'

Stanley leaned forward, took the picture and unfolded it, holding the paper loosely in his hands and turning it slightly toward the nearest streetlight to get a better look. It was definitely the kid from the other night.

'Why you wear them cotton gloves with no damn fingers, Stanley?'

Stanley glanced at Dusty and then back at the picture. 'They *padded* cotton gloves, Dust, and I wear 'em the same reason why you wear something on your damn feet, bro, cos the hands do the walking around here.' The kid certainly was in a better condition than when he'd last seen him, all done up like the high school jock he probably was, and Stanley wondered how the hell he'd ended up looking like a bum in Santa Monica.

'That him, Stanley?'

'What?'

'That the kid in the leather coat?'

'Might be.'

'So call the man's number, man!'

Stanley turned the paper over and saw the ten digits neatly written on the back. There was a payphone just down the street . . .

'You goin', or what?'

181

'What if this guy's one of the guys kidnapped him,' Stanley flicked the picture, 'you know, like in the first place?'

'What the hell *you* care?'

Well, true, what the hell did he care? Jamming the piece of paper under his left leg, Stanley twisted the right wheel back and the left wheel forward, stopped them both when the chair had done an exact 90° turn and then powered off down the pathway.

Gartner looked at his cell, sitting silently on the table in front of him, its light blinking. He picked it up and put it in his pocket. 'A watched pot . . .'

'You think that guy'll hand the message over to whatsisname, Stanley, and that Stanley's going to call?'

'He's gonna pass up free money? I don't think so, Matheson.'

'You never said how much.'

'Didn't have to. He'll figure it's got to be more'n I paid his stinky friend. He'll call.' Gartner signaled the waitress for some more coffee. 'Want some?'

Matheson shook his head. 'I have anymore, I'm going to have to glue my eyelids shut tonight.'

Gartner was stirring a second spoon of sugar into his cup when the phone vibrated into life in his pocket. He left the spoon in the cup, took his cell out and checked the incoming number. Not one he recognized.

'Hello? Oh, right, hi Stanley . . . you work a long day, man.' Gartner looked at Matheson, circling a finger over the table and pointing his thumb at the waitress, telling him to pay the bill. 'You have some information for me? Good, good. So what do we do here, you come to me or I come to you?'

Gartner watched Matheson schmoozing the waitress, a sharp, fake blonde, as he listened to the voice at the other end of the connection. 'Okay, I got no problem with that. I'll come down to the . . . what's it called – Hot Dog Stick? Right, Hot Dog Stick, in five, ten minutes.'

Matheson sat back down opposite his boss as he put the phone down on the table. 'Was it him?'

'Yeah, we meet the man over by the pier. Let's go . . .'

Dusty watched the two men go back to the black Mercury Sable, heard the engine roar into life and put his hand up to shield his eyes when the twin beams were switched on. 'How much he give you, Stanley?'

'Enough.'

'He gonna be pissed, he ever finds out you lied to him.'

They both watched the sedan back up and then drive off.

'How'd you know I lied?'

'You said to him the kid went down toward Venice when you know he went th'other way.'

'How'd you know that, Dust?'

'I watched him.'

'You watched?' Stanley wheeled his chair around to face Dusty, who was trying to match the two pieces of his $20 bill together.

'Di'n't do nothing else, Stanley . . .' Dusty looked up, suddenly aware that the mood had changed.

Stanley moved closer to Dusty. 'Do anything like that again and you will be so sorry. I got no beef with that kid, no reason to shaft him any worse'n he already has been . . . all I did was fair exchange, the man didn't pay *that* much and I didn't tell him *that* much. I got money, you got money and you say one more word to anyone about it and –'

183

'Lips zipped, Stanley . . . no problem.'

'Knew there wouldn't be . . .' Stanley wheeled himself off toward the park. The 100 bucks in his pocket, which he had to admit had been a lot simpler to get hold of than he'd figured they would be, were not going to change his life; but he wondered if there might be a way he could get some more to keep them company.

Jaxon was still out when Tee and Cam got back to the house, which was good, because it put off the evil moment when he'd realize Cam still hadn't gone. And it was bad, because he and Tee were alone. Together.

Pact or no pact, it made life complicated and there was nothing Cam could do about it. Except try and keep his distance, which wasn't easy, even in a house as big as Jaxon's. He knew he should be concentrating on his problems and what a solution might look like — planning, figuring out strategies and stuff — but all he could think about was Tee and nothing else. He was suffering from a totally one-track mind, but actually couldn't care less.

'You gonna follow me around like a dog from now on?'

Cam's brain snapped back into now mode. 'Say what?'

'Say how about you go play a computer game, watch TV, read a book or something?'

'Oh, right . . .'

'No offense, but I need time out before I have to face Jaxon.'

'Know what you mean.'

'I think you do.'

Half an hour later, in the lounge, looking out of the window where Tee had stood next to him and kissed him, Cam heard Tee's cell phone ring and then came the sound of her walking up the stairs.

'That was Deke, Cam.'

'Yeah?'

'He and Sarah are coming over.'

'She found some stuff?'

'Apparently. They thought we – you – might want to know right away.'

'Know exactly what about what, guys?'

Tee, who had been standing with her back to the stair-well, moved to one side, and Cam saw Jaxon, just visible, leaning against the wall where the stairs turned a right angle to go down to the hall. 'How the hell long have you been here, Jax?'

Jaxon pushed himself off the wall and walked up the steps. 'Who's Sarah?'

'She's a friend of Deacon's – were you spying on us?'

'Don't be so dramatic.' Jaxon walked across the room and flopped into one of the loungers, looking over at Cam. 'Still here?'

Cam shrugged, shaking his head, not knowing what the hell to say and wishing he was right now on another planet or alternate reality where Jaxon didn't exist.

Tee circled Jaxon like he was prey. 'Are you *jealous* or something?'

'Sure I'm jealous. It's my house, you're my girlfriend, why do I have to bother with *his* problems?'

Before he could get his answer the entryphone buzzed and Tee went over and looked at the screen. 'It's some guy in a wheelchair.'

Jaxon yawned. 'I don't know anyone in a wheelchair. Don't answer.'

Cam walked to where Tee was standing and looked at the

small black and white screen. It was that man ... what was the name on his badge? Stanley? What the hell was he doing here, now?

Chapter 29

Santa Monica Beach; Saturday March 1st, 8.20 p.m.

Cam opened the front door and stepped outside, pulling it almost closed behind him. 'Hi Stanley. How'd you find me?'

'Watched where you went the other night. But I think you might be more interested in *why* I came and found you, man.' Stanley, his face deeply shadowed in the harsh overhead light, twitched his wheels left, right, up, down. 'Much more interested.'

'Okay, why'd you come and find me?'

'Can I come in, you know, do the business *in* the house?'

'This is business?'

'Ain't nothing less than, bro . . . everything business where I come from.'

'This was my house, I'd invite you in – but it isn't and I think it'd be a whole lot better if we did whatever it is you want to do out here.'

'You okay, Cam?'

Cam looked around to find Tee watching him from the half open doorway. 'Fine. There's just something I have to sort out. This is Stanley, by the way, he kind of helped me the night I arrived here.'

Tee did a short wave and a half smile. 'Hello Stanley. Take your time, Cam, there's stuff I have to sort out myself, you know, upstairs . . .'

As the door closed Cam could hear that Tee had just pushed it to, without setting the lock, and he turned back to Stanley knowing he was part of the stuff she was going back to sort out.

'She your girlfriend?'

'Not really . . . no, not at all. Look, let's cut the crap, okay? What's the scam?'

'No scam, bro, no scam at all, just a simple trade is all. I got something I think you might want, you give me something *I* want and I hand it over.'

'What d'you want?'

'Fifty bucks.'

Cam laughed out loud. 'What makes you think I got fifty bucks, man?'

'You ain't got it, you can borrow it, from your not-really girlfriend or the man with the big red truck parked up here.'

'And if I can get the money, what d'you have that I might want that bad?'

Stanley smiled, his teeth, those he had left, all snaggled and grey. 'I got information and I got me a business card from some people they out looking for you.'

Cam went cold, like iced water had been dripped down his spine. 'They're here?'

'No, they gone, man, I ain't stupid.' The wheelchair twitched. 'I'm on *your* side, bro.'

Cam nodded; yeah, right. He knew he had more than fifty bucks in his pocket, he also knew he was being led on by a street professional, but if Stanley had really talked to some people who were out there looking for him, he needed to know about it. And Stanley probably needed the money more than him as well.

'Okay, I'll pay.'

'Show an' tell?'

'What?'

'Show me the money and I tell. Then you give me the money.'

Cam reached into the pocket of his jeans and took out the money clip, checking what was left in it after paying for the coffees and stuff that afternoon. He peeled off two twenties and a ten.

'Nice clip, man.'

'It's silver. Want that instead?'

Stanley gave him the snake-eye. He could see from where he was sitting that the clip was worth a lot more than $50; real silver did not shine in a cheapjack way, it glowed. 'You shitting me?'

'I don't want it.'

'You have yourself a deal.' Stanley reached out.

'Uh-uh, now the tell.' Cam took his money out of the clip, putting the bills back in his jeans.

'The man had your picture.' Stanley reached under his leg, pulled out a creased, grubby sheet of paper and handed it over. 'There's a cell phone number on the back.'

Cam unfolded the paper and saw himself in the picture his parents had had taken last fall. He turned it over and looked at the number, but it didn't register. 'What else?'

'This.' Stanley took a business card out of his pocket. The man had given it to him, saying he should call if he remembered anything else, or, even better, saw the boy again. He held it up between two fingers. 'Now the clip.'

Cam froze. He recognized the card. Handing over the

money clip he took it and read the name, not one he recognized: Thomas Gartner; he was VP for Personnel and Security for a company he certainly did recognize – Contxt Inc.

A quarter of an hour later Tee found Cam sitting at the dining table, staring at the picture of himself and the business card. 'Where'd you get those?'

'From Stanley.' Cam sat back. 'He was paid to *not* tell the police if he saw me again, but to contact this man,' he held up Gartner's card, 'who works for my father and has been out showing around this picture.' He waved the black and white print of himself. 'What is going on?'

The entryphone buzzed in reply.

'That should be Deke. Maybe we'll find out.'

Cam wanted to ask what had happened with Jaxon, but now was obviously not the time and he'd probably find out soon enough anyway. Moments later Deacon and Sarah walked in, followed by Tee.

'Hi again.' Cam got up. 'Didn't expect to see you guys so soon.'

Sarah put a plastic file case on the table. 'I got lucky.'

Deacon smiled and sat down. 'And I got curious and had to come along too. Where's Jaxon?'

'Upstairs.' Tee went through to the kitchen. 'Who wants anything? Coffee, snacks?'

'Something to graze on would be nice.' Deacon reached over and picked up Cam's picture. 'So that's what you really look like.'

Cam was about to go and offer to help Tee when Jaxon walked in, pulled out a chair and sat down.

'So, the gang's all here.' He looked up at Sarah, frowning.

'Except you're new.' He put out his hand. 'I'm Jaxon, and you are –?'

'Sarah Baldwin.'

'Nice to meet you, Sarah. You'll be glad to know I'm on my best behaviour this evening.'

'Right . . .' Sarah smiled in that way people do when they're not sure about things.

Deacon tapped the table with his knuckle. 'Don't be scary, Jaxon. Sarah's here to help.'

'So what've you got, Sarah?' said Tee, putting a tray with what looked like half the refrigerator on it down on the table.

'Does anyone here know what eugenics is?' Sarah looked around the table at three blank faces. 'Okay, simply put, it's kind of racial cleansing, like only allowing certain people to breed?'

Deacon sat forward, elbows on the table. 'Like the Nazis?'

'Like them and others.' Sarah opened the file and took out a sheaf of papers.

'What's that got to do with the Doctor Corporation?' Cam shifted uneasily in his seat.

'Okay, first off, remember I don't have everything, but what I do have is fact, not conjecture.' Sarah sifted through the pages of paper and separated out a few of them. 'And secondly, I don't know what all of this means, and what you're getting is like a brain dump. So, from the top, Cam, your father and mother like *own* the Doctor Corporation – did you know that?'

'Own it?' Cam looked stunned. 'My father owns a communications company.' He picked the business card off the table and showed it to Sarah. 'Why would he have anything to do with a medical facility? And my *mother*? She hasn't worked a day in her life, far as I know.'

'Well, you just have to keep on digging to find the information. Your mother's quite upfront about her charitable connections to the business, but behind a couple of front organizations.' Sarah pushed a sheet of paper over the table toward Cam. 'You'll find them as the majority shareholders.'

'My mother had that thing put in my arm?'

'Your *parents* had that thing put in your arm, Cam.' Deacon reached over and took an olive off a plate on the tray. 'At least that's what it looks like.'

'So why did you start this whole thing off by asking us if we knew what that, you know, eugenics was?' Cam glanced down at the sheet of paper in front of him, taking in nothing else but the fact that both his parents' names had been marked in bright yellow highlighter.

'Because the Doctor Corporation, which is, as far as you can tell from the outside, just your standard upscale private medical facility, has a kind of subsidiary company called Birth Sciences Inc., and Birth Sciences Inc. is a whole other story.' Sarah referred to a sheet of print-out in front of her. 'I nearly missed the connection, would've too if I hadn't figured that they shared certain accounting services.'

'And what is it with this Birth Sciences?' Tee said. 'What do they do?'

'I'm not entirely sure,' Sarah looked up, 'but it seems to me like they make babies to order. Nice white ones, with good IQs and a very clean bill of health.'

Jaxon smiled and looked straight at Cam. 'Woof, woof . . .'

Sarah ignored Jaxon, straightening all the papers up and putting them back in the file case. 'I have to go now, but I'll leave this stuff for you to look through.'

'You're going? Ah . . .' Cam looked confused, '. . . can't we like talk about this?'

'Sure you can, but not with me right now. I have to make a move.'

'Which means I have to go, too.' Deacon got up. 'We could meet up tomorrow?'

'Look, Cam, don't think that's it, that's all I'm going to do.' Sarah pushed the file case over toward him. 'This was just the first tranche of information. I'll give you a call Monday, okay?'

'Are you saying this eugenics has got something to do with me?'

Sarah looked across the table at Cam. 'I'm just a researcher here, I gather facts, I don't generally dispense opinions . . . but you want my opinion? Yes, I do.'

Chapter 30

Santa Monica Beach; Sunday March 2nd, 1.25 a.m.

Cam sat in the lounge, long after Jaxon and Tee went to bed, reading the twenty or so sheets of print-out Sarah had left behind, most looking like they came from websites. Some were about the Docto® Corp. and Birth Sciences Inc., but the bulk of them had something or other to do with eugenics, which a dictionary he'd found on a shelf said was '*the science dealing with the improvement of hereditary qualities*'. The word, he found out from one of the print-outs, had been coined in 1883 by a man called Francis Galton, a cousin of Charles Darwin. It was the root of the name Eugene, and it came from the ancient Greek and meant, said an article, 'good birth'.

Cam looked at the two words, good birth, thought about the implications of improving hereditary qualities, and picked up the next sheet of paper.

At the beginning of the twentieth century it was widely believed you could inherit genius, and for the exact same reason you could obviously also inherit the bad stuff, so therefore Nature could – and should – be given a helping hand by completely eliminating certain types from the gene pool. The scientific theory of eugenics – that you could get rid of everything from criminality, alcoholism, idiocy and poverty, and even epilepsy, by preventing criminals, drunks, stupid people and the poor from having children by forcibly sterilizing them – became hugely popular at the time.

Cam was well aware that you'd be crazy to believe everything you read on the web; any fool could post all kinds of trash, and frequently did. But Sarah's material came from primo sources, like the very mainstream kind of magazines and newspapers his father read, and also various university sites. And none of it was the really rabid stuff, written like an illiterate sermon, that shouted at you off the page. There were no multiple, or even single, exclamation marks.

During the year 1910, according to one piece Cam read a couple of times, Theodore Roosevelt had said that 'the inescapable duty of the good citizen of the right type is to leave his or her blood behind him in the world', while in England Winston Churchill, who wanted to compulsorily sterilize the mentally handicapped, said he felt 'the source from which the stream of madness is fed should be cut off and sealed up before another year has passed'.

Churchill, who Cam knew would later become the English leader who'd declared war on Hitler and the Nazis, didn't get his way, and obviously changed his mind about how good a notion racial purity was. But ex-President Roosevelt's ideas appeared to have been more popular, as by 1927 many US states, apparently, had passed laws in favor of compulsory sterilization; the article said that, by the time the laws were abolished, more than 100,000 people had been operated on.

Cam sat back, dazed. All this information. What the hell did it have to do with him? Read alongside all the stuff about the corporations his parents were involved with, he couldn't see what the connection was, although Sarah seemed convinced it was there. But nothing fitted. Why had he been kidnapped? By whom? What had *really* happened outside his uncle's house? Why had he still not called home again? And why were people from his father's company – the only one he'd known about till now – handing his picture out and asking questions about him? And not wanting the police involved?

His head was beginning to hurt and he could feel a sense of panic rising up, fed by his complete inability to understand what was happening to him. His life was coming apart so fast it was like he was being hit by a tornado, punched and pummeled by circumstances and events, none of which was helped by the way he was feeling about Tee. The fact was, in a world where he didn't really know who to trust, he couldn't even trust himself . . .

No longer able to focus on the print, Cam gathered the papers together and traipsed up to bed.

'Did you know, they were still sterilizing people in Sweden up till 1976 – can you believe that?'

'Exactly *how* late did you stay up last night, Cam?' Tee poured a couple of mugs of coffee and brought them to the table where Cam sat with the file case in front of him. 'And are you now like the world expert in racial cleansing, or whatever it's called?'

'It's just I can't get my head around some of the stuff I've been reading, Tee . . . I mean, we think it was the Germans who kind of invented all this racial purity stuff, but it was happening here first, right here in the US. Man, the Germans *got* a lot of their ideas from us, they just took them a whole lot further.'

'And fascinating though all this is, you know, historically and all? What has it got to do with you . . . I mean, what's *happened* to you?'

'I have no idea . . .' Cam looked away, 'but that company, Birth Sciences? Sarah found connections . . .'

Tee sat down opposite him. 'With what, or who?'

'With other organizations, people who still think this eugenics stuff is a good idea.'

'And?'

'And I don't know, I don't know *what* the hell to think . . . I mean, my *parents* own a corporation that has links with some pretty damn weird types, you know? People who think Hitler had the right idea . . .'

'You think the Doctor Corp. and this Birth Sciences place might be doing something about it, like actually *doing* something?'

Cam nodded.

'What information did Sarah get about them?' Tee asked.

'Not too much. She said she'd do some more digging around today.' Cam looked past Tee and out at the beach. 'D'you think Deacon might let me crash with him for a couple of days, till this all gets sorted out?'

'Deacon?'

'I can't stay here, Tee, it's driving me nuts.' Cam looked around, half expecting to find Jaxon standing behind him, smiling. 'It's not fair on anyone, least of all Jaxon . . . it is his house, and why should he have someone here he doesn't like?'

'It's a big house, Jaxon's a big boy, he can deal with it. We talked.'

'You might have, but we haven't . . .' Cam stood up. 'Is he awake?'

Tee nodded. 'What're you going to do?'

'*I'm* going to talk to him.'

It hadn't taken long, and it hadn't been what you could call a 'bonding session', but Jaxon, whom Cam had found in his office surfing the net, had been surprisingly cool about him staying for a few more days. As long as he knew Cam had no intentions of making this a permanent thing, he'd said, he agreed with Tee that it was good karma to let him hang out for a bit longer. Cam, he'd added, would just have to put up with the jokes.

'That was it?' Tee looked surprised. 'Jeez, maybe he does listen . . . oh, right, Sarah called, wants you to call her back.'

'What'd she say?'

'To call her back.'

'Okay . . .'

'Honest, Cam, that's all she said. The number's over on the pad by the cordless.'

Cam dialed the number and waited. Fifteen rings later he was about to call off when Sarah picked up. She'd obviously been running.

'Hi . . . sorry . . . who's there?'

'Cam. You okay?'

'Yeah, yeah . . . just out in the yard, forgot to take the phone with me. Thanks for calling back.'

'You found something?'

'I have.'

Silence.

'What is it?'

'Not something I can tell you on the phone, Cam . . .'

Cam frowned and Tee shrugged questioningly. 'Hang on, Sarah . . .' He put his hand over the mouthpiece. 'She says she's found something and can't tell me over the phone.'

'Ask her to come over.'

Cam went back to the phone. 'Can you come over here?'

'Is that jerk going to be there?'

'Jaxon?'

'The one with the bad case of ego.'

'Probably, but he's okay with things now.'

'Good for him . . . I can be with you in about half an hour, is that all right?'

'I'm not planning on going anywhere.'

It was more like forty minutes by the time Sarah arrived. After waiting for fifteen minutes, Cam, who couldn't keep still, went for a walk on the beach, coming running back when he'd seen Tee waving at him from the deck. Taking the steps two at a time, he'd arrived, panting, to find Tee and Sarah sitting outside at the table.

'My turn to be out of breath . . .'

'I'll go make some coffee or something.' Tee got up and left the deck before Cam had a chance to say anything.

'Subtle,' he said, looking at Sarah.

'I asked her if she could leave us alone for a few minutes.'

'Jeez, this is like some daytime soap and you're going to tell me I have a terminal disease and only days to live.'

Sarah smiled. 'Nothing like that.'

'Then what?'

'How much do you know about your family?'

'I don't know . . . the normal stuff. My dad's folks came from LA, where my uncle still lives, and my mom grew up in

New Mexico, moved to California when she was in junior high, when her dad got a new job. What else is there to know? They got married, came down to San Diego where I was born.'

'They never said anything else?'

'About what?'

'About you . . .'

'No, what should they've said?'

Sarah took a deep breath and sat back in her chair. 'There's no easy way to do this, Cam . . . believe me, I checked *everything* and I wouldn't be saying this if I didn't think it was the absolute truth: you are adopted.'

Chapter 31

Santa Monica Beach; Sunday March 2nd, 1.25 p.m.

Cam felt like all the air had been sucked out of his lungs. All he could hear, as he sat staring at Sarah, was a buzzing in his ears. Adopted? For a moment he couldn't even work out what the word actually meant. *Adopted?* As in his mother and father weren't his real, biological parents? Not possible . . .

'Cam, are you okay . . . Cam?'

Sarah's words forced their way though the buzzing and Cam's eyes finally focussed on her. 'What did you say?'

'I said you were adopted, Cam.'

'Yeah, that . . . that's what I thought you said . . .' Cam looked out at the ocean, moving like it was the calm, regular heartbeat of the planet. He could hear it, soft and clear, and right now it sounded like it was sighing. 'How do you know?'

'I hacked into some files held at Birth Sciences.'

'You went looking to see if I was adopted? Why?'

'I just went looking, Cam, to see what I could find . . . *I* didn't know what would be there, but their defenses were pretty extensive so I figured it'd be worth my while getting in, you know, on the principle the higher the walls and the bigger the dog the more there is to guard? And I was right.'

'Why make such a big thing, such a massive secret out of the fact that I was adopted? Why is it such a big deal?'

'Because it wasn't only you.'

'What d'you mean, not only me?'

Sarah leaned forward and touched Cam's arm with her hand. 'Look, I've still only found out a tiny part of the story and all I can give you are the bare facts. This is like trying to reconstruct a living face when you only have the skull; I know the outline, but none of the detail that'll tell us what we're really looking at, and it's going to take time to work out what all this is about.' Sarah squeezed Cam's arm. 'What I meant by it's not only you is that there were other names in this particular file, the one where I found your name. You were seventh on the list and there were twenty-four others. I found another three similar files, too, but I didn't have time to get anything off those.'

Cam caught sight of Tee moving around in the kitchen, trying to look busy. She must be wondering what was happening, but he needed space to take on board everything Sarah was telling him. 'What did you get off the one I was in?'

Sarah took some folded sheets of paper out of her backpack and put them on the table. Cam could see the top sheet had the words 'GENERATION 1' on it. 'As far as I can tell, this is a record of your conception and birth, and of all the others who appear to make up what they refer to as "Generation 1". From what I can make out, only eight of you are still alive.'

Pushing the sheets of paper away, Cam stood up. 'You telling me I have seven brothers and sisters? I'm some kind of *clone*?'

'No, nothing like that . . . nothing like that at all. These other people aren't related to you, you're all just part of the same program.'

'Great. Out of the blue, no family, but at least I'm part of a damn program.' Cam kicked at a chair and then slammed his fist down on one of the wooden deck supports. It hurt and, for a moment, took his mind off what he was finding out about himself.

'I'm sorry . . .'

'It's not your fault, don't shoot the messenger, right?' Cam sat back down at the table and pointed at the papers. 'What does it say about me . . . who am I?'

Sarah picked the sheets up and flattened them in front of her on the table. 'You mean who are your real parents?' Cam nodded. 'That may be difficult, if not impossible to find out, although I can tell you that your mother was from Norway and your father was of German origin. But I didn't find anything that would tell me who they actually were.'

'German?'

'Yup, and Norwegian.'

'Jeee-zus . . .' Milling around in Cam's head were a hundred different thoughts, all clamoring to be taken notice of, none of which were particularly nice things to think about. It was as if his life-slate had been wiped clean and he'd been handed a new one with a few scant details scribbled on it, and a feeling of helplessness flooded over him. How were you supposed to go forward with the rest of your life if where you'd come from was a complete lie? He stood up, stretching to try and unknot the painfully tight muscles in his neck and shoulders. 'I need a drink . . .'

Even a beer buzz did little to take the edge off his troubles, so he stopped drinking and feeling sorry for himself and wondered out loud, as he paced around the kitchen, what the hell he should do.

Tee looked at him. 'I should think that's fairly obvious.'

'What is?'

'What d'you say, Sarah? He should go confront his parents, right?'

Sarah nodded. 'I think that certainly should be done.'

'Just call them up and say, "Hi, guys, I think it's about time we had a talk about who I really am"?'

'That's one way,' Sarah nodded, 'but . . . look, I don't know how to say this without seeming totally heartless, except there's something going on here that's more than just about you. I mean it *is* about you, but it's also about all the others as well. From what I've found out so far, it's fairly clear that Doctor Corp. and Birth Sciences are in the business of producing perfect children . . . nice, white WASP kids for people who want a nice, white WASP world and are prepared to pay for it.'

'And that's what I am?'

The atmosphere in the room became like one of those cold, cold winter days when everything has frozen and you stand on the ice hoping it's thick enough to take your weight, listening for the tell-tale sounds that'll warn that it's too thin and you're in danger of falling through. Everyone could tell, Cam, Sarah and Tee, that they were all on the thinnest of ice here. Cam felt like he could spin off the entire planet right then and there, Sarah knew she could have lost Cam so totally she'd never get near him again, and Tee wished she had an emotional lifebelt to throw, but couldn't find one anywhere.

The silence elongated, Cam the only person in the room

who wasn't wondering when, not whether, it would reach its snapping point, because no silence can go on forever.

Tee watched him, trying to read his face, attempting to look through his eyes and see what he might be thinking, but she couldn't translate the language, couldn't see past the blank stare. Slowly he seemed to calm and center himself, looking at the floor for a long moment, then raising his head, a curious expression on his face. Sad, insightful, focussed. He looked like he'd grown up an awful lot in those few minutes, thought Tee.

'Okay.' Cam looked directly at Sarah. 'What do you want to do?'

Sarah checked her watch, then checked the battery status of her cell phone. 'Remind me of your parents' first names, Cam.'

'Gordon and Eleanor.' Cam reached for a cookie from a plate on the table. 'You sure it's okay to use that phone, Sarah? I mean, they can trace any call they want, and this is like my dad's business – he's bound to know how to find stuff out, right?'

'It's unregistered. They can trace all they want but they won't find a name or anything.'

'Where'd you learn all this shit anyway?'

'What shit?'

'Hacking into mainframes and using unregistered cell phones and stuff.'

'I'm a researcher, Cam.' Sarah smiled. 'You think I ask nicely and people just give up all the things I sometimes want to know? I wish. And a lot of these corporations make it so easy, they're lazy, and when some bullshit IT guy sells them a piece of off-the-shelf firewall software they believe everything'll be hunky-dory. Lots of them never think to check or upgrade, and their security is Swiss cheese . . . you can even drive by in a car and pick stuff up with the right equipment. They deserve to be hacked, most of them.'

'It was easy to get all this stuff about me?'

'No, this information was a bitch to get.' Sarah made to pick up a cookie, then thought better of it. 'I had to get some serious pro help to get in there. They did *not* want people snooping around in their back yard.'

'Everything you do legal?' Tee asked.

'Depending on your moral viewpoint, everything's legal . . . until you get found out.' Sarah shook her head. 'My memory's shit – what was your mother's name again, Cam?'

'Eleanor.' Cam caught sight of the whiteboard and went over to it, looking at the second and third lines down – 'CAS/ETS' and '7/25/Gen1' – the two they had yet to decipher. 'My middle name's Alistair, and my mother's middle name is Theresa . . .'

Tee joined him. 'And?'

'See?' Cam pointed. 'CAS, Cameron Alistair Stewart, and ETS, which is Eleanor Theresa Stewart.' Cam looked over his shoulder. 'I don't know why, but I kept on seeing the word "cassettes" when I looked at it before. And Sarah, didn't you say something about my name being seventh on that list in the file?'

'I did.'

'So that's the last line.'

'What is?' Tee frowned.

'7/25/Gen1 . . . it means I was the seventh of twenty-five in Generation 1, whatever that actually is. So that's the whole story: when I was conceived and born, who I became, who became my mother, and where I fit in the plan . . . seven of twenty-five, kind of like that *Star Trek* character.'

'Except you're a guy and Seven of Nine was a cool babe with a body to die for.'

'Except for that.' Cam smiled, which felt good.

'Guys?' Sarah waved at the two of them. 'Okay, I'm going to need some quiet while I make this call.' She looked upward. 'Could one of you make sure whatsisname doesn't come busting in in the middle of it?'

'Jaxon, his name's Jaxon. He went out while you were on the deck with Cam. Won't be back for a couple of hours, he said.'

Sarah smiled awkwardly. 'That sounded so rude . . . I'm sorry Tee, I just forgot his name.'

'Yeah, and I know he can be a jerk.' Tee glanced at her watch. 'Make the call, he'll be some time yet.'

Reading the digits off the piece of paper Cam had written them on, Sarah dialed the Stewart number, picked up the cell phone's hands-free unit, put it in her ear and waited.

Chapter 32

San Diego; Sunday March 2nd, 3.07 p.m.

Luiz Binay was glad to be out of Seattle. That climate would drive him nuts if he had to stay there much longer. And now the whole team was together – everyone Inverdale had hired for the job. This, he knew, wasn't part of the plan, but events had dictated a change and here they all were in sunny San Diego, except Joey Esposito. Pity about Joey, he'd have liked it down here, but that was the way the cookie crumbled sometimes. Although, Luiz had to admit, getting offed by some 17-year-old kid with a damn aerosol can was one weird way to go. So now Joey was going to be in Seattle forever, unless someone found where they'd dumped him, which Luiz felt was unlikely. Municipal garbage furnaces did a pretty good job of blitzing stuff.

Luiz had left Ed Barry watching the Stewart house over in La Jolla, figuring since when did it need two people to do a job like that? And he had had it with sitting in cars and the back of vans. Even being stuck in a damn office, on a Sunday afternoon, was better. At least here there were peo-ple to talk to who could string a sentence together; in fact he could do a lot more than just sit around and chat with that Sheila woman. She was eye candy, with brains.

Getting up, Luiz went to look out the window – not that there was what you could call a view, basically just empty downtown streets – but after spending more hours with Ed in the Seattle house than he cared to think about, it was good to look out of a big window at anything. He was contemplating nothing in particular, idly wondering how Sheila would react to him asking her out for a drink, and thinking that, if he was any judge, she'd go for it, when that nerdy Twinkies freak Alfredo came running into the room like his pants were on fire.

'Where's Inverdale?'

'Downstairs, went for a nicotine fix. Why?'

'Jesus, you are not gonna *believe* the call I just taped – *I* can't believe the call I just taped . . . I have to go make a file copy and set it up. Would you mind going down and getting him? He is gonna want to hear this baby . . .'

'I look like a bus boy? Go get him yourself, man.'

Alfredo, who had assumed Luiz would do what he asked, stopped on his way back to the room where all his equipment was and looked back at the man. He did not appear to be in the mood for a discussion. 'Fine, I'll go.'

'Sure you will.'

'Play that last part again.' Inverdale leaned toward the speakers. 'Have you done all that filtering shit and cleaned it up? Sounds crap.'

'I told you,' Alfredo punched a couple of buttons and rewound the digital counter to the position he'd noted down on his pad, 'she's using a cell and she must be in a shitty reception area.'

'Or using some kind of filter of her own, to disguise her

voice,' said Sheila, noticing how Luiz kept looking at her. No doubt about it, he was a man with ideas.

'Whatever.' Inverdale waved his hand. 'Just play it.'

Alfredo pressed another button and a woman's voice came out of the speakers.

'. . . *you can act as dumb as you like, Gordon – d'you mind if I call you Gordon? I've been backgrounding you so long I feel like I know you. Anyway, like I said, the production company I work for is putting together this documentary about test tube babies, and your operations seem to have a very different way of helping certain childless couples.*'

'*Who the hell are you? What operations? I think you must have the wrong number, lady. I'm in telecommunications.*'

'*Yes, I know, Contxt, right? Systems design, manufacture, management and installation? But it's not that company I'm talking about, Gordon, it's the Doctor Corporation and the other one, um . . .*' the woman appeared to be referring to some notes for a moment, '*. . . here it is, Birth Sciences Inc. Are you trying to say that I'm talking to the* wrong *Gordon D. Stewart – you are married to Eleanor, and have a son called Cameron? Well, I say "son", but according to my research neither of you is his biological parent . . . Mr. Stewart?*'

The hiss of static came out of the speakers and you could just hear the sound of someone breathing. Inverdale sat back and nodded at Alfredo. 'You can stop it for now.'

'Sounds like she knows pretty much everything.' Sheila flicked her lighter on and off an couple of times.

'How the hell, though?' Inverdale wasn't talking directly to anyone, more out loud to himself. 'How the *hell* did this woman, whoever she is, get hold of all this information? I know this operation, it's sealed up tighter'n Scrooge McDuck's wallet.'

Luiz screwed up the paper cup he'd been drinking water out of and arced it straight into a trash can the other side of the office. 'She doesn't know about us.'

'We don't know that, Luiz. She just didn't *mention* us in that call.' Inverdale shifted in his chair, took a cigarette out of his pack and lit it. No one thought it a terrifically good idea to remind him that he shouldn't. 'Who knows what she knows? If *that*,' he pointed at all the Mac equipment, 'is the extent of her knowledge, it's bad enough – when did she get him to agree to see her?'

Alfredo checked his notepad. 'Tomorrow, six in the evening, at the Doctor offices.'

'Can you believe that? He just rolled over and gave her everything she wanted.' Luiz smiled at Sheila, hoping she'd get the message he'd do the same for her.

'What's Stewart gonna do, Luiz? Tell her to go away and not bother him?' Inverdale looked at the cigarette in his hand, like someone had put it there without him noticing, glanced at the smoke alarms on the ceiling and stubbed it out in a used coffee cup. 'No, it was a good move, he's getting her out in the open. Where we can see her too . . .'

'Awesome, Sarah . . .' Tee grinned like a maniac and did a drum roll with her fingers on the table. 'You played him like a big fish, man!'

'You going to see him tomorrow . . . my dad?'

'Got to go in while I've got him off balance, not give him much time to get his act together. Best way.'

'What about me? When do I see him?'

'Okay, here's the thing . . .' Sarah stopped for a moment,

and it seemed she was checking off a mental list. 'I'm kind of making this up as I go along, which I figure you must've already worked out, so forgive me if this is a tad ragged around the edges . . . but how would you two feel about coming with me tomorrow? If I go in with my "team", it'll look more professional.'

'Professional . . . like with me with a bag over my head so's my dad won't instantly recognize me?'

Tee raised her eyebrows. 'Stop sounding like Jaxon – disguise, man. Baseball cap, hoody, dark glasses and stuff, right Sarah?'

Sarah nodded. 'Like that, and you hang in the background, act like a gofer and he won't even give you a second look. Believe me, I've been there, no one takes any notice of the help. And when the time's right, I'll introduce you and we'll see what his reaction is to that.'

Cam chewed his lip. The sudden prospect of facing down his father was giving him an empty, nervous, vertigo feeling in the pit of his stomach, like you get when you have to stand up in front of everyone at school or whatever and read something out. 'Okay . . . that's cool, that's cool . . . What's, um, what's Tee gonna be doing?'

'Can you operate a camcorder, Tee?'

'Me? Yeah, sure. Point'n'shoot, zoom, pan, fade, cut, print, right?'

'In a manner of speaking, Tee. I want Cam's father to think this is hand-held *verité* stuff we'll be using in the documentary, so you'll have to play it real straight, nothing fancy.'

'I can do simple.'

'Good.' Sarah pushed her chair back. 'I have to go and sort some stuff out, like getting tomorrow off work at short notice. I'll pick you guys up at like midday?'

Tee saluted. 'We'll be here, boss.'

Sarah stood up. 'It'll be fine, Cam . . . you're going to have to do this sometime, and tomorrow's as good a time as any. And this way you're not on your own.'

'Yeah, thanks.' Cam put on a smile. Except that, however you looked at it, he was on his own now, totally, and that's what he always would be – no way of ever finding out who his real parents were.

'Did you call Gartner yet?'

'Why would I call Gartner, Eleanor? This isn't something he needs to know anything about. I did, however, call the sorry bastard who is *supposed* to have installed the best available online security measures money can buy and told him to get his ass down to the facility – find out how that bitch got in there.'

'You're going to have to tell Gartner something, aren't you? You'll surely need back-up tomorrow when you meet her.'

'I will have back-up, Eleanor. You.'

Chapter 33

Police HQ, San Diego; Monday 3rd March, 9.10 a.m.

Mike Henrikson and Tony Matric walked into the Detectives Room together, having met in the parking lot. In the elevator on the way up they'd both agreed it kind of put the cap on things that neither of them had had a single phone call from the Stewarts over the weekend. Not a peep. It lent a new meaning to the phrase 'concerned parent', Mike had said. So what were the concerned cops going to do? Tony had asked as they got to their respective desks.

'Pay these people a visit and see if we can't get some damn straight answers, that's what. Just as soon as I've had my coffee.'

'I don't get this whole thing, Mike.' Tony popped the top off of his take-out cup, emptied a couple of sachets of white sugar and stirred them in with a pencil. 'Nothing makes any kind of sense. You talk to the people who witnessed the kidnapping and it sounds like the real deal, but the damn parents – the mother at least – acts like she doesn't give two bits and what's all the fuss about; the boy, who it turns out has been taken all the way up to almost *Canada*, escapes and then doesn't go to the police. And when he does call his parents, they don't tell us. What's that all about?'

'You tell me.'

'And they faked a ransom note.'

'We've agreed to assume all those things.'

'We did . . .' Tony picked up a fat envelope from his desk and looked inside.

'Cell phone records?'

'Looks like it.'

'Do 'em later, I'm gonna call Stewart.' Mike looked at his watch. 'I think it's time we put some cards on the table, don't you?'

'I think it's time we did bad cop/bad cop and see if we can get them to tell us what the hell's going on, because I am unhappy at being given the runaround, I truly am . . .'

Cam was surprised to find Jaxon up and fixing some cereal and coffee in the kitchen when he came down; no sign of Tee. Could he really be making her breakfast? Cam supposed anything was possible.

'You missed her.' Jaxon didn't turn around, but spoke to the coffee maker. 'She's gone to the mall or the nail bar or whatever, I wasn't paying attention. Said she'd be back in time, was the message. I do remember that.'

'Okay . . . right . . .' The idea of having to spend the next couple of hours 'hanging out' on his own with Jaxon did not appeal. Conversation was bound to be somewhat forced.

'She told me what you guys are gonna do, like spook out your dad? And have you in disguise and then kind of *reveal* who you are, all on tape, like some reality show. Isn't that what whatsername, Sally –?'

'Sarah.'

'Right, Sarah . . . isn't that what Sarah works on, a reality show?'

'Yeah, that's what she said.'

'I thought so . . .' Jaxon took his breakfast over to the table and sat down.

Cam was at a loss as to what to do or say. He hated the feeling of being unwanted, of having to ask Jaxon's permission to get some food, but this was his place and that was how he was making him feel. He remembered how it felt to walk into Kenny's house, or Ted's, and just graze in the coolbox, not even thinking about asking . . . still, he'd be gone in a couple of hours and, whatever happened, he wasn't likely to be coming back. He could hack it for a bit longer.

'Mind if I . . .' Cam waved a thumb in the general direction of the grill.

'Sure, why not . . . kinda like a Last Breakfast, right?'

'Yup.' Cam split an English muffin, put it under the grill and switched the machine's timer on. He turned around. 'You'll be glad to see the back of me, right?'

'Yup.'

'You don't go in for pulling punches, do you.'

'Nope, never quite seen the point.'

The grill dinged behind him and Cam got some butter and a carton of milk out the fridge. Jaxon got up and put his cereal bowl and coffee cup in the sink. 'Jeez, ten o'clock, I gotta go out. Tell Tee I'll see her when she gets back.' Jaxon turned to look at Cam. 'I told her she was dumb to go on this stupid trip.'

'Oh . . .' Cam concentrated on trying to spread some rock-hard butter on the muffin.

'You think she'll come back?'

'What?'

'You heard.'

'Yes, she'll come back. Why wouldn't she?'

Jaxon smiled and looked out at the ocean, then, as he walked past Cam he punched his arm, just below where he'd been shot. A short, sharp jab that looked friendly, but didn't feel it at all. 'Yeah, why wouldn't she, right? Me, I can't think of a single, solitary reason.'

Cam watched him leave the room, his arm, still tender and not quite healed, aching like shit. There was no way Jaxon hadn't done that on purpose. He wanted to curse and swear, but he would have to wait until he heard the front door close as there was no way he'd give Jaxon the satisfaction of knowing how much he'd hurt him. Only when he heard the truck start up did he allow himself to let the pain out, loudly venting his hurt and anger.

Then he threw away the cold muffin and toasted another one, topping it with two eggs and some strips of bacon on the side. Brewing some fresh coffee, he sat at the table and ate what he considered was a proper Last Breakfast. With no one watching him do it.

When he'd finished and cleared up he looked at his watch: 10.45. He should go around the house and collect what little stuff he had and put it in one of those paper grocery bags he knew were stashed under the sink – be all ready to go.

It was up in the lounge that he found the photo of Tee. Discarded, on the floor under a magazine rack. It was a dusty Polaroid which looked as if it'd probably been taken in a restaurant; grainy, a shot that looked like the flash hadn't gone off, it was of a girl with her hand held in front of her face, palm in, and you could only really see her hair and make out one eye. Defiantly mysterious, but you could still tell who it was. The jewelry, and the attitude, unmistakable.

Was it stealing to take it? It wasn't like it was precious, in a frame or anything. Without it he'd have nothing physical to remember her by – except the flattened penny – and he didn't just want this picture, he needed it. In the end it would be all he had to remind him of the last five days.

He took it with him upstairs.

Tee came back at 11.45. She'd been down in Venice, she said, seeing a girlfriend to talk about the possibility of moving into her apartment.

'You serious, Tee?'

'Never more so.'

'He thinks you're not gonna come back from San Diego.'

'He say that?' Cam nodded. 'Well, he's right and he's wrong . . . I am coming back, but only to move out. Time to refocus and reposition.'

'Right . . . yeah, I suppose I've kind of got some of that to do myself . . .'

'It'll be okay, Cam, really . . .'

One moment they were two people standing in the hallway, waiting for Sarah to ring the door, and the next they were together. Who'd moved first, Cam couldn't say. They kissed, they held each other, like if they didn't they'd disintegrate, and then they slowly moved apart, in silent admission that what had hardly started was now finishing.

When the doorbell did go, the sound cut the moment like a knife and then they were two people in the hallway, waiting for a ride. Tee went and opened the door.

'You guys ready?' Sarah asked, smiling, completely

unaware of the tiny, intense drama that had just played out in the hallway.

'Cam's packed,' Tee pointed to the supermarket bag on the floor, 'we've brushed our teeth, we're wearing clean underwear and both of us promise not to ask you if we've got there yet, at least till we're way past Anaheim.'

'Fine.' Sarah walked back down to where an old, blue Toyota sedan was parked.

Cam picked up the bag, took the battered leather coat off the chair and followed her, waiting as Tee set the alarm and closed the door. Goodbye Santa Monica . . .

Chapter 34

San Diego; Monday 3rd March, 4.45 p.m.

As they came down the 120 miles of 5, Cam, in the back seat of the Toyota, could feel his nervousness and tension rising. The nearer they got, the more familiar the names on the Interstate signs: Oceanside, Carlsbad — he had an old schoolfriend, Haley, in Carlsbad, had lost touch when she moved and not seen her for years — on past Encinitas and Del Mar. And then he saw the first sign for La Jolla. But Sarah didn't turn off, kept her foot down and they were going past North Claremont, Mission Bay.

Cam had wanted to tell Sarah to take the La Jolla off-ramp and drive him to his house, to take him home. His mother would be there. He could demand an explanation from her and not have to go through this whole charade of disguises and shit with his father. Not that his mother was the soft option — he just wanted to be on familiar ground for the first time since he couldn't remember how long, and he didn't really care who he got answers from as long as he got some.

In fact he couldn't imagine how he'd face up to his mother about this. She was the kind of person who could silence you with a look. His mother had always been the strictest, never cutting him the slack his father did, always pointing it out when he didn't quite make the grade she considered he should have. He'd never really thought about it before, her attitude toward him, but with what he knew now it looked like all she really cared about was his achievements. He'd always figured she was proud, got a buzz out of him winning, coming out on top and stuff, but maybe that was exactly what he'd been designed to do.

But the fast lane of the freeway wasn't really the place to negotiate a change of plan, plus, as they approached the complex road layout where two Interstates met – where there were off-ramps to everywhere it seemed like – Sarah started to ask him for directions and somehow they managed to find themselves going east. Rather than still going south. Great. So much for his claim that they wouldn't need a map with him in the car.

'What do we do now, Cam?'

'It's okay . . . sorry, Sarah, I wasn't paying attention.' Cam sat forward, kicking his concentration circuits into gear and referring to the diagram of San Diego he had in his head. 'Keep going . . . it's okay, we're going to come to another intersection in a moment, right? And you just have to take the exit going south and that'll take us straight down, almost to where we'd have gotten off for Broadway anyway.'

'You sure?'

'I'm sure . . . I was just, you know, slightly freaked at being back here and about to do what we're about to do . . .'

Tee swiveled around to look at Cam. 'How'd you feel?'

'Like I wish it was tomorrow and this was all over . . . and I knew everything and was out of this limbo. Pretty much like that.'

Sarah took her right hand off the wheel and pointed ahead. 'Is that the exit coming up?'

'Yeah, can you see the sign? Stay in this lane and we'll feed straight onto the freeway going south.'

'Did it say we're going past the zoo?' Tee asked. 'I *always* wanted to go to the zoo here, I never made the trip yet.'

'Yeah, we're going through the park, Balboa, which the zoo is in.' Cam sat back, watching the late afternoon sky as the sun started making for the western horizon. Thinking. Thinking about the zoo, and other places like it. Places where a lot of the animals, unlike in the wild, were the product of human intervention. You take this big old male tiger and put him with your choice – not his – of female tigers; and, if you know your family trees and stuff, you get yourself nice, strong little cubs which you can sell to other zoos. Hey! Waddaya know? Wasn't that kind of like how come *he* came to be here?

How could his parents – or at least the two people he'd grown up *thinking* were his parents – be involved with anything as weird as running what amounted to a breeding program for human beings? He'd been to the San Diego Zoo more times than he could remember – birthday treats, school trips, everything – and each time he'd had no idea that there was a connection between him and so many of the animals there behind the bars and glass screens. Alive and breathing not as the result of chance, like it should be, but because someone had plans. If this story ever became public knowledge, would he become an object, like the monkeys and the pandas, something to be looked at and kept for research? Would there be a zoo just for him and the others like him?

'Cam . . .?'

'What?' Cam looked around to find Tee staring back at him.

'Where were you, heading off into the wild blue?'

'I was thinking about what they did.'

'Who?'

'My, um . . . my ah, parents . . . I mean, Jaxon wasn't far wrong, was he? Like when he said I'd been leading a dog's life? I'm the result of a damn breeding program . . . selective, just like they have in the zoo. When were they gonna tell me, ferchrissake? *What* were they going to tell me?'

'Won't be long now before you can ask.' Sarah glanced back. 'What happens next?'

'Far as I remember, we go underneath the freeway and follow the signs, which I hope will be there, for Broadway . . .'

Luiz was back on stake-out again. And this time everyone was involved, except Twinky-dink Alfredo, who had to stay back and look after the communications. No loss there.

Inverdale had bossed it up and grabbed the easy gig, sitting in the front window of a coffee shop that had a reasonable view of the generic downtown block where the Docto® Corporation had its offices. With Sheila. Big surprise, Luiz had got to watch the back of the building.

He wanted to think all this was overdoing things. I mean, wasn't Ed going to be following Stewart in from La Jolla anyway? But Inverdale had insisted no chances were taken and, having already lost the boy up in Seattle, Luiz really couldn't blame him for wanting everything to be totally tight. His position, he supposed he'd do the same, for sure.

Around five after four his cell had gone and it was Ed in the tail car: Stewart, plus his wife, were a couple of minutes away in the silver Mercedes, he'd said. Wife driving.

Luiz called Inverdale and told him what was happening, then he sat back and waited. The entrance to the basement parking facility was at the rear of the building, so the car was bound to finish up here. A couple of minutes later a late-model silver Merc slid around the corner, came down the street and turned into the steeply sloping parking entrance. Just the wife, no sign of Stewart. Luiz fast-dialed Inverdale as the trunk of the car disappeared from view.

'It's me. I got the wife, no Stewart. Should I be worrying?'

'No. She stopped in front of the building and let him out, he went straight up. What did she do?'

'Parked, in the basement.'

'Stay put.'

For another two hours? The woman wasn't due till six, but Luiz knew there was no point in wasting his breath asking what the point was. 'Where d'you want Ed to go?'

'Tell him to park up, nice and legal, and meet up with you.'

Mike Henrikson was so angry he wanted to rip something apart. Instead, from where he was standing, he slammed the phone's handset down so hard it jumped off its cradle and landed on the desk. Tony could hear the buzz of the dial tone. Whatever tiny amount had been left of his partner's sense of humor, it had obviously finally packed up and left for the day.

'What did they say?'

'They said . . .' Mike screwed up a sheet of paper and proceeded to tear it to shreds, '. . . they had the goddam nerve to tell me that he'd just called in from his car to say that he wouldn't, after all, be going into the office today.'

Tony looked at the shreds of paper on Mike's desk — which, considering Mike's mood, he thought was lucky not to have a hole punched out of it. 'Pity we can't put out an APB, get some help in tracking him down, right? All he's doing is not returning calls, though.'

'He has got *no* idea the trouble he's going to bring down on his head for doing this.' Mike swept the bits of paper off his desk. 'Wasting a whole day of my time . . .'

Tony nodded. While not 100 percent true, it did seem like most of what Mike'd done was leave messages, talk to secretaries and maids and get nowhere with this particular case. 'Your phone's still off the hook, Mike . . .'

Mike leaned down and picked it up, dropping it back in place. It immediately started to ring, like it was complaining about the treatment it'd been getting recently. Mike snatched it up. 'Henrikson . . . What? A call about the Stewart boy? Who is it?' Mike waved at Tony to get ready to pick his phone up when he told him. 'Caller says it's anonymous for the moment . . . okay, put him through and see if you can get any kind of trace on it . . . yeah, sure, I'll keep him on as long as possible.' Mike indicated to Tony to pick up. 'Hello, Mr. . . .?'

'Can you guarantee no one will know it was me made this call?'

'That all depends on what you're going to tell me, sir.'

Tony smiled. The voice at the other end of the line didn't sound old enough to warrant being called 'sir', but it was a nice touch.

'I know where he is.'

'Who?'

'Cam Stewart.'

'How do you know we're looking for him, sir?'

'He's been like kidnapped, right?'

Mike sat down. 'We believe so. Where did you say he was?'

'I didn't yet. Is there a reward?'

'I'm sure his parents will be only too grateful to show their gratitude in getting their son back, Mr. . . .'

'Yeah, I'm sure . . .'

'But we neither of us are going to get much further if you don't tell me something.'

'Ah shit, screw the money. Look, he's gonna be at some place called the Doctor Corporation, okay? Pulling some kind of trick on his father.'

'When?' Mike, scribbling on his pad, looked like he'd just been told he'd won free pizza for a year.

'I think six this evening. Yeah . . . I'm sure it's six.'

'Thanks for that, that's great. Now if we need to get back in touch, Mr. . . .'

'And he said he killed someone up in Seattle.'

Dial tone.

Tony and Mike both put their phones down in synch. Mike scratched his head. 'You think there really is a Santa Claus, and he's just delivered what he forgot to give me last year?'

'You think that was on the level?'

'Man, he knew a *lot* of stuff . . . yeah, I think it's kosher.'

'He said the boy killed someone, you think that's true also?'

'We'll ask him when we finally get to meet in about . . .' Mike looked at his watch, '. . . an hour from now.' Mike's phone rang again and he picked it up, listened for a couple of moments and put it back down.

'Did they get a trace?' Tony asked.

Mike nodded. 'A number in Santa Monica. Regular land-line, registered to a J. Colby.'

Chapter 35

San Diego; Monday March 3rd, 5.41 p.m.

At about twenty to six Inverdale left Sheila in the coffee house and went over to the Docto® Corp. building, telling the helpful lady at the main reception desk that he was early to meet his wife; they were, you know – and here he looked at the ground – going up to the tenth floor for an appointment? He wondered if she would mind if he waited here in the lobby for her?

  The receptionist'd only been at this job a couple of months, and though she knew the Docto® hours were 8.30 to 5.30, she wasn't sure if they did late appointments. They did a lot of fertility work up there and she was very under-standing about letting this nice, quite nervous man wait for his wife. She looked over at the man, sitting now on one of the two sofas in the lobby. Giving him an encouraging smile, she went back to cleaning out last month's emails from her computer.

Sarah circled the block. They'd found the building, all they needed to do now was find a damn parking space. Why didn't offices offer valet parking? At ten to six Sarah found a meter in a street a good way from the office block, which meant that a couple of minutes after six found them all arriving, slightly out of breath, outside the building's street-to-ceiling plate glass entrance.

'Right, are we all clear what we have to do here?' Sarah fanned herself with the document case she was carrying. 'Cam?'

'I stay way in the background.' Cam rubbed his chin, itchy with a day's growth of stubble. 'You know, make busy, look bored and keep my back to my dad as much as possible.'

'Right, and you, Tee?'

Tee pointed to the large camera case Cam was carrying. 'I get Cam to help me set up and then I keep focussed on his father, maybe the occasional shot of you.'

'Okay, let's go.'

'Wait a second.' Tee grabbed Sarah's arm. 'Cam, put on your shades, man, and the baseball cap.'

'Right, right . . . I forgot.' Cam put the camera case down and got the sunglasses out of the hooded jacket Tee had borrowed from Jaxon without asking him. Taking the cap out of his back pocket he tugged the bill down low. After he'd finished, Tee pulled the hood up and stood back to look at the result.

'Your own mother wouldn't recognize you.'

'Just as long as his father doesn't,' said Sarah, walking toward the doors.

Inverdale checked his watch again. He was beginning to wonder if they'd missed a call or something and the whole deal had been called off. Then he noticed the woman, quite attractive, interesting-looking.

The woman, who looked a bit flustered, stopped outside

228

the building with a couple of younger people, a guy and a girl – her kids? No, no, they were too old. The woman was facing him, fanning herself with what was probably a leatherette document case, and talking to the other two, who had their backs to him. They looked to have been running, or at least walking fast.

Inverdale was bored and this was like a little piece of theater, so he carried on watching. The woman then tucked the case under her arm and started to walk toward the doors, the guy turning to follow her. The girl grabbed the woman's arm as she moved and stopped her, the guy turning back to look at why she'd done it.

But not before Inverdale had seen his face.

Jesus H! It was the Stewart kid! He was totally damn sure of it. Inverdale's brain dropped a gear and accelerated with major wheel spin – first off, the woman didn't look anything like she sounded, and second, how come the Stewart kid was with her? How the *hell* come? Inverdale knew that Cameron had seen him up in Seattle; he'd still been a bit groggy from the sedation, but there was no way he wouldn't recognize his face. He stood up and turned away from the street, making a deal of looking at his watch as he got out his cell and called Luiz, figuring the woman at the reception would assume he was calling his wife. Behind him, as the connection was made, he heard the doors open and footsteps cross the lobby. Luiz answered.

'Just hold on, Luiz, I can't talk right now.' Nodding like he was having a conversation with someone, Inverdale strained to hear what the woman said at the desk, and sure enough she told the receptionist she had a six o'clock with a Mr. Stewart at the Docto® Corporation. Inverdale waited till the footsteps went over to the elevators. 'She's here, Luiz, gone up to the offices, but she brought a little extra something for us.'

'Why're you whispering, man . . . extra what?'

'The woman from the TV company's here, and Cameron freaking Stewart's just gone up to the tenth with her.'

'Serious?'

'Am I known for my love of practical jokes?'

'Okay . . . what next?'

'Leave Ed out back and come meet me at the coffee shop.' Inverdale closed his cell and turned to the nice lady at the desk, shrugging. 'That was my wife, she's been delayed. I just called, you know, as she was late? She told me she'd had a flat and she won't be able to make the appointment.'

'I am sorry, sir.'

'Well,' Inverdale, who could just see Luiz down the street, crossing over to the side where the coffee house was, pointed at the doors, 'I'd better go see if I can help . . .'

A couple of minutes later, having checked the receptionist wasn't looking his way up the street, Inverdale crossed the road and slipped into the coffee house. He sat down at the table opposite Luiz, who had the chair next to Sheila.

Luiz nodded at the street. 'We gonna wait and pick them up as they come out, tail 'em back to LA?'

'If it was just her, that would've been the thing. I mean, she would be walking right out of there, I'd've said half an hour from now. All Stewart thinks he's gonna be doing is stonewalling her and trying to find out how much she knows and how come she knows it. But she's got the kid with her, plus someone else, so she has other plans, Luiz, she has other plans . . . she's gonna mess with him, and it's going to get a tad unpredictable.'

'So?' Luiz picked up an empty sugar sachet and began folding it in half and then half again.

'I want that boy back.'

'So we lift him as they come out,' Luiz shrugged, 'or take him on the street, whatever.'

'Whatever's not good enough . . .' Inverdale drummed on the table top with his fingers, frowning, a strained expression on his face. Luiz thought he looked like he was constipated. Then Inverdale focussed on Sheila. 'We gotta go in – you and me.'

'Go in where?' It was Luiz's turn to frown.

'The clinic. It's containable up there, more private.'

'Why you two? Shouldn't it be me and Ed?'

'You two look like you're trying for a kid? Like you would be going up to some fertility clinic? I don't think so, Luiz. Maybe in San Francisco, but not here.' Inverdale glanced at Sheila. 'You got your piece, right?' Sheila patted her shoulder bag. 'Let's go, then . . .'

It was only ten blocks from the SDPD building to 4th and Broadway. They could've walked, Tony thought, but decided not to share this opinion with Mike as they stood on the sidewalk and waited for the patrol car to come and pick them up. As they waited he watched the uniform finishing writing up the citation for the blue-rinse citizen who had driven into the back of them at the lights at the intersection with 12th.

He felt sorry for the lady, but wasn't this just absolute proof of Murphy's Law? What with them being on a schedule and all? The last thing they'd needed was to be rear-ended, and the back of their car truly looked like the Hulk had punched it. He looked at his watch: 6.10; he looked at Mike: keeping it together, just. And then he saw the patrol car coming down the street toward them, Mike walking toward it, impatient. They'd be later than they'd planned to be arriving at the Docto® offices, but it wasn't the end of the world.

Tony followed after Mike and reached the patrol car as it came to a halt to pick them up. Mike took the front passenger seat, leaving Tony to sit in back, behind the grille, and, he had to be honest, it gave him a creepy feeling to be sitting there, even without cuffs on.

'You want full orchestra?' The driver looked over at Mike.

'What?'

'Siren and lights, sir.'

'Just get there without crashing, okay?'

'Yes, sir.'

'And wait outside for us.'

Chapter 36

San Diego, Monday 3rd March;
6.05 p.m.

The knot in Cam's stomach was a gut-crunching, physical thing, and getting more intense as the digital counter flicked up through the floor numbers, *1 . . . 2 . . .*

What the hell was he doing?

Out of somewhere the quote leaped front of mind, '*. . . it's 106 miles to Chicago. We've got a full tank of gas, half a pack of cigarettes, it's dark, and we're wearing sunglasses. Hit it . . .*' Only he wasn't Dan Ackroyd or John Belushi, he wasn't in a movie and he didn't have a personal R'n'B soundtrack; for him it was just four floors to go and counting, he looked like a skanky home boy, it was six in the evening and he was wearing wraparound shades. Shit.

What they were about to do was crazy, totally certifiable. *Why* had he agreed to do this? Up in LA everything had made sense, it had had a logic that seemed to work. Not here, though, no way it was working here. As *7* changed to *8*, Cam had one of those moments of frightening clarity when everything clicks into place and you can see exactly what you've done and realize at the same time what you actually *should've* done. He'd been taken by the moment, shocked by Sarah's revelations about him, and, fueled in equal parts by fear of the future and anger about his past, he hadn't thought anything through. Heart over head. Completely lethal emotional combination. *9 . . .*

What was Sarah getting out of all this, anyway? And what was Tee doing here, about to video the whole thing? The questions wouldn't go away. *10 . . . ding!* Oh jeez, this was it . . .

The elevator slid to a halt and the doors sighed open to reveal a warm-white up-lit corridor, carpeted in a mottled blue; all very restful. There were framed prints on the wall, the kind of pastel abstracts designed to have a calming effect on visitors. Out of the blue Cam had an instant hit of déjà vu, a realization that he almost remembered being here before. He found himself staring at a sign saying 'Welcome!' with a friendly, rounded arrow pointing to the left, and the moment passed as quickly as it'd come. He watched Sarah and Tee walk out into the wide corridor, but stood rooted to the spot, unable to move.

'Cam?' Tee beckoned, but all he could do was shake his head. The doors began to close again and Tee held them back, trying to stare through the impenetrable black plastic insect eyes of the sunglasses for clues as to what was happening. 'Cam, what's the matter?'

Sarah glanced down the corridor, down at her watch and then up at Cam. 'You don't have to come in, Cam. You can stay in the lobby, I can nail this without you being there in the room.' She put out her hand, motioning him out of the elevator.

'You can?' Cam felt the weight that was holding him back lift off his shoulders.

'Sure.'

234

Cam picked up the camera case and walked out of the elevator, Tee letting the doors shut behind him. 'I don't know why I'm here, Sarah, really . . .' He looked over at Tee. 'Or you.'

'You're here to get answers, Cam, and Tee's here to help.' Sarah glanced down the corridor again.

'It'll be okay, Cam.' Tee touched his hand, tentatively linking fingers.

Cam didn't say anything, but held tight and started to walk.

Gordon Stewart looked at the clock on the wall. She was late. Still, thank God she hadn't been early; it'd taken a lot longer than he'd anticipated for Eleanor to get everyone out of the place. This wasn't something he could have effectively done, as only the senior consultant, whose office he was now in, knew who he was, and he wanted to keep it that way. But members of the staff were familiar with Eleanor, from her charitable work and in her role as a trustee. It was a good cover and meant she'd been able to oversee the timely exit. He sometimes wondered about people's credibility; Eleanor had told the office manager that she was having the whole suite feng shui'd and needed it empty. No one had batted an eyelid.

And now everyone had left. Gordon looked around. It had taken a long time to build this up, a lot of money, a lot of sweat, and to have everything they'd planned and worked for threatened now was like a really sick joke. It was *not* going to happen. They had been putting this together for over twenty years and nobody, *nobody*, was going to screw it up now. Not even that bastard Marshall Inverdale.

Just thinking about Inverdale made him hyperventilate.

What he was up to, trying to muscle in, was just damn piracy! He had no idea how the cheap, shyster gangster had found out about them, but the man had known enough to strike at the very heart of what they were doing by kidnapping Cameron. The man was unbelievable . . . not only had he demanded a ransom for Cam's safe return, he'd also wanted to become what amounted to an equal partner in the business! Gordon's left eye twitched involuntarily at the thought of what might have happened if Cam hadn't escaped, how near he'd been to agreeing to all Inverdale's terms and conditions.

But this wasn't just about money – although he couldn't deny it was lucrative – it was about trying to keep a part of the world clean, uncontaminated. White. Gordon drummed his manicured nails on the green leather desktop, an automatic, stress-indicating gesture, then realized what he was doing. Glancing at his reflection in the computer screen, he smoothed his hair and straightened his flawlessly knotted tie. He'd been holding this all together since Cameron had been lifted, wondering, now, where he was and if he'd ever see him again . . . all that investment of time and money, all gone.

Of the eight Gen 1 survivors, Cameron was without doubt the best. Perfect pedigree, perfect school record, perfect temperament . . . they'd chosen well, got the biology absolutely right, and they'd done the parenting well also, even if he often thought Eleanor was being a little hard on the boy. Cameron's had been a totally normal upbringing, he had no idea he was so special and was all the more balanced for that.

He was truly the perfect combination of nature and nurture, and a terrific endorsement, even advertisement, for their product. He was worth a fortune, like the finest Arab studs. Which, as it happened, was a very appropriate simile.

This was a world full of disease – from AIDS and drug-resistant clap to every damn kind of psychosis – and a society that seemed determined to allow everything to be thrown into the melting pot and then let even the aberrant survive . . . so, in a world where morality had gone to hell in a handbasket, who wouldn't pay a lot of money, really *a lot*, to be guaranteed a son or daughter you could be totally proud of? Because, you know, sometimes you couldn't trust your own gene pool. He was secretly actually quite relieved, with what he'd found out about Eleanor's family, that she hadn't been able to have children.

Going around being vocal about their beliefs would only have brought unwanted attention. Practice what you preach, but don't make a circus out of the preaching, that was how to do it. All their connections with other like-minded people were also as well hidden as was possible, because this was not your regular business. A lot of what they were doing wasn't illegal, although some of it most definitely was. Like what you could call their quality control, for instance.

Some of the children they'd helped create weren't as good as they should have been, especially early on. You know, weren't up to scratch mentally or physically, or showed some unacceptable, unexpected ethnic traits. That meant they'd had to remove certain children from the program, permanently, which was unfortunate. But you had to have standards, right? Otherwise what else was there? Chaos, like the situation they were trying to get away from. They'd lost a lot from Gen 1, but had made their processes better since; practice really did make perfect.

It had been tough – he liked kids and he didn't know how

he'd have felt if Cameron had turned out bad and had had to go. He'd thought about that particular scenario, especially recently as Eleanor had become tougher with Cam. If he'd failed to match up, what would she have wanted to do? God knows, her maternal instincts had never been as strong as her business ones.

And now this Sarah woman . . . what was her name, Baldwin? Like that writer, the gay, black one. Gordon fleetingly wondered if she was both black and gay herself, and thought he wouldn't be surprised. Whatever she was, he would, though, be charm itself, make every effort to disabuse her of these strange ideas she'd gotten hold of about the Docto® Corporation. As well as trying, as subtly as possible, to find out where the hell she'd gotten them from in the first place . . . and being very direct, in a non-threatening way, about what the legal consequences would be if she'd been sharing them in the public domain.

As Gordon pulled back the sleeve of his dark blue blazer to check the time again, he heard the buzzer go out in the lobby, and then the sound of someone knocking. Eleanor must have locked the door to stop anyone coming back in. He stood, did up the center button on his blazer and went to greet this Sarah Baldwin.

Alone in the lobby, with its light, floral scent layered over a slight medical sharpness in the air, Cam felt distinctly weird. Just as Sarah had predicted, his father hadn't given him a second glance, ignoring him and instead focussing entirely on Sarah, while at the same time sneakily eyeing up Tee. To keep him distracted, put him off his stride, Sarah had asked Tee if she'd mind undoing an extra button or two on her blouse. Cam hadn't believed his father could be that shallow, but dammit if he wasn't. But hey, he'd hardly been able to stop from staring himself.

He caught sight of himself in a framed picture hanging on the wall. He didn't recognize the person looking back, his face thinner, dark glasses hiding his eyes, face framed by the cap and the hood. He was even slouching in that couldn't-give-a-shit way. A voice from the old life said 'Straighten up!' but he ignored it. It wasn't relevant, if, he thought, it ever had been.

Looking around, Cam felt more small pieces of memory slide into place, adding to but in no way completing a picture of when his mother had brought him here. With the hushed whisper of the AC the only noise, there was a strangely dream-like quality to it . . . like his whole life at the moment. Every so often he would find himself wondering if he was going to wake up and find it had all been a hysterical nightmare, but knowing, deep down, this was it. Reality, no matter how strange.

A tap on the door behind him made Cam turn and look. The other side of the glass panel was a smiling Asian-looking woman, and behind her, his back to Cam, he could see a short, balding man who looked kind of familiar, but he couldn't think why. The woman was waving and making gestures that made it clear she and the man wanted to come into the clinic.

Cam shrugged, palms out. What was he supposed to do? This wasn't his place, there was no one else here, he couldn't go letting people in. He shook his head. The other side of the door he saw the woman frown and push the doors, hard, and then he heard the sound of a cell phone ringing and saw the man putting one to his ear.

* * *

'Inverdale?' Luiz, stirring some Sweet'n Low into a latte, carried on looking across the street toward the Docto® building. 'Look, just so's you know, a patrol car's just parked up outside and two plain clothes have gone in . . . no, can't see what they're doing now, but the car's staying put . . . yeah, only the one. Where are you? Just the boy, no sign of the woman? What're you gonna do?' Luiz took a sip of coffee, listening. 'Fine, we'll be waiting . . .'

Luiz cut the connection and made a new one, waiting as the call went through and was picked up immediately.

'Ed, s'me . . . yeah, look, slight complication . . . cops . . . no, stay put, I'll be right over . . .'

Chapter 37

San Diego; Monday 3rd March, 6.25 p.m.

It was hard to ignore the fact that there were two people out in the corridor trying to get in. To make it easier to pay them no attention, Cam went over to a low, glass-topped table and picked up a *National Geographic*, sitting down in one of the chairs that faced away from the door. Rude, but he did not feel like going over and engaging the woman in some useless conversation. *Really* did not.

And then the almost silence was broken by a loud spitting sound. Cam looked over his shoulder to see the woman pushing the doors open and calmly walking past the front desk. She was holding what looked like an Uzi machine pistol in her right hand, its stock folded forward and a thin plume of greasy smoke coming out of its barrel. The smell of burnt cordite wafted across the room as the man, to the woman's left, came in behind her, also with a gun in his hand: square-barreled, snub-nosed and silenced.

This was totally surreal, like some kind of absurd practical joke. Who could be *that* desperate to see a damn doctor?

Smiling, as if this was the way he normally entered a room, the man moved into the middle of the lobby.

'Hi there, Cameron,' he said, nodding. 'Long time, no see, buddy . . . man, have *you* led us one merry dance.'

In a state of shock, Cam stared at the gunman, speechless. It was the guy from Seattle, the one who'd come into the room to check him over when he'd woken up. What the hell was he doing here?

'So, are you going to make a fuss, or come with us, nice and easy?' The man didn't wait for an answer, just raised his gun until its barrel pointed straight at Cam, then beckoned with it. 'Move, Cameron.'

Eleanor had just gotten into the ladies' room when she'd heard the entrance buzzer; the Baldwin woman must have arrived. The lobby was way down the end of the corridor, and she was desperate to go. Gordon could answer it himself.

Some few minutes later, finished, freshened and sucking on a breathmint, Eleanor was nearly back at the lobby when she heard voices: men's voices. There should be no men here, apart from Gordon, and he ought by now to be in the senior consultant's office with that woman. Opening her shoulder bag she reached in and took out a tiny little .32 Beretta Tomcat automatic, the Titanium model Gordon had given her on their last anniversary. It didn't pack much weight, the man in the store had said, but it sure did pack a punch. And it fit in her hand just right. Eleanor slipped off the safety, put her bag down and began to walk very quietly up the corridor.

She stopped, just before turning the corner, arranged a smile on her face and walked into the lobby, her right hand out of sight behind her. In that microsecond she took in the scene playing out in front of her – a young man, she couldn't see his face, dressed in that way some boys will do, copying what was called 'ghetto style', and to her left a middle-aged, balding man and an Asian woman. Both, she realized too late to back out, carrying guns. The man's was pointing directly at the boy.

Eleanor took a calming, deep breath. 'Is there a problem?'

The young man looked around, the flush-mounted over-head spotlights bouncing glare off his sunglasses, said 'Mom?' in a disbelieving voice and started toward her; the man's gun followed him, the Asian woman moving back into a two-handed covering pose.

'One more step, Cameron, and she gets shot.'

The man's voice was calm, quiet – there was no way Gordon would be aware anything was amiss . . . and then Eleanor realized what he'd just said. This scruffy boy was *Cameron*?

Eleanor readily admitted that she had just about zero maternal instinct, but her talents for personal survival and the protection of an invaluable asset were highly developed. Somehow Cameron had managed to find his way back, and now this man and his accomplice were threatening to take him away again. Just not going to happen a second time.

If there was one thing Eleanor had always excelled at it was learning things fast. Exactly as her gun instructor had taught her, she suddenly dropped to one knee, at the same time swinging her torso sideways and raising her gun arm, steadying it with her left hand. Having both surprised the intruders and provided them with a much smaller target, she immediately started firing. Eleanor's first two shots had hit the man in the chest and neck, the third making the woman flinch, before her luck ran out and she took a bullet in the shoulder from the short burst the Asian woman fired.

It slammed her to the ground like she'd been hit by a wrecking ball, blood spattering back onto the pale walls in a delicate arc.

Sitting behind the desk Gordon felt things were pretty much going his way. He was blocking and returning the questions like a top seeded tennis player; the Baldwin woman — neither black nor, as far as he could tell, gay — had up till now not managed to even dent his armor. The toughest job so far was keeping his eyes off the camera-operator's tits and his mind on what he was doing. She did have a truly great pair, and she *kept* on bending over . . .

'Mr. Stewart,' the Baldwin woman interrupted his train of thought, 'what would you say if I told you I have document-ed evidence that you are creating racially "pure" babies on a commercial basis, and that you cull children who don't match up to your standards and expectations?'

'Excuse me?' Gordon didn't quite understand, for a moment, the sudden change of tack.

'And what if I were also to tell you I have proof that your own son Cameron is, in fact, a product of your eugenics business?'

In the silence that followed the questions, all Gordon could hear was the whirring of the zoom motor on the video camera. *What had she just said?* He was struggling to put together some kind of reply when the gunfire started.

The girl with the video almost threw it on the carpet and made for the door, yelling 'Cam!'

Sarah Baldwin, seemingly just as open-mouthed as he was, stared straight at him. 'What the hell was that?'

'How the hell should *I* know?' Gordon pushed his chair back. The only other person in the office, apart from that gofer they'd brought with them, was Eleanor . . .

Tee couldn't believe what she saw as she came crashing out of the office and ran into the reception. Cam was over to her left, kneeling down by someone – a woman – on the ground; over to her right, also on the ground, was a guy, and just behind him was a smartly-dressed Japanese or Chinese woman. With a big gun. And a bloody left ear. Amazing what you could take in when you needed to.

Skidding to a halt, Tee didn't know how to react – go to Cam, which was what she wanted to do, or get out the way of the gun. Before she could make her mind up, behind her the air seemed to explode and, as she dove for the ground, her ears ringing, she saw a vase of flowers behind the Asian woman disintegrate, pottery, leaves, petals and water spraying out in all directions.

Looking up, Tee saw the woman turn and disappear through the office doors. She pushed herself off the ground, ran over to where Cam was still kneeling and crouched down beside him. 'Are you all right?'

'Yeah . . . yeah, I'm, uh, I'm fine . . .'

Tee looked at the woman on the ground, a well-dressed, older woman with elegantly coiffured hair, precisely applied make-up, expensive jewelry and what looked like half her shoulder blasted off. 'Who's that?'

'My mother.'

'Is she . . .?'

'Dead? No, she's alive.'

Now Tee looked, she could see the woman's chest rising and falling very, very slightly, though her face was almost paler than the paint on the walls.

'Cameron? Is that . . . is that you?' Gordon looked puzzled.

Tee stood up, between Cam and his father, noticing the gun hanging down in his shaking hand. 'I hope you and your wife are proud of what you've done,' she yelled at him, '*real* proud!'

Behind her she could hear Cam get up, felt his hand grip her shoulder. 'Hi, uh, Dad . . .'

Tony watched the floor counter, kind of mesmerized by the way the red dot-matrix display walked the numbers across the tiny screen as the elevator moved upward. According to the building's log book, someone called Sarah Baldwin – '+2', as she'd written by her name – had gone up to the tenth floor at 6.05; one of those '+2' had been a young male. If their informant was right, it must be Cameron Stewart. The lady at the front desk had told them that, about seven or eight minutes later, a man and his wife had insisted on going up, even though she'd told them there was no one there anymore. They were, she'd said, probably on their way down right now.

They'd find out if Cameron Stewart was up there in one floor's time, and then they'd hopefully get some answers to their many questions. For the life of him Tony had no idea what direction this case was taking, and he didn't believe Mike had anymore of a clue either; all that seemed to be driving him was an intense personal dislike of the boy's parents. Give him a regular break-in or embezzlement, Tony thought, or even a straightforward murder, any day.

As the elevator doors opened the unmistakable perfume of a firefight hit him and Mike at the same time, and they came out of the elevator fast, ducking low, guns drawn, one checking right, the other left. It was left, the way the sign for the Docto® Corp. was pointing and the shouting was coming from. As he followed Mike, Tony was aware the elevator next to the one they'd come up in had begun to operate, but down the corridor was where the problems lay.

Fifteen yards or so up ahead Tony could see the doors to the Docto® offices and he and Mike dropped below the eyeline of the glass panels, and ran up to them.

'Someone was in a hurry to see the physician.' Tony pointed out the bullet-shattered lock.

Mike prairie-dogged, looked through the glass panel and ducked back down. 'Looks like two down, let's get in.'

They took a door each, Mike leading, Tony covering, and went through into the lobby area, both doing an instant appraisal: no guns pointing their way; two victims, one male, one female; four adults also present, and apparently unhurt, including Gordon Stewart. Who Mike suddenly saw was carrying heat.

'Drop the gun, Stewart! Now!' Mike pointed at the man, the victim nearest them. 'Check him, Tony, looks like he could be a DOA – then call the paramedics. I'll take the woman.'

Tony knelt down by the man, removed the silenced pistol still gripped in his right hand and felt for a pulse. Nothing. As he got out his cell and hot-dialed the paramedics he saw the small wound in the man's upper neck and another in his chest. Didn't look like lucky shots to him. Whoever had had this man in their sights was good, and had meant to kill. As control picked up, and he started to give them the location, Mike yelled over at him from where he was squatting down by the woman.

'Tell 'em to bust a gut getting here, we got a live one – and tell 'em to send a couple more cruisers.'

'More cruisers?'

Mike nodded. 'There's another gun still loose in the building, apparently – female, Asian, about 5'2"... she ran out just before we arrived. Get onto the uniform out front, warn him as well.'

Sheila's ear hurt, although she did seem to have just about staunched the bloodflow. She was damn lucky to be alive. That bullet only had to have been another inch or so to the right and her brains would've been wallpaper.

The elevator was on its way to Lower Ground, a.k.a. the garage; she could exit the building that way and Luiz would be there with the car. From her bag she took out a red plastic crocodile grip and quickly fastened up her shoulder-length hair, then pulled out a pair of dark glasses. Taking her dark blue jacket off, she turned it inside out to show the pale lining and hung it over her arm; pulling up the collar of her blouse she inspected herself in the chrome panel to the left of the doors. Okay... sufficiently different to probably fool anyone with only a sketchy verbal description of her.

Shame about Marshall Inverdale, though, but that's the way the dice roll – if your number's up, you die. She didn't feel at all guilty for not putting up more of a fight – there was nothing in her contract that said she had to lay her life down for the job. What she did have was an obligation to herself to get out and not get caught.

Chapter 38

Police HQ, San Diego; Monday 3rd March, 9.07 p.m.

Tony watched Mike up at the whiteboard, writing stuff under four headings – which they'd decided should be *G. & E. Stewart, C. Stewart, S. Baldwin* and *John Doe* – just to get things straight in their heads. There was nothing under *John Doe*.

As the situation stood right now, Eleanor Stewart was in hospital, probably still being operated on. The bullet, a hollow-point, had made a real mess, but hell, reflected Tony, wasn't that what they'd been designed to do? Expand on impact and make a bigger hole going out than going in. The woman was lucky she hadn't caught the slug elsewhere in her upper body . . . she'd likely be dead if she had.

Gordon Stewart was being held overnight while the DA and his crew of lawyers worked out if this was going to have to go Federal or would stay State; on top of which they had to decide exactly what they were going to charge him with. And there was going to be quite a lot to choose from, if half of what the Baldwin woman had told them turned out to be true.

'You think she's right, Mike?'

'Who?'

'Sarah Baldwin. You think they've actually killed kids who didn't come out the way they wanted? You can't quality control *kids* . . .'

'You kinda have to, if you're selling perfection.'

'Sick bastards.'

'There are a lot of them out there in the Land of the Free, Tony. How long you been a cop? You should know that by now.'

'What's gonna happen to the kid?' Tony yawned and rubbed his eyes; he was truly beat.

'Short term, there's nothing we want him for; long term, he's gonna have to deal with the inevitable shit storm when this whole story breaks, which, if Ms. Baldwin has her way, I guarantee won't be too long.'

'And the thing with him supposed to have killed someone up in Seattle? What about that?'

Mike put down the dry marker. 'He's saying nothing about it, right?' Tony nodded. 'Seattle PD have squat, so we've just got the word of what turns out to be the righteously jealous boyfriend of the foxy Ms. Taylor Philips.'

'Yeah . . .'

'And Cameron says he stayed undercover because the incident outside his uncle's place freaked him, with only his father knowing he was there and all. He thought, for whatever reason, Stewart'd told the kidnappers where to find him, runs away, and then some suburban cowboy shoots him.'

'There's a paranoid logic there, and jeez, after all he'd been through, he's allowed that.' Tony flicked through a couple of pages of his notebook. 'Gartner has admitted he was up there that night and that they were the people he ran away from.'

'Shame Mrs. Stewart was such an ace shot,' Mike turned to look at the whiteboard, 'because we've got precisely nothing on the dead man . . . no credit cards, just cash, plus a fake driver's license and Social Security number.'

'Cameron says he was the main man up in Seattle.'

'Yeah, well until we get the results back from the Fed's fingerprint database, that is *all* we know about him and what this whole kidnap thing was about, except that he kept some pretty dangerous company.' Mike reached up and wrote 'Seattle' under *John Doe*. 'That woman he was with wasn't carrying anything that would fit neatly in a purse. She was pretty serious.'

'Yeah . . .' Tony snapped his fingers, '. . . did I tell you there's CCTV footage of her exiting via the underground garage? Changed her appearance just enough to be missed on the first run-through, but that's it, nothing else . . . although it looks like she was hit, there was some blood on the elevator carpet.'

'Way to go, Mrs. Stewart! Three shots fired and three hits. If she wasn't going to jail, I'd say she could've looked forward to a career in the SWAT team . . .'

Cameron was almost numb with shock. His mother, who wasn't his real mother, was in the hospital – liable, said the doctor when he'd called, to lose her arm, and lucky at that. His father, also not his real father, was in custody. He, on the other hand, was free.

Although the cops had asked him direct whether it was true that he'd killed someone up in Seattle, he'd kept his cool and straight out lied, figuring he had enough to deal with without that as well. And the further away from the incident he got, the more he felt kind of justified in having done it and the less of a crime it seemed. Wrong? At the moment, who cared.

It was when he'd told the cops the actual address of where he'd been staying in LA that they'd let slip it was where the tip-off phone call had come from. Jaxon had goddam dropped a dime on him! Tee went ballistic when he'd told her. He maybe shouldn't have, but hey, she knew what Jaxon was like so there was no way she was going to be totally surprised. Still, maybe he shouldn't have. Truth? He'd only done it to stitch the guy up, and he didn't feel one bit better for doing it. Probably worse.

He stared at the walls of the visitors' room the officers had put him in to wait, while they checked about him with Social Services, they'd said. His head was turned every which way, random thoughts firing off so he couldn't keep his mind focussed on anything very long. He'd begin to try figuring out what some future plan might be and then he'd suddenly get this clear-as-day memory coming back. Like when he was sitting with a bunch of friends, all complaining what jerks their parents were, him saying 'These people *cannot* be my mom and dad . . . I gotta be like *adopted*, man!', everyone laughing and agreeing they thought the exact same thing. He remembered, after his parents had pissed him off about something, actually thinking that it had to be true. And now it was.

Part of him also felt this was his fault, that he should've known something was wrong with his life, known he was adopted. There must've been signs, surely . . . had he just not been paying attention his whole life? How could he not know, not feel the truth about this most central thing: who he was. What he did feel was like some kind of weird amnesiac or someone with a bad case of False Memory

Syndrome. Like he was a complete fake.

The sound of a squeaky door handle being turned made him look around to see Tee coming into the room on her own.

'Where's Sarah?'

'She went.'

Cam frowned. 'I thought she was going to like give you a lift back to LA?'

'We had a disagreement.'

'About what?'

'About that I told her she should hold off on breaking the damn story.' Tee pulled out a chair and sat down. 'Like give you some time out?'

'And what'd she say?'

'Screw you, basically . . .' Tee looked away. 'Whatever else your father is, he was *not* wrong about journalists.'

'It would've got out anyway, right? The shooting and everything.'

'That's what *she* said. Bitch!' Tee hit the table with the flat of her hand. 'From the moment she figured there was a story, we were doing things to *her* agenda . . .'

'Hey, none of this is your fault, it *was* Plan B, right? Never quite as good as Plan A.'

'How can you be so damn calm about all this, Cam?'

'You know, I wondered about that myself?'

'Are you being sarcastic?'

Cam shook his head. 'You know, it's only been like six days since I was kidnapped? Not even a whole week – can you believe that? I don't think I'm calm, Tee, I think I'm just too stunned by all the shit that's happened. You want to know what's real weird?'

'What?'

'It's my birthday next Tuesday, and I have no idea if it's my *actual* birthday or just some date my, you know, my parents picked out?'

'Ask them. You gotta have questions from here to Tijuana you want answers to.'

'I did see my father.' Cam stood up and stretched. 'They let me talk to him for a couple of minutes. I asked him why they put a chip in me, treat me like some pet? All he did was say I wouldn't understand because I didn't know every-thing, but that if I did – *when* I did – I'd realize they'd done it all for all the right reasons.'

'And did he say *when* they were gonna get around to telling you?'

Cam smiled, shaking his head. 'When I was eighteen. Next week.'

Chapter 39

La Jolla, San Diego; Monday 3rd March, 11.07 p.m.

The tail-lights of the rental disappeared as it turned right at the bottom of the street. Cam stood, watching the space where the car had been, feeling empty. Not in a way that had anything to do with hunger – empty in a way that felt like something had been physically removed from his spirit and he was less of the person he had been. Whoever that person was.

Tee had decided she *had* to go back to LA and sort out her life and she had to do it *now*. She hadn't asked him what he thought – why should she? – hadn't told him what she was going to do, where she was going to go after she'd done it, whether he'd see her again. Ever. Why should she? She had a life to lead and why did it have to have anything to do with him? It had *nothing* at all to do with him, except that – and he could only say this to himself in the privacy of his own head – man, he loved her. Really. And it hurt, burned like a flame, that she'd gone, maybe for good.

Cam dug into his jeans pocket and took out a flattened oval that had once been a coin. 'I love you' it said on it, and that was about all he had left.

As he walked up the steps to the front door of his house, small lamps set in the side of the walkway came on as he went past them. He'd rung ahead to check someone would be there, not having any keys to get in, and as he reached the porch Consuela opened the door. He didn't know how much she knew about what was happening, but from the way she looked at him, enough.

'Hello, Mister Cameron,' she smiled, 'glad to see you . . . I was worried.'

'Thanks, Connie.' Cam hugged her, somehow sure she'd been the only person in this house to have been worried about him for the right reasons. He hugged her tight, as she really was all he had left of his old life . . .

'You hungry?'

'All I've had since about breakfast is a cup of San Diego Police coffee. I am starving.'

'You freshen up, I got something going in the kitchen.'

As he went upstairs he could smell whatever was 'going in the kitchen' and realized he wasn't starving, he was ravenous.

He decided to take a shower, have a shave, change everything he was wearing. Get rid of the smell of gunshots and paramedics and police squad rooms that seemed to be clinging to him, reminding him of everything he'd seen and heard. His mother on the floor, lying in an expanding pool of blood; his father in one of those gray interrogation rooms you see on TV cop dramas, a place where the walls seemed to have soaked up fear and guilt until you could taste it. He'd lost his parents twice, first when he'd discovered he was adopted, and now, from what the cops had told him, they weren't likely to be coming home any time soon.

Cam stood in his bedroom, in the house he'd been trying to get back to almost from the moment he'd been kidnapped, and felt weirdly homeless. Like he didn't belong here anymore, and in some ways never had.

As he took some fresh towels into the bathroom he heard the phone start ringing. He could take it in his parents' bedroom, but decided to let Connie deal with the call. What he wanted to do right now was stand under pounding water that was almost too hot to bear, so he did. Having someone who could answer the phone for him was probably going to be one of the first things to disappear from his life . . .

'Boy, that smells awesome, Connie!' Cam, now dressed in old warm-up pants and a soft-from-a-hundred-washes polo shirt, slid onto a stool next to the breakfast bar. 'By the way, who was on the phone?'

'No one you want to talk to.'

'How'd you know?'

Consuela didn't answer and concentrated on attending to the pots on the stove top.

'Consuela?'

'A reporter.'

'Already?'

'I told him you weren't here . . . I make chicken, vegetables, gravy and cornbread, okay?'

Cam nodded automatically, his mind trying to process the fact that the media was on his case before he'd had even a day to prepare himself for the onslaught. Then he glanced up and saw Consuela looking at him.

'Sorry . . . chicken, yeah, sounds great . . . '

'Don't answer the phone, okay? My job.'

'Right . . .' Cam was about to thank her when the door

bell sounded and they looked at each other, knowing they were both thinking the same thing: they're outside, now . . .

Consuela took off her apron. 'The door is my job, too.'

He watched her walk out of the kitchen, this person his parents paid to be ordered around, who seemed to care more about him than anyone else, and thought about the last few days. A week ago he had a family, a place in a world he understood and a future that, even if he didn't work very hard, was fairly much assured because everyone had assumed, him included, that he'd join the family business. Right . . . Cam ran a hand through his still-damp hair . . . except, as it turned out, he *was* the family business.

And now, like a sandcastle on the beach, his life had been swept away, foundations and everything. He took a deep breath, pulling himself back from the brink of total self-pity. On the bright side, if there was one thing he'd learned about himself it was that he was nothing if not a survivor. Cam looked around the familiar room . . . he'd get through this, though where he'd end up afterward was another matter.

He glanced at the Tag on his wrist, which he still hadn't changed for his spare Swatch – 11.45. Who the heck was Connie having to deal with? Cam cleaned the crystal glass face with his shirt. He knew a part of him was wearing the watch like a kind of scalp-trophy, but he also felt he needed a constant reminder of the reality of what had happened to him, otherwise it could so easily become like he'd imagined it. He checked the time again. Maybe he should go see if she needed help.

When he turned the corner into the hallway he saw Tee standing outside the front door, her way blocked by Consuela.

Despite being able to clearly hear the clock up on the wall ticking, it felt just like someone had paused the action. Neither of them moved, nobody spoke, although inside his head a voice was screaming, '*She's come back!*'

It was Consuela who broke the silence. 'She says she isn't a reporter, that she knows you, Mister Cameron.'

'She isn't . . . she does . . .'

'Can she come in?'

Cam couldn't speak.

Tee was watching Cam for a reaction. 'Is that all right, Cam?'

'Is that . . . wha— uh? Yeah, of course, come in – what are you –'

'I was almost onto the freeway,' Tee interrupted, and then stopped.

'And?'

'And . . . and I, uh, I had to . . . look, I have *no* idea whether I was acting like a coward and *couldn't* go back up to LA and sort the Jaxon situation out, or if I *needed* to come back here. I sat outside for ten minutes before I rang the bell.'

'Needed to come back?'

Consuela ushered Tee inside the house, closed the door behind her and double locked it. 'Okay if I go to my room now?'

'Connie! Jeez, I forgot you were there – sorry – yeah, sure . . . thanks. See you tomorrow.'

'Goodnight, Cameron, goodnight, Miss . . .?'

'Tee . . . Tee Philips.'

'Goodnight, Miss Tee.' Consuela walked past Cam. 'There's plenty of food for two, I'll put out another plate . . .'

Cam watched her go, then looked back at Tee. '*Needed* to

259

come back?'

'I'm not saying I'm *never* going up to LA, just that if I go back now Jax'd probably be *out*. And I knew you'd be here, on your own.'

'I thought I'd never see you again . . .'

'You nearly didn't. I so almost got totaled by the guy behind me when I decided not to get on the freeway.' Tee was still standing just inside the door, the space stretching between them filled with awkwardness and possibilities. 'What happens now?'

'You're asking me?' Cam shrugged. 'I have no idea . . .'

'I mean, do we eat, or what? I am *so* hungry I was nearly chewing on the steering wheel.'

'Oh, right . . . I thought you meant . . .' Cam could feel himself reddening. 'I'll get the food.'

'I know what you meant.' Tee, like she'd suddenly been freed, moved quickly across the hallway to Cam. 'Let me help get the food ready.'

Cam, instead of doing what he thought he'd do, which was reach out for Tee, now she was so close, did the opposite and walked into the kitchen. It would, he knew, be so, so easy just to ignore the thoughts in his head and surf the emotional wave, but if he didn't say this now he probably never would.

'What's the matter, Cam?' Tee asked as she followed him.

'My grandpa, my dad's father? He told me once . . . he said, no one ever tells you the *whole* truth.' Cam wanted to look straight at Tee, but his eyes kept flicking elsewhere. 'He was a nice guy, but I guess he was a cynical old bastard at heart . . . I just wanted to say that I love you, Tee, I still would even if you hadn't come back. That's the whole truth. And please don't tell me I'm like a kid or anything.'

260

'A kid?' Tee reached out, pulled Cam tight to her, kissed him, hard, and then stood back slightly. 'Believe me, I would *not* do that to a kid, okay? The truth. And . . . uh, and since you didn't ask, I love you too.'

'You do?' Cam smiled. 'I'm glad that's all straightened out.'

'Wanna know something else?'

'What?'

'It's my birthday next week also.'

'Yeah?'

'Sure, the fifteenth, Saturday . . . for four whole days we'll be the same age.'

Cam, about to begin serving out the food, stopped. 'You're *eighteen*?'

'Sure.' Tee smiled. 'What, I look like an old lady or something?'

'No . . . no, it's just I thought, you know, you were kind of like twenty-three.' Cam spooned food from each of the pots onto the two plates, adding a piece of warm cornbread to each. 'Why didn't you tell me before?'

'Other things on my mind, know what I mean? So it was the *idea* of an older woman that attracted you . . .'

Cam put the plates on the bar. 'Honestly?'

'Seeing as that's the mode we're in.'

'Yeah, a bit.'

'Cool.' Tee dipped her piece of cornbread in the gravy. 'That's two fantasies fulfilled – *I've* always wanted to be someone's Mrs. Robinson.'

For several minutes they sat and ate in an easy silence, the kind of situation, when it happens, you wish would never end. Cam knew it had to, because 'Happy Ever After' is from fairy tales and he surely wasn't living in one of those.

'So,' Tee forked up a piece of chicken, 'what does happen next, with you?'

'You know, I hoped we could leave that till tomorrow?'

'No point.'

Cam got up, went to the fridge and got out a couple of his father's premium imported beers. No one to ask, no one to tell him not to. He opened them both and handed Tee one, knowing that even good evasion tactics have to come to an end sooner or later. He took a long sip.

Tee did the same, putting the bottle down. 'Well?'

'What d'*you* think I should do?'

'If you mean, what would *I* do if I was in your place – I'd take whatever chances came my way to be the person *I* wanted to be, not who *they* wanted me to be.'

'Okay . . .' Cam wiped his mouth on the back of the hand holding his beer. 'You're telling me to get a life, right?'

'Guess I am.'

Cam drank some more beer. 'Guess I'll have to do that.'

'Can we go upstairs now?' Tee watched Cam's arm stopping in midair as he put his bottle down. 'I kinda want to find out if all that good breeding is everything it's cracked up to be.'

Epilogue

San Diego; Tuesday March 11th

On the advice of legal counsel supplied by the Federal
Bureau of Investigation – who had taken over the Docto®
Corporation/Birth Sciences Inc. case from the California State
Prosecutors, because offspring from their 'breeding program'
were documented to be in 23 of the 50 States – Cameron
Stewart legally changed his name to Jeffrey Leonard.

If anyone had asked him, he'd have told them that he'd
chosen Jeffrey in memory of his girlfriend's dead father, and
Leonard came from his favorite writer, Elmore. But no one did.

As March 11th was Cameron's birthday, the trust fund set
up in his original name became available to him. The funds
were immediately transferred to a new account in the now
sub judice, legally protected name of J. Leonard.

Four days later, after Taylor Philips had acquired a driver's
license and Social Security card under the name of Sophia
Moore from a contact in Venice Beach – her choice of names
had a lot to do with movies – she and the newly christened
Jeff Leonard went to Deacon Mayhew's apartment for a
champagne brunch, then left LA, and California, for good.
Neither trusted a journalist ever again.

Deacon Mayhew qualified as a veterinarian, eventually opening a very successful Beverley Hills practise with his partner, Bruce.

Jaxon Colby finally got his movie deal with a script he wrote titled *Hell Child*, a schlock-horror, B-movie-style picture about an evil cloned boy called Cameron. It became a cult hit, spawning four sequels.

It was deemed the wisest move to keep details of the Docto® Corp./Birth Sciences Inc. case under wraps as it was a real political hot potato – if it ever made it to open court no one would benefit and a lot of lives would be permanently blighted. So a deal was struck. The two plaintiffs would be dealt with in separate closed sessions, their absolute and continuing silence guaranteeing them reduced charges.

Gordon Stewart was sent down to serve a minimum twenty-five years of a number of concurrent fifty-year sentences for a variety of largely unspecified violations of the US Penal Code – mainly, in fact, falsifying birth documentation.

Eleanor Stewart, who did lose her arm, was released from a Federal penitentiary after serving five years for aiding and abetting a felony. Her husband's claims that the whole business had been her idea in the first place were completely discounted by the judge. She divorced her husband soon after her release.

Although the prosecutors were positive that a number of children, whom the records showed as having died, were in reality the victims of unlawful killing, these charges had to be dropped as they proved impossible to verify.

After protracted legal arguments, a local LA news channel had to pull 'the story of the damn decade', as a senior VP had called it, and hand over every single piece of tape, film, and paper to do with the story concerned to the FBI. Even so, Sarah Baldwin kept her new position as an investigative reporter.

Detectives Mike Henrikson and Tony Matric were reassigned to new cases and told to forget all about Gordon and Eleanor Stewart, the Docto® Corp. and Birth Sciences Inc. and what they may or may not have been doing; they were discreetly informed it would harm their future career prospects if they tried to find out. And, as Mike told Tony, the truth wasn't worth losing a pension over.

The John Doe body was IDd, through fingerprints, as that of Otto Bartoli, a kidnap and extortion specialist who operated under a number of aliases, one of which was known to be Marshall Inverdale. Even after his identity was verified, no one claimed the body, which was later cremated at the State's expense.

Sheila Ikeburo formed a successful partnership with Luiz Binay as online security specialists, incorporating a company called Control/Alt/Del. Alfredo Perro and Ed Barry were both put on the payroll.

Art Kellaway Jr., whose complete lack of marksmanship was entirely responsible for the eventual discovery of the truth behind Cameron Stewart's kidnapping, never did join a gun club, but remained a life-long member of the NRA.

Stanley Terrill invested the bulk of the money he made selling the silver and turquoise money clip Cam had given him in a sure-thing bet on a horse. It lost. He did, however, buy a *Fantasy 5* Lotto ticket on the same day. It won him $50,000, an amount of money which did change his life.

The body of Joey Esposito was never found, having been incinerated. An autopsy, had one ever been carried out, would have shown he died from a cardiac arrest following a dysrhythmia event, possibly brought on by the inhalation of an unusually large quantity of a volatile solvent or aerosol. An unfortunate accident.

GRAHAM MARKS

The thing about a Graham Marks novel is that you never know quite where he's going to take you – but you always know you're in for an intense, exciting ride. In *Radio Radio*, he gave us a *Lock Stock* style caper about city kids attempting to set up a pirate radio station. Ditching the conventional fiction format, Graham structured *Radio Radio* as a screenplay. Fellow novelist Eoin Colfer was amongst the book's many fans, calling it 'a shot in the arm for YA literature'.

The characters of *Radio Radio* lingered in Graham's imagination and two of them provided him with the idea for his next book *How It Works*, a gritty urban fairy tale which follows Seb's 'long dark night of the soul' through the seamy streets of contemporary London.

Graham has two sons, 'one just out of his teens, the other in the midst'. He acknowledges that 'a side-effect of this cohabitation (was) to reintroduce me to my own teenage self, someone I'd almost forgotten about. This was an important connection for me, to be able to look out through another pair of eyes, to recapture some of the passion, the couldn't-give-a-shit attitude, the fearlessness and the frailty of standing on the edge of the rest of one's life. Waiting for your go.'

In *Zoo*, Graham has created a page-turning, high-concept thriller, with a touch of *24* and *The O.C. Zoo* puts an utterly contemporary spin on the age-old issue of a teenager distrusting his parents. Set in the USA, *Zoo* follows Cam Stewart's journey from San Diego to LA. It's a journey Graham himself made, taking photos and making notes as he travelled. Research and the quest for authenticity is always part of his creative process.

When he's not writing fiction himself, Graham is still deeply immersed in the world of books. He is children's book correspondent for *Publishing News* magazine and has interviewed just about every major author and illustrator in the field. Even when Graham goes home, there's still one more author to see — he is married to journalist Nadia Marks, now the author of two books for teenagers herself.

Find out more about Graham Marks @
www.bloomsbury.com/grahammarks
www.marksworks.co.uk